THE HAYBURN FAMILY

THE HAYBURN FAMILY

GUY McCRONE

EDINBURGH
B&W PUBLISHING
1996

First published 1952
This edition published 1996
by B&W Publishing Ltd
Edinburgh
Copyright © 1996 Guy McCrone
Asserting an Author's Moral Right
ISBN 1 873631 58 8

06902376

British Library Cataloguing in Publication Data:
A catalogue record for this book is available
from the British Library.

Cover Illustration: *After the Play*
by Arthur Melville (1855-1904)
Photograph: Bridgeman Art Library,
by kind permission of
the Fine Art Society, London

Printed by Werner Söderström

Introductory Note

THE following pages were written to stand by themselves, quite independent of what had gone before. But this being my fifth Moorhouse book—there were three in *Wax Fruit*, and *Aunt Bel* made a fourth—I feel it is time I set down the pattern of the Moorhouse clan for those who may want to refer to it. I feel, too, that a note is better than a formal family tree, for thus I need not go into useless ramifications.

Here they are, then. When I give a number after a name this is to indicate the character's age in the year 1900, which is when *The Hayburn Family* opens.

The elder Mungo Moorhouse, farmer of the Laigh Farm, Ayrshire, was killed in an accident in 1870. He left six children. Mungo, Arthur, Sophia, Mary and David were by his first wife. Phœbe by his second.

Mungo, 65 (the Ayrshire Moorhouse), farmer and landed proprietor, married Margaret Ruanthorpe, 61, only surviving child of Sir Charles and Lady Ruanthorpe of the Duntrafford estates in Ayrshire. They have one son, Charles, 21.

Arthur, 63, wholesale provision merchant of Grosvenor Terrace, Glasgow, married Isabella Barrowfield (Bel), 54. Their children are: young Arthur, 29, Isabel, 27, and Tom, 25. The first two are married.

Sophia, 62, married William Butter, 63, commission agent of Rosebery Terrace, Glasgow. Their children are young Wil, 37 (who married his cousin Polly McNairn), and Margy, 35, also married.

Mary, 60, married George McNairn, soft-goods agent, formerly of Albany Place, Glasgow, who died in 1880. Their children are George (Georgie), 35, John (Jackie), 32, and the twin daughters Anne and Polly, 26. Anne is unmarried.

David, 53, of Aucheneame House, Dumbartonshire, married Grace Dermott, 51, daughter of Robert Dermott, chairman and founder of Dermott Ships Limited. Their children are Robert-David, 20, and Meg, 14.

Phœbe, 40, married Henry Hayburn, 45, of Hayburn and Company, shipbuilders and engineers, of Partickhill, Glasgow. There was a stillborn child in 1880. Henry has a natural son, Robin, 19, whom Phœbe has adopted.

I would again remind my readers that all the above people and those who move through the pages with them are friendly shadows in my own mind. They have no other reality of any kind.

And for this book. I have taken the word Creole in its first meaning; that is, one descended from the French or Spanish colonists to those lands washed by the Gulf of Mexico or the Caribbean Sea. His blood is unmixed European, and he may be a person of much distinction.

G. McC.

Chapter One

HENRY HAYBURN, shipbuilder and engineer of the city of Glasgow, stood at the corner of St. Vincent Street and Renfield Street waiting for a tram-car to take him to his home out west.

The year was 1900 and the month was November. It was a drab, nondescript night, foggy, a little, and cold, with a threat of snow.

Henry, who was the master of a prosperous shipyard on the River Clyde at Partick, had found himself forced to come into the centre of the city late this afternoon to settle some transport squabble in the goods-office of a railway company, and, having on the whole been worsted in the settlement, was in no very good temper.

He stood now under the lamp at the stopping-place, a spare figure in an Inverness cape and a tweed helmet—strange coverings, perhaps, for a man of affairs, but ones which Henry was not to be kept from wearing—nursing his annoyance and waiting for the tramway-car to come.

"Paper, sir?"

Henry dug into a trouser pocket for the necessary coin, and received an evening paper from the urchin's hand. He was glad to see that the car coming just then was half-empty. He need neither stand hanging on a strap inside nor go upstairs to the bleak inhospitality of an outside seat.

He jumped in, sat down, paid his money and opened his paper with a lack of interest.

The same news as the morning. The dragging South African War. The clothing factory of Mann Byars in Virginia Street had been gutted by fire. Failure of a great firm of brokers in New York due to defalcation. The ageing Queen's health seemed to be precarious, but she was still giving audiences, was still seeking to do her duty.

Nothing fresh. He raised his eyes, looking for a moment at the others in the lighted vehicle. Men and women sat huddled in their winter coats and wrappings, anxious like himself to be home. Having nothing better to do, he looked once more at his paper. Advertisement columns. Short paragraphs of comment. City entertainments.

A short poem of three verses. He looked through it idly. He knew nothing about poetry, but it seemed all right to him. Though why a commercial paper such as this should want to publish lines about the rattle of November leaves being the death-rattle of the dying year, he could not see.

Henry looked at the name printed beneath the lines, then folded his paper and stared once more about him. His mind was still given mainly to his altercation with the railway officials. The name of the writer of the verses was, indeed, so very familiar to him that he had quite failed to take it in. But now it began to penetrate.

Quickly he snapped the paper open again. Yes, there it was! Robin Hayburn! The name of his own son. With quick annoyance Henry folded it into a hard square and sat staring at the poem. One or two nearby passengers wondered for a moment at the flush of intense displeasure on the lean, clean-shaven face of this odd-looking, tweed-clad man.

What the devil was Robin up to? Writing penny-a-line trash for an evening rag like this! Or, indeed, writing for anything at all! What was his own son doing writing poetry? And putting his name to it! Robin was nineteen now, and a man. He was quite a good student and, if he would learn to give his mind to things a bit more, he had the makings of quite a good engineer. Henry crammed the paper indignantly into his pocket. He would see his son about this. It was beneath the boy's dignity, if it was nothing else. Beneath the dignity of the name of Hayburn!

The tram ran on. Between the bright lights of Sauchiehall

Street. Through Charing Cross. Past the handsome terraces known as "The Doctors' Row", since Glasgow's medical specialists were, as now, gathered together into this quarter. Then on, farther westward, clanging its bell and running faster as the traffic became less.

Henry Hayburn sat staring before him. Robin. He wished that Robin were stronger. He didn't want a delicate son. A boy should have a good, hard body at nearly twenty, so that he could get on with his training and stand correction. Delicate young people, especially if they were a bit smart, could use their disabilities to slip through the fingers of discipline.

He remembered that Robin had not come down to breakfast this morning. He had been forced to hurry off before he had discovered why.

A quick stab of apprehension drove itself into the bowels of Henry Hayburn, for he loved his son. Could something really be wrong with Robin? Was this persistent coughing more than the remains of a drawn-out, common cold? Should he take the boy to see a doctor?

But as Henry trudged the last part of his way home under the dark, leafless trees to his villa in Partickhill, his mind came back to Robin's verses. Ill or not ill, he was going to tell Robin what he thought of this poetry-writing.

Robin was the son of one Glasgow engineer and the grandson of another, the heir to a great tradition. It was in the direction of engineering that his star lay, and he would not be allowed to forget it.

II

The carpeted entrance hall was warm and quiet as he shut the front door. It was dimly lit by a shaded oil lamp. There was no light from the landing upstairs. No light on the staircase itself. No sounds came from the kitchen quarters.

The grandfather clock beside him began to strike. Henry

3

stood in the middle of the hall until it had finished striking six strokes.

Again there was silence. Where was everybody? On another evening he would have made nothing of this. He would have hung up his outdoor things and shouted to discover his wife's or his son's whereabouts. But now his mood would not let him.

He crossed to the door of his study and threw it open. A great, heaped fire was blazing, filling the room with a bright red glow, lighting up his shelves of books, outlining his work-desk and gleaming on the worn leather chairs. For a moment he did not see his son standing there to one side of the fireplace, an arm on the mantelpiece, his brow resting upon it, his gaze turned to the dancing flames.

As Henry shut the door behind him, Robin raised his head, turned round and said: "Hullo, Father." His shape was outlined by the firelight now. It was the shape of a tall, too slender young man in a box jacket.

The fragility of his look had some effect, perhaps, upon his father's first words. Instead of exploding, as he might have done, all Henry said was: "Hullo. Have you been at the University today?"

To Robin, his father's voice sounded sharp and threw him on his guard. He shook his head and merely said, "No."

"Not feel well enough?"

Robin put back a strand of dark hair, that had fallen on his brow, and once more said, "No."

Still in his rough cape, Henry stood looking at his son. The boy's handsome features seemed white and, somehow, weary. But he couldn't quite tell in the firelight. "What are you doing in here?" he asked, rather to make Robin talk, than because he wanted to know.

"Warming myself."

Robin was in one of his defensive moods—moods that made Henry angry. Now he drew the hard square of folded newspaper from his pocket. "Look here, did you write that?"

Robin took it from him, read it, smiled with pleasure at

4

seeing words written by himself standing there for the first time in print and said: "It's got my name underneath it, hasn't it?"

Henry hated the boy's smile. He hated the look of pleasure. He had expected somehow that Robin would look embarrassed and caught. And here he was, pleased with himself!

He turned to fling off his heavy cloak, then faced his son. "Well, once and for all. We don't want cheap scribblers in this house! Penny-a-liners!"

"But I've got to begin somewhere."

"Begin? You've got to stop! Now!"

Robin stood crestfallen, his hair down on his brow again, staring ruefully at the little poem of three verses in his hand. He thought of the enthusiasm, the dear trouble that had gone to the making of them. And the paper had liked them and published them! He had worked hard at these twelve lines. Moved words back and forth. Tried others. Laboured to get them smooth; to express exactly what he felt.

"It's the University that's your affair! You've a career to study for! Not this nonsense!"

Without raising his head, Robin said: "I would like to show this to Mother."

"Rubbish!" With an impatient gesture, Henry Hayburn snapped the paper from his son's hand and thrust it into the fire. For Henry the action was nothing more than a gesture of extreme but temporary irritation.

To Robin Hayburn it was something quite other.

They were standing facing each other, the boy's face hot with something very near to hatred, the man still angry but self-conscious, and now, perhaps, anxious to defend what he had done; when once again the study door was opened, and Phœbe Hayburn, his wife, stood there, a slim figure with furs drawn about her shoulders. *Her* face, too, seemed white in the red glow of the firelight. Her strange, slanting eyes, big with anxiety, reflected its flames.

5

"Hullo, I thought I heard someone in here. What is it? Is anything wrong?"

Neither answered this question. But the tension relaxed as they dropped their eyes and turned towards her, shamefacedly, as it seemed to her now. She came into the room, taking off her furs.

"I've arranged for you to see a specialist tomorrow, Robin," she said. Then, turning in deep concern to her husband: "Has Robin been telling you what happened last night, Henry?"

Chapter Two

IT was the following afternoon. Robin dumped the pile of obsolete *Punches* together, set them straight on the shining table and got up.

The black marble clock on the black marble mantelpiece of the sombre waiting-room chimed the three-quarters. They had come at three. Since then he had undressed, had been examined, sounded, and Heaven knew what else, had put on his clothes again and forthwith been banished in here. Now his father and the consultant doctor were discussing his condition.

Robin began pacing the thick Turkey carpet. No. Three-quarters of an hour wasn't much for all that. Nerves were making him impatient. He wasn't well, of course, but he would be all right. Anyway, he had better await the verdict before he allowed himself to think anything silly.

At a window he stopped to look out. Already a thin curtain of Glasgow fog was threatening to shorten still more the short November day. No. He mustn't think anything silly.

But now, intensely conscious of himself, he drew a hand from a trouser pocket and fell to examining it. Did it seem transparent? Did the veins show blue through the skin? Didn't other young men of twenty have stronger, browner hands? He spread out his fingers, noting, not for the first time, that they were long and thin, with odd, spatulate ends. Last year an arty lady, reading hands at a church bazaar, had told him he had the hands of an artist, that he felt things more intensely than most. This had been meat and drink to Robin's self-awareness, his secret hopes, his vanity. Remembering her words, he smiled a little, put his hand back into his pocket and began once more to pace the room.

But now he could hear a door-handle turn and the doctor's voice say: "Well, you'll tell the laddie's mother just what the trouble is, Mr. Hayburn. And what I've advised you to do."

The doctor was professionally cordial as he helped this important Glasgow engineer into his Inverness cape, and his son into his overcoat, while the attendant maid, whose duty it was to do these things for lesser patients, was allowed merely to stand by and presently to throw open the front door.

"Dear me, Mr. Hayburn! Do you mean to tell me you've got one of these things? Well, don't go and blow yourself up!"

Just across the pavement, at the doctor's carriage-stone, a French automobile was standing, a strange horseless vehicle like a large open chair on wheels with a seat of buttoned upholstery, gig-lamps and a steering-bar.

The doctor put a friendly hand on Robin's shoulder.

"You're a brave boy, Robin, to let your father drive you about in a thing like that." Then, answering a look in the young man's face: "I've been telling your father what I think. He'll let you and your mother know. Mind now, it'll be all right." He turned to shake a quizzical finger in the direction of Robin's father, who had, by this time, mounted his motor-car and sat resting his hands on the steering-bar. "Now, Mr. Hayburn! Just you remember that ten-mile limit!"

And presently, on this second grey afternoon, Henry and Robin Hayburn were to be seen making their progress out of Woodside Terrace, along the farther end of Sauchiehall Street, past the West End Park—its grounds already desecrated by scaffolding and other preparations for the great exhibition that was to be held in the coming summer—past the new Art Galleries, not yet open, and on, up into Partickhill, the strange petrol carriage spluttering as it ascended.

Immediate curiosity about his condition had left Robin. He did not know why. His father seemed tense, somehow. Thus Robin was content to sit beside him saying nothing; content to wait until a joint explanation should be given to his mother

8

and himself. It would be better to receive the doctor's verdict at the same time as she did.

II

"Hullo, Phœbe! I've just run up to ask for Robin. How is he today?" Mrs. Arthur Moorhouse closed the door behind her and crossed the Hayburns' Partickhill drawing-room.

Bel Moorhouse was a woman of fifty-four, handsome, carefully corseted and smart. Following the dictates of the infant century, Bel, always careful of fashion, wore a very wide cinnamon-coloured coat, its collars and cuffs of lavish sable. Her hat was a small affair of brown ostrich feathers, and she carried a small round muff. These things suited her. They underlined the fact that Mrs. Arthur Moorhouse was a person of some importance. Her figure, as she bent to kiss this sister-in-law she had come to see, might be none too flexible, but at least it was regal. Yet, if tight lacing and an instinct for right deportment had made Bel's movements formal, there had been nothing of formality in her voice, nothing, indeed, but affectionate concern, as she asked Phœbe Hayburn her question.

Phœbe did not reply. With a quick "Hello, Bel" and a motion that almost seemed like a drawing-away, she turned and moved across to a window.

Unperturbed by this, Bel sat down in a fireside chair, opened her coat, laid aside her muff and pulled off her gloves, all the while contemplating Phœbe's back as she stood staring out. Phœbe seemed upset by her question. It must be serious with Robin. Queer creature, Phœbe. She always behaved oddly when she was in trouble. And she was so hard to get at. So hard to comfort. Bel had known this half-sister of her husband's since she was a child of ten; had brought her up from then, indeed. But even now she could not claim quite to understand her. Yes, a strange girl.

9

Girl? Phœbe must be forty now, although Bel could scarcely think so as she sat looking at the back of that thin figure, over there in the window. The shirt-blouse, the dark, bell-shaped skirt, braided with a band of black velvet, the broad leather belt enclosing an almost too slender waist. Phœbe must feed up a bit, Bel decided irrelevantly. It wasn't good to have a girl's figure at forty. If she wasn't careful, Phœbe would suddenly look skinny. And that would make her look old. As it was, there was a white thread or two in her shining black hair.

But she must really force her to say something. She couldn't be allowed just to stand there for the rest of the afternoon, staring from this hilltop drawing-room at the distant chimney-pots of Partick, the far-away cranes by the docksides and the ships moving on the river.

"Well, Phœbe? What about Robin? I hope his cough is no worse, dear?"

With another quick movement Phœbe crossed to the fireplace and stood over her sister-in-law. "There was blood on Robin's handkerchief the night before last, Bel," she said in a tone that sounded almost accusing.

Bel looked up. She could see that Phœbe's beautiful face was dark. A stranger would have called it sulky. But Bel knew it was not that. Phœbe's odd, Highland eyes were pools of trouble.

Surprise and alarm made Bel's next question sound foolish. "Blood, Phœbe? Blood from his coughing?"

"Do you think I would have told you, if he had only bitten his tongue?"

At once Bel discounted this retort. Its hard ungraciousness was only a further sign of unhappiness. For a time she lay back in her chair, watching Phœbe as now she paced back and forth like a caged animal. What was she to say to her? Attempt the task of sympathy? At times like this, Phœbe could be so difficult, so unpredictable. You had to be ready for anything.

But Bel was not ready for Phœbe's next question.

10

III

"I suppose the family has always known that Robin is Henry's real son?" The younger woman was standing now, stock-still in the middle of the room, looking fixedly at her sister-in-law.

Bel felt her colour rise. This was bewildering. "What on earth makes you ask that, Phœbe?" she said, playing for time.

Her memory went back some twenty years to a very young Mr. and Mrs. Henry Hayburn stepping down one December evening from the train that had brought them back on the last stage of their journey from the city of Vienna. She remembered her surprise at the sight of a child in Phœbe's arms. Typically casual, the Hayburns had given no warning of its coming. She remembered Phœbe's short, defensive explanation. "His parents were burned in the Ring Theatre fire, Bel. He's our baby now." The Hayburns had lost a child of their own. This adoption was natural. Bel and her husband had asked no more questions.

Thus strangely, and with little further talk, had Robin become one of the large Moorhouse circle. If others had gathered together to gossip, neither Bel nor her husband, Arthur Moorhouse, had joined in.

But now Phœbe was pressing her for a reply. "You all know about Robin, don't you?"

"Phœbe, my dear! We know nothing! We took you at your word! At least, Arthur and I did. Why should we have done anything else? It was your business, not ours."

"Yes, it was our business."

"Besides, Phœbe, Robin has never looked at all like Henry. Well, now that I come to think of it, there may be a look, but I mean—"

Phœbe was bending over her writing-desk, taking an envelope from an inner drawer. She opened it and held out a photograph.

"Do you see any likeness there?"

11

Bel took it into one hand, and held her hand-glasses elegantly with the other. It was somewhat thumbed, and there was a faint streak of red where a stick of opera-girl's face-paint had once smudged it. "Where did you get this?" She looked up.

"It was given back to us, along with Robin's mother's clothes, after we claimed her at the mortuary. Her own parents, Robin's grandparents, were in the audience. They died in the fire, too. He had nobody left." Phœbe was silent for a moment, busy with memories, then she added: "Robin's mother was gassed. She wasn't burned. That's how we got her clothes and this photograph. She had it in the theatre with her."

It was past Bel's comprehension why Phœbe should only now, after so long a time, tell her of these things. She examined the photograph with great curiosity. It was a cheap print of a foreign-looking young woman, pert, very pretty and in the style of twenty years back, holding a baby in her arms. "Robin and his mother?"

Phœbe nodded. "You can see a strong look of Henry in the baby's face, can't you? But he's grown up like his mother, hasn't he?"

"Yes. Exactly!" Bel held the card, fascinated. Robin Hayburn's fine features, his quick dark eyes, his thick black hair, his odd, foreign look, were all here. The young woman's face was round and merry. Now, at what must be about the same age, her son's face was thinner, more refined perhaps, and male. But it was the same face.

Bel looked up once again at Phœbe. "Who was she?"

"Do you remember the name Klem? People we lodged with in Vienna just after we were married?"

"Yes, I think so."

"She was the girl Klem. She was a singer."

"And Henry—?" Bel stopped. No. She had no right to ask that. It was for Phœbe to tell the story, if she felt she must. Bel turned to look into the fire, avoiding her eyes. But what had happened? Her mind went back, seeking to remember the

12

Hayburns' return to Glasgow. In these first days, Phœbe and Henry Hayburn, having no home of their own, had stayed with herself and Arthur in Grosvenor Terrace. It was easy to explain Phœbe's obsession with this foundling baby. Her own child could never be replaced, they said. But Henry? There had been no signs of coldness between Phœbe and her young husband. Rather the reverse.

Bel knew Phœbe as much as anyone could know her. She was a strange, passionate creature with a stiff pride and little compromise. What circumstances had joined themselves together to make it possible for her to forgive her husband and to take this child of his unfaithfulness into her arms?

But now, after a time, Phœbe was answering Bel's unfinished question. "Henry? I had left Henry alone too long, Bel. You remember I stayed on here at home after I lost my own child. It was cruel of me. It was his child as well as mine who had died."

"But, my dearest, you were ill!"

"I should have been ill in Vienna near Henry."

Bel did not try to dispute this. She remembered, uncomfortably, that her own behaviour had, at that time, not been above reproach. She had been too possessive of Phœbe. Had not bothered to consider the young man who had been left in exile.

"Henry told me at once; whenever I got back to Vienna; told me he had been with the Klem girl." There was a trembling moment before Phœbe added: "I couldn't forgive him!"

Again Bel looked up quickly. An extraordinary thing had happened. Phœbe, whom she had scarcely ever seen weep, even as a child, stood before her weeping quietly. She was twisting a torn handkerchief in her fingers and letting the tears run unchecked. It gave Bel a measure of Phœbe's present anxiety.

"Dearest! But why didn't you come home to us?"

"No, Bel! I wasn't going to ask help or tell anybody at home. One day I saw the Klem girl in the street, and knew she was going to have a child. I knew then what it meant to

13

be jealous!" Phœbe took a step or two, tearing her hand-kerchief to ribbons as she went on: "I couldn't forgive him, Bel!" She pointed at the photograph still in Bel's hand. "That poor girl had to be carried out of the burning theatre and laid dead at my feet before I could forgive him!"

"Phœbe! You were very young! And, after all—" Bel got up and made to go to her.

But the younger woman eluded her, saying: "No, Bel. I am a fool!" Phœbe turned once more to the window, hating her own weakness.

Bel stood pondering for a moment, then she sat down again. It was possible for her now to fit together this strange story that had taken twenty years to tell. Frustrated and affronted maternity. Anger. A stiff pride. Jealousy. Hatred of another woman who could bear her husband a living child. And then the breakdown of these things. The splendid victory for pity in Phœbe's burning heart.

"Now you see what Robin is to me, Bel. Why he's as much my child as if I had had him. More, I sometimes think."

Bel saw. Phœbe had known no travail of the body to win this boy. But there had been a great travail of the spirit.

"You've been a long time in telling me this, Phœbe," was all she could find to say.

"I didn't think I would ever tell anybody. I suppose it's because I'm worried off my head this afternoon, that I'm telling you now. Henry and I haven't even mentioned it to each other for years. We're just like any other husband and wife, and Robin is our son."

"Have you told Robin?"

"No. Why should we? We let him think we're both his adopted parents."

The rattle of a strange mechanism stuttering to a halt came up to them from the road outside.

"There they are!"

"I'd better go, Phœbe."

"No, Bel. You had better stay to hear what the doctor says."

14

"Do you want me?"

"You had better stay."

Bel understood and was flattered. In her own fashion, Phœbe was begging for support. "Put that away again, dear," she said, as she took up the photograph of the Viennese girl and her baby, thrust it into its envelope and gave it back.

IV

Bel Moorhouse had never been certain whether she liked her brother-in-law Henry Hayburn or not. This was not surprising, perhaps. Placed as she was at the centre of a large and ever-widening family circle, her interests were feminine and personal; her affections warm.

He baffled her. As the head of a flourishing engineering firm of his own founding, his preoccupations were constructive, executive and male. She knew he liked men better than women, and took care not to be mixed up in family politics, seeing them merely as a waste of time. He was bound up, indeed, more with things than with persons.

To Bel, Henry was a limited sort of creature, rather cold, and from a woman's point of view not very interesting. In these twenty years she had often wondered what Phœbe saw in him. Now, however, as he came into his own drawing-room, followed by Robin, a spare, loose-boned man of forty-five in his weather-beaten cape, she found herself looking at him anew. There were, obviously, all kinds of things about Henry Hayburn she had missed. She was by no means sure she liked him better for what his wife had just told her, but the knowledge that the boy who followed him was the son of his body and not merely of his adoption gave wings to her interest.

"Well, we've got back, Phœbe," Henry looked old. Bel caught a strained casualness in his voice. "Hullo, Bel. Where have you come from?"

Bel took this as a dismissal. Once again she got up. "You've

15

got things to talk about. I'll hear what the doctor says about Robin later."

"No. She mustn't go. Must she, Mother?"

"I've already told her to stay, Robin," Phœbe said.

And this boy. He had come across to Bel and kissed her artlessly and engagingly. His manners were easy and had much charm. Even now, at this moment of tension, he thought of them. Bel's own more downright children had been known to say that Robin Hayburn's manners were too easy, too plausible. But Bel, liking good manners, had disagreed. They must remember, she had said, that Robin's blood was foreign, however Scotch his upbringing.

But knowing now that his blood was only half foreign, that the other half of it came from this man who stood beside him, questions crowded into Bel's mind. Robin looked frail today, frail and tired, yet, even so, he looked very like the young woman whose photograph she had held in her hand a moment ago. How would this boy develop? And what would become of him?

There was a pause. It was typical that the three Hayburns should be standing there together lost, somehow, inside the circle of their trouble. Phœbe seemed uncertain what she dare ask. Henry seemed uncertain what he dare tell her.

Bel's quick sympathy rose up to help them. But she could not help without being firm. "You had better tell us at once about Robin, Henry," she said.

Without bothering to take off his cape, Henry sat down on the edge of a chair, placed his bony fingers on his knees and said the few words he had to say awkwardly and without addressing anyone in particular. "The lungs are not very good. He says the boy's to go south to a warm climate, if he's to have a chance."

A chance?

Henry spoke bluntly, as though, indeed, his son were not in the room. But they knew it was the stress of his feeling that had made his tone harsh.

For a time no one spoke. Bel looked at the Hayburns. All three had become dumb and wooden. And as she looked, the room began to swim before her vision. Taking hold of herself, she got up briskly.

"Well, things might be worse, mightn't they?" she said. "If Robin has to go south to get better, you can afford to send him, can't you, Henry? There's nothing very difficult about that."

Again it was typical of this odd trio that they did not show emotion. They had found support in Bel's words. If Robin were ordered south, then south he must go. And in time he would be cured, of course, and come home again. They must take hold of that. Thus they could go on.

Not for the first time in their lives did the Hayburns have reason to be grateful to Bel Moorhouse.

V

Robin climbed the narrow stair to his bedroom. He went up carefully, for his breath was not good these days. On the little top landing he halted, holding his door-handle as support for an instant, then he turned it and went inside.

His room was at the top of the house. The upper part of its walls sloped inwards, following the slope of the roof. It had two dormer windows, one on each side, whence, in good weather, Robin could see the Campsie Fells to the north of Glasgow, and to the south the Clyde, the Renfrew hills, and even, when it was very clear, the peaks of Arran. It was a large room, occupying all the available space up there immediately under the slates. It had perhaps, been intended as a billiard-room or a nursery. It was painted white and warmed by a studio stove. Here was Robin's kingdom.

An intruder with some talent for deduction could have learnt many things about Robin merely by looking round. The floor was carpeted to the walls with thick grey felting, and in front

17

of the stove, the doors of which could be thrown open to show the blaze, there was, in addition, a large rug, made of tweed and tartan rags, that Phœbe had once brought back from a Highland holiday. At one side of this was a deep wicker chair well supplied with cushions of rough mauve linen. The bedcover and curtains were of the same stuff and decorated with square, New Art leaves and roses. Like the woodwork, the furniture was painted white. Behind the door was a thick dressing-gown, and by his bed a pair of fleece-lined slippers.

The bedroom, one would say, of a cherished only son, who had no objection whatever to being cherished.

But the room had still more to tell about Robin. On his work-table under one window were one or two books on engineering and dynamics, together with several notebooks bearing Robin's name. There was a current number of the *Glasgow University Magazine*. Robin, then, was a student, studying subjects that would fit him to enter the family firm of Hayburn and Company, Shipbuilders and Engineers.

But his bookshelf and the pictures he had bothered to hang showed other facets. Prints which might be called provincial and arty. An Aubrey Beardsley. An engraving of a full-throated pre-Raphaelite damozel. A Japanese scroll. His shelves contained some unselective romantic poetry, some modern novels, many classics, most of Stevenson, a published play or two by the up-to-date Mr. Shaw, a brown-papered covered book which, had the visitor pulled it out, would have revealed itself as the writing of Oscar Wilde. Several books of comment on literature and painting.

And had the stranger had the further bad manners to rummage in the drawer of Robin's table, he might have come upon a sheet or two of verse in Robin's own scrawl; verse that was curiously sultry, and should, the stranger might feel, have been written in a language other than English. He might have found, too, a half-finished short story, not ill written.

The room of a young man, then, whose life was directed towards achievement in practical affairs, while his nature reached towards books, pictures and the passions, or at least the pleasures, of the mind.

Robin came in, shut the door and leant against it, a little picturesquely, perhaps. He was feeling very conscious of himself, conscious of his breathing, conscious of his heartbeats. He told himself that his life was in danger; in such danger, indeed, that he must leave home. He had, he told himself, come to a parting of the ways.

And yet he was not utterly cast down. He felt, in some measure, as though he were standing aside, watching that poor sick boy propped against the door there, examining his feelings one by one and savouring, not without interest, his predicament. A poor sick boy, he told himself a little falsely, who could not now go on with his life's work, but must of necessity follow the paths of easy indulgence rather than take the harder and more manly way. It is nice, at twenty, to feel oneself unusual.

Where would they send him? To Italy? The French Riviera? Robin left the door and, wandering across to the stove, threw it open and sat down in the large wicker chair, warming his hands.

But now reality came upon him unawares. This was his room. He would miss it. He would feel strange away from it. And his foster-parents. Those two downstairs, who had brought him as a tiny baby from Vienna. He called them Father and Mother. They were the only parents he had known. He had taken them for granted, as children do. He knew that he loved them, particularly his "Mother".

And his "Father"? He loved him, too, he supposed, though he had been near to hating him last night. Yet more and more, Robin, as he grew up, was coming to diverge from Henry. Why was it that now so often he found his father out of sympathy, found their ideas clashing?

Not for the first time in his life, Robin sat thinking of his "real" parents. They had been musicians, killed in a terrible fire, he had been told. They must have been young and quick

19

and Viennese. What were other Viennese like, he wondered? He pictured them as persons of infinite charm. But he had never met any, except a rather pompous banker from Vienna who had visited them once when he, himself, was ten or twelve. A heavy, dark man with formal manners whom Robin hadn't much liked.

It is common, they say, for children to imagine themselves to be young princes or princesses, weaned, somehow, from glory, and forced to live with a man and a woman who are too fond of discipline, who do not understand their royal feelings. Robin had known something of these imaginings; and the knowledge that had been allowed to come to him, gently and with tact, that he was not a Hayburn but an Austrian foundling, had kept these imaginings alive.

He might not be a prince, indeed, but it pleased him to think that he was quicker, more intense and of finer stuff than those he called his parents.

And yet when the door opened presently, and Phœbe Hayburn crossed over to him, went on her knees on the hearthrug and looked up anxiously, searching his face, Robin bent to kiss her with all the familiarity of a young man, who bends to kiss a much beloved mother.

Chapter Three

THE following morning was cold, and there was a light rain falling, as Henry Hayburn left his house on the top of Partickhill and took his way down into Partick proper, where the not unimportant offices and yards of Hayburn and Company lay, fronting the busy river.

It was seldom that Henry missed this half-hour's walk between home and work. It was, indeed, difficult for him to avoid it, since no public vehicle came up into Partickhill. Besides, the drop down the footpath into Peel Street, and thence to Dumbarton Road, was easily accomplished by his long legs. And although it was inevitable that Henry, being an engineer with a natural interest in every new contrivance, should have one of the new motor-cars, he never thought to keep his petrol carriage at home. It must be kept at the yard, where its unpredictability might be constantly under the eyes of the yard mechanics.

His long figure, striding along in the weather-worn Inverness cape and the old sportsman's tweed helmet, was a sight to set clocks by; so little did his progress vary between half-past eight and nine. Partick housewives would turn from their work to watch this odd creature, his square, clean-shaven, pug-nosed face usually set in deep thought as he passed. Some of them, indeed, wondered how he got along without knocking into things, so little did he seem to notice where he went.

But this half-hour of walking was one of the most productive times of Henry's day. It was now that he did his thinking, attacked problems, fixed the day's duties.

The misty autumn rain wet his face, its fine particles made a white, watery bloom on the rough tweed of his cape. His feet, dropping down the incline, squelched mud and dead leaves on the little footpath. There was a smell of soot, of decaying vegetation, of the coming winter.

Henry Hayburn had, people said, a touch of genius. A true son of his city, he was a brilliant engineer, creative and practical. In the twenty years since his return from Vienna he had built up and made himself master of an important shipyard. The South African War was then being fought, and Henry's firm, it was known, had been doing special work. Some said that his name, young for honours though he still might be perhaps, would one day soon be laid before the Queen.

And yet he was a simple creature, whatever his brilliance in things technical. He accepted his wife and son, and loved them. That was what wives and sons were there for. That his family had been strangely put together had long since ceased to occur to him. He had been grateful to Phœbe for the part she had once played, deeply grateful, indeed. But, thanks to her and to these years of healing and forgetting, there was nothing much left in Henry's mind to forget or to heal.

Now he was striding along the sodden pavements of Dumbarton Road thinking of his son's illness. The boy must get well. No other thought was tolerable. The doctor had given a grave warning. Graver than he, Henry, had allowed Phœbe or Robin to know. But there was money enough. Money surely to buy his son's health back and allow him to follow out the plan laid down. Let him go anywhere that was best, then: anywhere that would cure him. But when the cure was made, he must come home to his studies, to Hayburn and Company, to his career, to his heritage.

Now Henry halted at a side street while a lorry, loaded with steel plates and tubing, turned from the main road, making for the shipyards of a world-famous competitor. Rapt though he was in the thought of his son, the upper layer of Henry's consciousness marked the team of giant Clydesdale horses straining round the corner with their load; marked that these plates must be intended for the sides of this ship, that these tubes must be used in the interior of that other.

22

When it was possible to walk round the end of this obstruction, Henry did so, leaving the pavement for a moment, looking from habit this way and that, then striding on.

But presently he was turning in at his own gates and nodding good morning to his gatekeeper. Now familiar things soothed him. The sense of being inside his own yard. The sound of hammers in a half-built hull. Packing straw. Oil-soaked mud. The shouts of workmen. The belching chimney of a tug, as it moved out there on the river, hazy in the rain. These and the very act of crossing to his own office took hold of him, forced him to think of the day that lay before him, and brought him a great measure of comfort in his trouble.

II

There were no frills about the offices of Hayburn and Company. Other firms might occupy palaces; particularly where their shipyards, ever creeping down the river, had taken in what had, in earlier times, been a pleasant riverside property. Then the handsome house, early Victorian, or, more likely, Georgian, now blackened with smoke and standing among sheds and coal dumps, machinery and cranes, might have its shabby, forlorn dignity pressed into the service of Glasgow's greatest industry, and become an imposing office.

Henry's private room was a mere box of a place, lined with cheap white pine, stuffy and absurdly overheated by a radiator connected to the works boiler. Visitors, unaccustomed, sometimes exclaimed at the heat, but Henry did not seem to notice and had not yet died of suffocation.

He took off his tweed helmet and Inverness and laid them dripping over the radiator, thus adding the smell of wool woven in Harris to the steamy closeness of the room. Thereafter he settled himself in his swivel chair and rang for his letters. They were brought, all of them opened and read by his chief clerk, as was usual, so that Mr. Hayburn need not be

23

troubled by what belonged merely to routine. One, however, was marked "personal", and the seal had not been broken. The flap of the envelope was embossed with the lion and the unicorn. The postmark was London.

Henry took it up, turned it this way and that, decided it was some official notice—there were many in these war days— laid it aside, and went through his other letters. This done, he rang for the heads of the departments to which the letters applied, discussed the contents with them, made decisions and gave his orders. It was getting on for eleven when the last man left him, setting him free to go out and have a look at the work that was in progress. Henry got up, looked through the window and saw that there was a gleam of bright sky, although it was still raining. He took his hat and cape from the radiator, noting with satisfaction that they were already quite dry. He put them on.

As he crossed the room the unopened envelope caught his eye. Standing there by his table, Henry cut it open.

It was a letter from Authority. Authority was aware of the service Mr. Henry Hayburn was rendering his country. And Authority wanted to be sure that, should the Queen see her way to offering Mr. Hayburn a knighthood, Mr. Hayburn would find no impediment to his name appearing among the New Year's Honours.

He drew out his chair again, slumped down in it and sat staring at the letter. Whatever others had whispered, such a happening as this had never once occurred to his simplicity. Whether he should accept or not did not yet concern him. For in Henry's mind, this, somehow, was as much an honour paid to his father's memory as to himself. His thoughts went back. If his father could know! A great engineer who had been at the making of Glasgow! Who had built up the first Hayburn and Company, but had died mercifully before it had collapsed with the City Bank disaster, killing his widow with shock and throwing his sons Stephen and Henry on the world.

And Phœbe? On the night of his mother's funeral Phœbe

24

Moorhouse had told him she would marry him and stand behind him while he rebuilt the ruined Company. Now this!

But how would her unconventionality take it? Would she want to be Lady Hayburn? Henry doubted that. Yet, like himself, she would, surely, be pleased with this recognition of work well done.

For a time he sat, staring before him. But at last an office-boy, coming in, roused him. He got up. "Get me my town coat and hat," he said.

The boy went to the white pine cupboard, took out a tall hat, a black overcoat and an umbrella and helped him to change.

Henry took the letter from the desk and crammed it into his pocket. "I'm going into the town," he said, stating the obvious. "I'll be back to sign the letters." He must consult with his brother Stephen and with his brother-in-law David Moorhouse about this.

III

No one quite knew how Stephen Hayburn occupied himself at his place of employment. But as Stephen's place of employment was the head office of Dermott Ships Limited, and as his close friend was David Dermott Moorhouse, the chairman of the company, how Stephen occupied himself did not, perhaps, matter very much.

At the turn of the century many great Scottish concerns, not yet having been turned into public companies, were still in the full possession of the men, or the relatives of the men, who had brought them into being. And thus, if the owner chose to maintain a hanger-on or two at the firm's expense, there was nobody to say him nay.

But from this do not let it be supposed that Stephen Hayburn was a fool. Quite the reverse. He knew that he was lucky. Brought up in Glasgow's industrial purple, he had

25

been destined by a fond, over-ambitious widowed mother for a gentleman's life of idleness. But the City Bank crash that had wiped out the family fortune had likewise wiped out any such hope for Stephen. Thus, he had become a shipping clerk. But not quite an ordinary one. For Dermott Ships then belonged to old Mr. Dermott, a friend of Stephen's dead father; and thereafter—in less than a year, indeed—to David Dermott-Moorhouse, the old man's son-in-law, who happened to be Stephen's close friend, and who, not unnaturally, saw to it that Stephen did not starve.

Stephen occupied a little office beside the Chairman's room. It was here that he conducted the business side of his bachelor existence. If you wanted a competent fourth for this new game of Bridge which was just beginning to be fashionable; if you were a hostess making up numbers for dinner and were seeking an unattached male with a sufficiency of light gossip spiced with enough pleasant malice to call forth little, gay scoldings; if you were a jaded weekender looking for a companion, tactful and distinguished, who knew how to fall in with your ideas of comfort and could swing a club without shaming you at Old Prestwick or St. Andrews, then all you had to do was to telephone Dermott Ships, Extension 6, and ask for Mr. Hayburn.

Stephen was sitting in his office, thinking idly of a sentimental letter he had received from London this morning—wondering how he could induce the firm to send him south this month, drawing stars and triangles on his blotting-paper, and asking himself at the same time if another, perhaps more intimate meeting with the sender of the letter might not be unwise. From these important deliberations he was roused by his friend the Chairman standing in their intercommunicating doorway.

"Here's Henry to see us," David Moorhouse said. "He says he wants our advice."

Stephen rose and followed David. He called "Hullo" to his brother as Henry came into view, standing hat in hand in the middle of David's large, Turkey-rugged room with its blazing fire and the fly-blown photographic enlargement of old Robert Dermott over the mantelpiece.

Why couldn't Henry wear his clothes properly? Stephen found himself wondering, as, indeed, he had wondered all his life. Henry looked bundled up, somehow, in his black city overcoat. A nondescript tie was working its way up the back of his "stand-up" collar, and his boots were heavy, like a workman's, and sticking with Partick mud.

"Sit down, everybody," David said, indicating two red leather fireside chairs. He went to his desk, took out a box of cigars, offered them, then, rotating himself in his own swivel chair, sat between them, sucking his cigar and placing the points of his fingers together.

David Moorhouse was pink and portly. Good living had left its mark upon him. Hair that had once been chestnut was now thinning on the top and turning to a sandy grey. And yet David was still a handsome and dignified man, with the well-cut features and high cheekbones belonging to the men of Moorhouse breed.

They were very old friends, the Hayburn brothers and he. There was an unbuttoning of the spirit when the three were alone together.

"What do you think of that?" Henry said, showing them each in turn Authority's letter.

Neither David nor Stephen were typical Glasgow business men. In the commercial world they were known for light-weights. In Dermott Ships itself, indeed, the Chairman and his equerry were known with indulgence as the Old Boys. The firm had David's nephew, Wil Butter, as its mainspring and hard-driving director. Yet now, however surprised the Old Boys might be, they did not show it, but fell back by instinct on the sententious bearing, the studied imperturbability of the pompous business Scot.

"This is an important matter, Henry," David said pontifically. He stopped sucking his cigar and rubbed his chin

27

thoughtfully. As was natural, perhaps, he now saw himself receiving the same offer. How much better his own poise and presence could carry a knighthood. His country place, down there at Aucheneame on Clydeside, with its lawns, its gardens and its stables. His gentle wife, Grace, and their carefully brought-up son and daughter. All of them well-bred, all of them pleasant to look at, all of them more than fit to support dignity.

"Yes, it's important," Henry answered eagerly. A large hand with a bony wrist stretched out to receive the letter back.

"Are you going to take it?" Stephen asked. A like notion to David's had passed through his mind. What a trim, self-sufficient bachelor knight he himself would make! Urbane, well-informed and easy. Very much in social demand and a favourite with everyone. And *his* tie wouldn't creep up his collar, and *his* fingernails wouldn't show black with machine oil.

"I've just come to ask what you think." Henry had always looked up to his elder brother Stephen. He had been taught to do so by his worldly mother, who disliked his own young awkwardness, and had constantly held up Stephen's polish for admiration and imitation. Although this was more than twenty years since, it had never occurred to Henry to make a revaluation. In all respects, he was worth a dozen Stephens, but nothing would have surprised him more than to be told so.

They smoked their cigars in silence for a time, David and Stephen turning the matter over in their minds. Each in his way was fond of Henry. To David, Henry was an old friend and the husband of his sister Phœbe. To Stephen, a brother to whom, despite the fundamental differences, he had always stood close. It was unthinkable that either David or Stephen should feel real jealousy. And yet there were wisps of it floating in their minds, causing each in turn to think of Henry's unsuitability to receive this honour. His lack of conventionality, his abrupt manners. Henry's brilliance as an engineer affected their deliberations strangely little.

28

Suddenly these were interrupted by a large, energetic man of thirty-seven or thereby, with a mop of black hair and a strong, mobile face. It was Wil Butter, David's nephew and co-director.

Wil was busy. He burst in with a sheaf of cost-sheets in his hand, shouting: "Look here, Uncle David!" before he became aware of Henry's presence.

David was glad to postpone the unpleasant duties that Wil's forceful tone portended, by hastening to call "Hullo, Wil. Come and give us your advice."

Wil slapped down the sheets, said: "Oh, hullo, Uncle Henry. Listen, Uncle David, I'm in a fearful hurry. I've no—" and was making to go out again, but for once David managed to assert some authority.

"No. Stay where you are, Wil. We want you. Henry, show him your letter. Your Uncle Henry wants to know what we all think about that."

Wil took Authority's letter from Henry, sat himself on a corner of David's great table, swung his legs and read the letter, emitting at the end a long, low whistle. "Good business, Uncle Henry!" he said, his large face grinning with delight and surprise. Wil Butter worshipped success.

"Your Uncle Henry's wondering if he should take it or not," Stephen said.

Wil paid no attention to this. He seldom paid any attention to Stephen Hayburn. Not because he disliked him, but because he saw no point in noticing him.

"What do you think, Wil?" Henry asked.

"About taking it? Of course you'll take it! Take everything you can get! It's all in the day's work!"

David and Stephen exchanged a look here, flinching a little at Wil's lack of perception when it came to the more delicate values.

"Besides, it's a wonderful tribute," Wil went on. "It shows you've really done something. And from everything I can hear you deserve it. What does Aunt Phœbe think?"

29

"I haven't told her yet."

"Haven't told her! Polly would murder me if she hadn't been told before everybody else that she might be Lady Butter!"

"I wanted to make up my mind first. Besides, your Aunt Phœbe's queer. You never know how she'll take a thing like this."

"She'll be all right! Don't bother about that. Write the acceptance and tell her after. Surely you know how to handle women by this time. 'Bye. Must see you about these cost-sheets before you go for lunch, Uncle David. Some of these charges are just getting a bit too funny! Can I tell Polly the great news, then, Uncle Henry?"

"I suppose so."

"Good." The junior partner of Dermott Ships went, banging the door.

Behind him, the Chairman's room settled back to peacefulness, as a mountain tarn settles back after a sharp squall.

IV

Henry took Wil Butter's advice. On that same afternoon he sat himself down in his office to reply to Authority's letter. He wrote in his own hand that Mr. Henry Hayburn was much favoured by Authority's communication, and that there would be no impediment whatsoever to his acceptance of the honour proposed. Having done so, he slid the letter into his pocket, put on his Inverness and, walking to the nearest post office, bought a stamp and posted it. What drove him to this odd, boyish secrecy he could not have explained even to himself. Had this letter gone downstairs to be posted with the others, it is improbable that his clerks would have been interested enough to notice to whom it was addressed. And it is still less probable that, had they noticed, they would have felt the faintest impulse to steam it open and read what Mr. Hayburn had written.

Henry had never been conceited. His engineer's enthusiasm and achievements had gone to form his character and build up his self-confidence and force. Yet tonight there was something in him that made him shy of telling Phœbe and Robin immediately he got home. A feeling of guilt, perhaps, among other things, that he had not consulted with his wife before replying.

But Robin's quickness told him that his father had something on his mind. He could not have said why. But for those who live close to us, an untypical gesture, a dry cough, a burst of humming, may reveal tensions.

Robin had spent a day that could not be called unhappy. He was a young man of vivid awareness. Awareness of himself, of events, of places, of people. An awareness that was, at most times, more detached than warmly sympathetic.

This, the day following the verdict, had been, in its way, a pleasant void. Void of everything but warmth, comfort, and the knowledge that he need, in the near future, do nothing he did not want to do. He knew that his illness was serious. But yet, perhaps from the very nature of that illness, he was neither greatly cast down nor worried. For Robin, it meant a truce in the battle with his father's ambition for him. Now he need neither study seriously nor—what he most loathed—work among the mess and rigours of the shipyard. Now he might wait to hear what was arranged for him, knowing it could be nothing unpleasant.

They were sitting at the dinner-table when Henry exploded the news.

"I've accepted a knighthood, Phœbe," he said suddenly, his colour rising.

"A knighthood, Father? From the Queen?"

"I was talking to your mother."

Quite unabashed by this, Robin sat taking in the situation with excitement. An excitement born rather of curiosity than

31

from any pleasure in the distinction his father had brought upon them. And what would his mother say? How would this affect her?

Phœbe, a steaming tureen in front of her, was ladling soup into plates. She stopped for a moment, the ladle in her hand. "Well, I suppose if you've accepted it, you've accepted it," was all she said.

"Aren't you surprised, Mother?"

"Of course I'm surprised! I've never even thought of anything of the kind." Phœbe went on with her ladling.

"You don't look particularly pleased," Robin said.

"Just what I was thinking," Henry put in, glad now of Robin's help.

She took her time. "I wasn't asked whether I would be pleased or not."

In the face of this important news, all three sat saying nothing for a moment. But now, Henry's experience understood better than his son's quickness what was passing in Phœbe's mind. He saw her rising flush, the gleam in her eyes as they turned to meet his own. He saw that now it was Phœbe's turn to remember old struggles; and that she was pleased for him.

Thus Robin was surprised and at a loss when, upon his saying: "You *must* be glad, Mother! Why shouldn't you be?" his father turned upon him sharply.

"Don't bother your mother, Robin! She'll talk about it in a minute.

"Does anybody else know?" Robin asked presently.

"Your Uncle David and your Uncle Stephen. And Wil Butter. I went to see them about it today."

"That means the news is round the family by now. They'll all be jabbering like magpies!"

Neither Phœbe nor Henry tried to censure this. The Hayburns lived a little apart, a little out of the main stream of Moorhouse politics. The boy had merely expressed a feeling shared by all three of them.

32

Chapter Four

NEXT morning, just after breakfast, Phœbe found Bel alone in the back parlour of her house in Grosvenor Terrace.

As Bel Moorhouse and her husband Arthur had long regarded themselves as the centre of the family, Bel was gratified that Phœbe should come to her thus at once. It was natural and right. But really, the girl—Bel persisted in thinking of Phœbe as a girl—was behaving ridiculously. Having given the momentous news, she was looking positively glum.

"But you must surely be delighted, Phœbe," Bel insisted.

"I suppose so. I know it's a good thing for Henry, anyway."

"And then, of course, it will mean all kinds of new arrangements. The Partickhill house won't be quite—"

"We're making no difference."

"Oh, no *real* difference, dear. I can see that. But you'll have to—" Bel hesitated. What she wanted to say was that the Hayburns would now have to pull themselves together, to stop being so easy-going, to look to taking their places among the pillars of their city.

"We won't let it make any difference," Phœbe said.

Bel gave up. "Why, exactly, was Henry offered this honour, dear?" she asked a little tartly. "Oh, we all know he's wonderful, of course. But why, exactly, now?"

"Something to do with the war."

"And what did you say when he asked you what you thought about it?"

"He didn't ask me. He consulted David and Stephen, then came home and told me it was settled."

This, too, displeased Bel. Didn't ask his own wife? And why David and Stephen? Why not Arthur? The idea of anything so important happening in the Moorhouse family with herself and Arthur left out of all consultation seemed to Bel like a slap in the face. Especially anything happening to Phœbe.

For a moment, as she sat looking round her prosperous and polished Victorian parlour, feelings of uncertainty, of unsureness, mixed themselves with Bel's annoyance. This room was in the best of taste, or so she had thought, twenty years ago. But now she wondered. Was that ball-fringed fireplace with the side drapings, was this mahogany furniture, round, solid, and covered with plush, becoming out of date? Were she and Arthur slipping? Were they, the centre of the family to whom everyone had so far turned for advice, approval, and a support, indeed, which had often been real enough to mean Arthur's signature in his cheque-book—were they now coming to be looked upon as getting old and past consulting?

Not if she could help it! Arthur was a vigorous sixty-three, and she was nine years younger. They were in the very prime of their lives.

She pulled herself up, smiling the smile which Phœbe, undeceivable in most things concerning Bel, recognised as a challenge. "Well, Phœbe," she said, "all this is simply splendid! I'm very proud, dear. And I'll tell you what. I must arrange a dinner-party for you at once. I'll telephone Henry to congratulate him and fix a date."

The family centre must not be allowed to move from Grosvenor Terrace.

II

That evening Bel hung up her telephone with a sigh of achievement. The knight designate had been difficult to pin down. But Bel, knowing her man, had been well prepared for this. Henry's: "It's very nice of you, Bel, but well, I don't just know how I'm placed," had been met with a firm: "Nonsense, Henry! I'm fixing Thursday of next week. Now, is there any reason why you can't come on Thursday?" Her question was shrewd. She knew that Henry's mind, quick in business, was slow in things social. His: "Well, yes. Yes, I daresay on Thursday. Anyway, you can speak to Phœbe," had been quite enough for his hostess to work on. "Splendid, Henry! Thursday." And so it was fixed.

Bel returned to the parlour, where her husband was sitting by the fire smoking his pipe and reading his paper. Arthur Moorhouse was, on the whole, well preserved. In the last years his hair and old-fashioned side-whiskers had changed to white, but his body was still lean and active. Tonight, however, he looked tired and his handsome face was showing, somehow, the first shadow of age.

They had, at their evening meal, discussed the honour accorded to Henry Hayburn. Then together, here before the fire, Bel and he had been remembering old times. How Phœbe, Arthur's orphan half-sister, still a little girl, had come to live with them. It must now be thirty years since. Her growing up. Her marriage.

Finding Arthur in a softened mood, Bel had put forward her idea of a dinner-party. And she had been gratified by Arthur's: "Telephone Henry, then, and see what he says." Gratified because she knew that her husband could not much be bothered with such things these days.

But now, tactfully, Bel did not announce her victory. She merely sat down on the other side of the fireplace, took up her sewing and said: "Anything in the news tonight, dear?"

"Another fifty men ambushed in the war."

She looked up. "Killed?"

"Aye."

She found it difficult to ask: "Anywhere near where Tom is?" Tom was their younger son.

"No. No, Bel. I wouldna think so."

Bel went on with her sewing, raging in her heart at the son who had insisted upon joining up. But Tom had always been impetuous; had always insisted on getting into scrapes. And why were we fighting in South Africa, anyway? She had never been able to understand, though she never dared say so. "I thought Mafeking being relieved was going to make all the difference," she said, without looking up.

"It didna finish the war, my dear." Arthur lowered his paper and looked across at his wife. A single tear splashed down and glistened on the hand that held her needle. Well, if your son insisted in going off to the war, it was more easy to bear if you didn't make a fuss. He folded his paper. "Ye havena told me if Phœbe and Henry were coming," he said, deliberately seeking to distract her.

Bel took her husband's meaning perfectly. And she was grateful. "They can come on Thursday. I'll try to get everybody for then," she said, determinedly regaining her composure. "And I've just been thinking, Arthur. After all, our family is so immense now, with nearly all the children grown up and some of them married. I think we ought only to ask the brothers and sisters with their husbands and wives. What the children call the Old Brigade."

III

It was the night of the dinner-party.

Young Robin Hayburn stood admiring the elegance of his own extreme slimness, fledged as it was in adult tails, white waistcoat, and pumps. It was reflected in the enormous mirror, with its gilded cupid frame and its marble shelf of ferns and palms, which covered and embellished almost an entire end of his Aunt Bel's drawing-room.

Robin, whose health in the last days had improved, superficially, if not fundamentally, from rest and enforced idleness, found himself standing here in the drawing-room alone. An untimely breakage in his Aunt Bel's kitchen and a telephone call for help had brought him across early with a substitute for what had been broken.

36

Robin was one who found interest and entertainment in almost anything. Now therefore he took to roving round the familiar room examining this and that.

The bearskin rug before the white marble fireplace. Robin noted that the hair was wearing on the bear's head. The handsome gilded clock beneath its glass dome. The knick-knacks on a table. Silly things, like a silver cowbell from Switzerland. An antique candle-snuffer; useless, since the room was lit by gas. A cut crystal box which held nothing. A genteelly expurgated copy of Robert Burns' poems bound in green suede, with gilt ends and a crimson ribbon for a marker. A heart-shaped Dresden box, the lid of which was covered with tiny china flowers. He opened it. It contained a penny stamp which had been stuck on a letter, then pulled off again, a hairpin and a bit of string.

As these things could not feed Robin's curiosity, he turned to look at the photographs of Aunt Bel's children. Young Arthur Moorhouse, whom Robin quite liked and who had been made by the photographer to look more important than he was. Arthur's wife, Elizabeth, with her two young children. His soldier cousin Tom Moorhouse in mess uniform. His cousin Isabel, who was married to an Englishman called Ellerdale and lived in London. A large photograph in a handsome silver frame of Aunt Bel's mother, old Mrs. Barrowfield, who had died some years ago.

Queer how these people were his relatives and yet not his relatives. Robin turned about absently. Now what were these little figures in the china-cabinet?

As he crossed the room to examine them, the door opened and his Aunt Bel came in.

"I say, Aunt Bel! You look tremendous!"

"I didn't know you had come, Robin. Who let you in?"

"The butler."

"Don't be foolish! You know he's only a caterer's man. You see, I thought that with fourteen to dinner—"

"But I say, Aunt Bel, you *do* look tremendous!"

Bel laughed. It was this kind of thing that made her like Robin. "Silly boy!" she said. "How can an old woman look tremendous!"

"But you do! And you're not old!"

"I'm more than twice your age."

"That's nothing. I say, your dress is awfully nice!"

"Like it?" Bel turned herself about.

"New?"

"Bad boy! Don't tell your Uncle Arthur. I've allowed him to think I got it last year."

"Told him, you mean?"

"I said *allowed* him to *think*. He never notices anything." Bel's eyes sparkled with mischief. She examined herself with approval before the great mirror. And indeed she could not disapprove of her reflection. Not many women of her age had a figure like that. Her shining dress of black satin lay perfectly to it. The lines were severe and it was cut low. But it had long, tight sleeves of some black transparency which added— or so her dressmaker had assured her—to its sophistication. On her corsage were dark velvet roses. No. She wasn't a bad fifty-four. It was remarkable what not too many potatoes, no toast at breakfast and careful corseting could do.

Robin was standing back apprising her as an artist might apprise a picture. "Yes," he said thoughtfully. "Yes. Very nice indeed!"

"You don't think it looks a little fast, do you?"

Robin laughed. "Fast! How could it on you, Aunt Bel?"

Bel turned to look at him. "You queer boy! I wonder where your parents got you?"

"I've often wondered that myself. There are so many possibilities."

Bel's colour rose. She crossed to the young man and patted his arm. "I'm sorry, Robin. I wasn't thinking. I wouldn't have said that if I had remembered."

"What? That I'm a waif and a stray?"

Bel stood beside him, confused now. Robin's frivolity had

38

led her into thoughtless talk. She was afraid she might have hurt him. "Don't say waif and stray, Robin," she said. "You know very well you're nothing of the kind."

There was something imp-like in Robin's look as he said: "I don't know. It's fun to feel your blood is a bit of a gamble. I know my Austrian parents were singers, but that's all. I don't even know if they were nice or nasty, whether they were honest people or rascals. Only think, my dear Aunt Bel; they may have been wickedly immoral!"

Better informed now of Robin's parentage than he was himself, Bel did not like this. She drew away from him, becoming a little chilly. "We'll hope not, Robin," she said primly, bending to rearrange the flowers in a vase. "I would hate to imagine you thought of your real parents with any-thing but sorrow and respect." Then, pleased with her own moralising, she went on: "Still, it won't do you any harm to keep your eyes open for the temptations that may be lurking in your blood, dear."

"Of course not, Aunt Bel."

Bel, enjoying herself, looked up from her flowers and took encouragement from Robin's naughty earnestness. "Always shun questionable company, Robin, even if it is amusing. And the great thing is always to be straightforward and truthful, dear."

"Never 'allow anyone to think' anything, Aunt Bel?"

Robin's face was still so serious that Bel, as she looked at him, did not at once catch the echo. But suddenly there was a smile which broadened into gay impertinence. Was he actually daring to refer to her innocent strategy with Arthur over this new evening dress? Couldn't he see that was some-thing quite different? Now she was far from pleased. "I must see what's happening downstairs," she said coldly and left the room.

39

IV

Smiling to himself, Robin remembered he had been on his way to the china-cabinet when his Aunt Bel had interrupted him.

The queer figures that had caught his eye were a row of little "moving" mandarins brought to Glasgow, no doubt, by Mr. Stuart Cranston, the tea importer who, following the vogue for Chinese and Japanese decoration, had extended his imports to include such things as oriental porcelain, Satsuma ornaments, and painted fans.

Robin opened the cabinet and set the little mandarins wagging all at once. One nodded his head wisely, as he read from a tiny painted scroll. One shook a warning finger. One kept bowing his head in the obeisances of a courtier. A fourth waved a fan. A learned mandarin in spectacles kept making gestures of instruction.

He was standing watching them when his cousin Anne came into the room.

"Hullo, Robin. Still like playing with dolls?"

Robin turned to look at her. "Hullo, Anne. What are you doing here? I thought it was to be only uncles and aunts. I was asked, of course, because the party is for us."

"I suppose *I* was asked because Mother hasn't got Father to bring her."

Caught by the dispirited tone of her voice, Robin turned to examine Anne McNairn's too-mature figure, her stupid, gold-fringed evening dress, and her round, freckled face. He did not see much of this cousin, and did not particularly want to. But now a show of sympathy might yield him some amusing talk from this twenty-six-year-old spinster. "Do you remember your father, Anne?" he asked.

"Yes. I was six when he died."

"What did he look like?"

"He was big, and had a beard, and I was a little frightened of him. I think we all were. The boys and Polly, too," she said, referring to her brothers and her twin sister, Mrs. Wil Butter.

"Are you sorry he's dead?"

"Of course! What a queer thing to say! He was my father!"

No. Anne was too conventional to yield much by these tactics. Robin changed his ground. "I have frightful rows with mine. Fathers are not always perfect, you know," he said. "And I don't think it has anything to do with only being adopted. It's because I want to do things that I don't suppose anybody in this family would approve of."

"What kind of things?" Anne's plump face looked at him a little blankly.

"Something, I don't know. Write. Do something original. Out of the ordinary." Robin began to wander about the room. "I wish I had a real, obvious gift," he added. "A singing voice. Or a hand that could use a paint-brush."

"No. You wouldn't be encouraged in anything like that in the Moorhouse family."

Robin turned in surprise to look at Anne. She was speaking with some heat. "Would *you* like to do something original?" he asked.

"I would like to do anything rather than what I am doing!"

"Anne! What do you mean?" He looked more solemn than he felt.

"Well—" Anne coloured, half turned away, then, speaking low and almost angrily, she continued as though to herself: "What have I got, living alone with Mother? Dull church meetings among old women. Shopping. Sewing. Housework. Visiting a twin sister, and seeing her happy with her babies and her husband. Oh, I'm not jealous of Polly and I love the children. But—" Here Anne stopped to dab an eye that threatened to become moist, and to gaze bleakly into a future that kept looking less and less promising.

All this was too uncomfortable for Robin. He didn't much like his Aunt Mary McNairn himself, if it came to that. A dull woman who was inclined to be sanctimonious. He quite saw

41

how Anne felt. But he didn't want the embarrassment of hearing about it.

"I wonder if you ever see the Moorhouse family as I do," he said, deciding to move to less personal ground. "The Old Brigade, I mean. Uncle Mungo, Uncle Arthur, Uncle David, Aunt Sophia, your mother, my mother. There they are, standing square to the world like the Guards at Waterloo. And they've got us, their families, well inside the square, protecting us and keeping us prisoners at the same time." He thrust his hands into his trouser pockets and took a further step or two. "Funny to think how I managed to wander into that square," he added.

"I don't know what you mean."

Robin turned away and continued to walk about. Anne's real trouble was that she was stupid. She had a certain sharpness of tongue—there was that remark about his playing with dolls—but she was blunt-witted. The only possible thing for her to do was to stay at home with Aunt Mary as her unpaid companion. But he could not tell her so. "You may not know what I mean, but you feel it. Just as I do," he said. "You feel the family pressure. Pressure of approval, pressure of disapproval, pressure of criticism, pressure of curiosity, of interest, of gossip, of poking their noses into what isn't their business. It's all so stuffy, so provincial!"

"Mother says we should all be proud to belong to a family that has always paid its debts and worked for what it has got."

Robin gave up. Really, if Anne couldn't do better than quote her mother's platitudes, what was the use of going on? Instead of replying, he reopened the glass door of Bel's cabinet and once again set the little mandarins wagging. "Look, they all just keep doing the same thing all the time." Then, turning to Anne: "Allow me to introduce you to the Moorhouses!" he said.

42

This thought was to amuse and sustain Robin through what would otherwise have been a dull family party.

Here, for instance, was his Aunt Mary McNairn coming into the room, followed by Aunt Bel. Now what would Aunt Mary do? How would she wag? Aunt Mary would be serene and entirely selfish.

The widow of George McNairn, sometime Baillie of the city of Glasgow, was a personable woman of sixty. Mary Moorhouse had once had the oval face of a Madonna. Even now, her eyes and her skin were fine. Her dowager black was set off by neat little cuffs and a collar of fine white lawn. A white cashmere shawl hung over one arm, to be fixed presently by Anne, her daughter and handmaid. Her still dark hair, parted in the middle and made sleek, was surmounted by a cap composed of many tiny, snowy frills.

"How are you, Robin dear?" she said, presenting an ivory cheek to be kissed. "I hear you haven't been very well."

"I'll be all right, thanks, Aunt Mary. How are you?"

Mary smiled a calm little smile with the right amount of indulgence in it.

"Oh, I can never say I'm *well*, Robin," she said. "You see, I'm getting old, and I daresay I've had more than my share of ill-health and sorrow. But—oh, I'm very happy, really, dear," she added, putting a brave face on it. "Anne, will you fix my shawl for me, please? And after that run up to the bedroom where we put our things and look to see if I left my spectacles. I may not have brought them, but please make sure, dear."

Anne interrupted the fixing of the shawl to say: "I'm certain you didn't bring them, Mother."

Robin marked the steadiness of Mary's voice as she said: "Go, Anne dear. When your mother asks you."

Yes. Aunt Mary was wagging exactly as he had expected.

And now here was his Uncle Arthur Moorhouse bringing in his Aunt Sophia and Uncle William Butter.

Uncle Arthur, for whom Robin had a wholesome respect, would be simple, distinguished, and noncommittal. Aunt Sophia would be talkative, scatterbrained, and untidy. Uncle William, her husband, would stand about and say nothing.

Sophia Butter, born Sophia Moorhouse, was flooding towards her hostess. "Bel dear! This is wonderful! Such a good idea! Just a party for all the funny old brothers and sisters to congratulate Henry and Phœbe. None of the young ones to take the shine out of us."

Bel disengaged herself from Sophia's untidy embrace, smoothed her new dress, and took another hasty, indignant glance at her own fashionable reflection in the drawing-room mirror. Which of the next generation shone so brightly, she wondered, that she, Bel, would be forced to become a mere moon in the younger, dazzling sunlight?

"Except you, of course, Robin dear. You're a guest of honour, aren't you? Oh, and I saw Anne going upstairs. How are you? Are you going to your father's investiture? Oh, but, Robin dear, you must! Mustn't he, William?"

Sophia's husband said nothing.

William Butter was a fat man. His grizzled, untrimmed beard and whiskers grew so luxuriantly that they covered the greater part of his face, thus depriving it of the ability to express joy or sorrow, pleasure, or pain. Indeed, after some thirty-nine years of marriage to their sister Sophia, the Moorhouse family still very much doubted whether William had ever felt any of these emotions.

But Sophia was going on: "There you are now, Robin! Your uncle says you must."

Arthur Moorhouse took one hand from behind his back, smoothed a trimmed, white whisker, straightened his discreet black waistcoat, rubbed his firm chin with elegant, bony fingers, looked at his patent-leather boots, at the ornate moulding round the gasolier, then at his wife, towards whom he directed the wraith of a smile.

Sophia should really get a new dinner-dress, Bel was thinking. She remembered a dress very like this one some eight years ago at the wedding of Sophia's daughter Margy. Not that Sophia at sixty-odd could ever attempt to be smart, but at least she need not look shabby—positively dirty, in fact.

"And, do you know, we heard the most awful story, the other day, about some man who was to be knighted! Didn't we, William?"

William made no remark.

"Yes. I can't remember who it was, but I'll remember in a minute. Somebody Scotch. Oh, dear me! A name we all know! At any rate, the Queen was at Osborne, on the Isle of Wight. And evidently you have to get a boat at Portsmouth—or is it Southampton, William?—Portsmouth, that's right—and cross over. And then they meet you with carriages and there's a great luncheon affair and everything. Well, this man missed the boat! Wasn't it awful? Fancy! Going to be knighted by the Queen and missing the boat! I would have died!"

"And what did he do, Sophie?" Bel felt impelled to ask.

"Well, I'm not sure, Bel dear. I suppose he would have to invent an illness or something. But I think he got his knighthood. Oh, I daresay they would just post him his medal or his certificate or whatever it is you get. In an envelope. Still, the very idea of missing—"

VII

And here were some more of them. His Uncle Mungo Ruanthorpe-Moorhouse and his Aunt Margaret. Now what would they do? Robin looked back at the little figures in the cabinet.

Uncle Mungo, the oldest Moorhouse, had always been

a countryman, and showed it. And Aunt Margaret, who was the daughter of a baronet and had heired the estates of Duntrafford in Ayrshire, would show her background too.

Margaret Ruanthorpe-Moorhouse was a sturdy woman. Her face looked red and weather-beaten, now that the hair that surrounded it was almost white. But her eyes were dark and commanding. The dress she wore had been put together by a village sewing-woman, but it was embellished with family lace, and it had the look, somehow, of being a kind of uniform she was used to. For ornaments she had her mother's handsome diamonds, old-fashioned and set in thick gold.

Her imperious tones were making themselves heard above the family din, as she greeted her host and hostess. "It was kind of you to want us to stay, Bel, but we knew you would have quite enough. And St. Enoch's Hotel is really perfectly nice. My dear, what is your news from South Africa?"

Robin could not hear Bel's reply.

But his Aunt Margaret's voice went on: "Well, soldiers' mothers must just keep smiling, mustn't they? We're having an awful time with Charles—" Margaret was referring to her only child, a young man of twenty-one—"You heard, of course, that the doctors wouldn't pass him? I was sorry for Charles about that. Soldiering is so terribly in his blood. All our family—" Her voice kept a bright, disciplined impersonality.

But Robin, who had come nearer, could hear his Uncle Mungo say: "Well, *I'm* not sorry. And the boy will just need to stop his girning and content himself. Oh, I'm not saying he wasna right to offer himself. But that was surely doing his duty well enough."

Uncle Mungo was stolid and downright. Dignified, and a Moorhouse in looks too. His farmer's body was broader, more filled-out and stronger than his brothers'. There was a slow confidence about him.

Looking at them, Robin's sharp wits wondered how this plain man had ever come to marry the heiress of Duntrafford.

46

VIII

"Mr. and Mrs. David Dermott-Moorhouse!"

Robin turned to look at his Uncle David and his Aunt Grace. They were easy figures in the row.

Uncle David would start pompous, but might, with luck, end up waggish and gay. Aunt Grace would agree with everybody. And that would be all about her.

Having greeted Bel and Arthur, David and his wife caught sight of Robin and came towards him.

Grace Dermott-Moorhouse gave him her hand. "Robin, I'm so glad to see you here. We heard you had been ill, and didn't think you—"

"Oh, I'm all right, Aunt Grace." Robin smiled back at this rather faded aunt, whose only attribute seemed to be gentleness. And then, finding his Uncle David standing over him, aloof and, Robin somehow felt, censorious, he added: "I've been bone idle, and idleness suits me."

David continued to look important. "It's a very bad thing for a young man to be idle for long," he said.

"Grace dear! I must tell you what Margy's wee Billy said the other day! He looked at his baby sister and shouted—" and the good-natured Grace was taken aside to endure the incontinent grandmotherhood of Sophia, leaving David and Robin together.

Robin gave the appearance of turning over David's pronouncement in his mind. "Do you really think so, Uncle David? Do you really believe that 'Satan finds some mischief still—' and all that sort of thing?"

"Certainly."

"Were you never idle when you were young?"

"Never." But now, at last, there was a gleam in David's eye.

"And didn't you ever get into any kind of mischief?"

"Never." David allowed himself a look of patronising amusement at Robin's presumption.

47

"What about the spangled ladies in the Old Scotia and the Whitebait?"

"Look here, Robin, who's been talking to you?" Uncle David had actually grown pinker and was throwing alarmed glances towards Aunt Grace.

Robin was delighted. "Only Uncle Stephen."

David had withdrawn into himself again, but this time he was on the defensive. "What did your Uncle Stephen tell you, Robin?"

"Oh, not very much. But I can't help guessing, can I, Uncle David?"

"Well, don't guess too much, Robin. For it won't be true."

"How can I be sure, Uncle David?"

"And take that innocent look off your face! Do you know what you are? You're an impertinent young monkey!" But David's importance was melted now. He twisted his nephew's ear and turned away laughing.

Robin was pleased with himself. He had succeeded in getting that Moorhouse mandarin to make his own characteristic nods in the row with the others.

IX

And now Uncle Stephen Hayburn. But he didn't count, of course. He wasn't in the row. Wasn't a Moorhouse.

There was something amusing and old-fashionedly foppish about him, with his sparse oiled hair, his black stock, and his eye-glass—an affectation he had the sense not to permit himself at the office—suspended on its broad black ribbon. He was so very unlike any of the others, was, indeed, as Robin well knew, held a little in contempt by them.

Robin liked this uncle. He liked his tolerance of life, his lack of striving. If the moon did not feel disposed to drop into Uncle Stephen's lap, then Uncle Stephen did not put himself to the trouble of crying for it. There was something of the

48

artist about him. Something that met Robin's sympathy. Of all his elders, his father's brother was the one to whom Robin seemed to come nearest. It was, almost, as though Uncle Stephen were his real uncle.

The boy watched him now, as, urbane and detached, he returned the greetings of the family. And he knew that Uncle Stephen was amused, even as he, himself, was amused.

No. Uncle Stephen did not belong to the Moorhouse row.

X

And those two strangers, Phœbe and Henry Hayburn? Now Robin tried to see his adopted parents as he saw the others tonight, apart and impersonally. But he could not.

As a little boy, he had taken it for granted that his mother was the most beautiful being in the world. And now, again, as he watched her, he told himself he had not been far wrong. She was, indeed, more "tremendous" than Aunt Bel. But you could never tell her so. You could please Bel with flattery, but you couldn't please Phœbe.

And his father. Everything about Henry Hayburn was now expressing excitement and force. His wiry, angular body. The clenched fist driven down on the palm of the other hand, as he sought to underline some point of talk. His bluff features. His cropped hair. There was a look of agelessness about him. In twenty years, probably, he would look and behave exactly as he was doing now.

Robin was afraid of him. Afraid of the enthusiasms, that were the mainsprings of his life. The enthusiasms of his inventive mind. They seemed to leave him so little personal life. So few softnesses.

Yet Robin could look back to a time when he had seemed different. When he had crawled about the floor, playing with his toys, mending, as it seemed, by magic, those that had gone wrong. In those days Henry had been Robin's hero.

Chapter Five

PHŒBE wished Robin had not come to see her off. For, though the afternoon sun was bright, here on the Riviera in early February it might suddenly become treacherously cold. She could have said goodbye to him in their hotel. There was no sense in taking risks.

But he had insisted upon bringing her here to the little Garavan Mentone railway station. And now, having brought her, seen to her luggage and found her sleeping-carriage, he was feeling the embarrassment of waiting until such time as that part of the train which came from Ventimiglia in Italy should appear, hitch on the sleeping-cars and start the long journey to Paris, the first stage of her journey home. But finding nothing more to say Robin had gone off to buy unwanted newspapers and seek needless railway information.

Phœbe knew why he had left her. This boyish, last-minute neglect did not wound her in the least. She took a slow step or two up and down the platform awaiting his reappearance.

She hated leaving him. This fortnight during which she had been with him here in Mentone had been a time of close affection. Their relationship in these silver days had been brittle, happy and, somehow, anxiously precious to her.

A faint puff of wind sent smoke across the open platform. A gardener was making a bonfire in a nearby garden. The air became blue and aromatic from burning eucalyptus leaves and pine-needles.

Now there was the rumble of a train in the distance. Phœbe turned, wishing Robin would come, and found herself face to face with a lady.

"I'm sorry, but I had to follow you up the platform! I think I know you! Do you know me?"

She was an elegant little woman, very well dressed in the blacks and greys that smart British women wore just then to show respect for their queen who was scarcely more than a week dead.

Phœbe was not particularly pleased to find herself thus addressed. Whoever this could be was, she felt, of little moment to her. But now memory was caught and she stood hesitating.

The other laughed gaily at her confusion. "Oh, Phœbe Moorhouse! Did you never hear tell of a farm at home that they caud the Greenheed?" Deliberately, in saying these words, the little lady allowed the accent of Ayrshire to blow across her speech.

Phœbe recognised her. "Lucy Rennie?" Now she remembered. There was a story attached to this woman. Phœbe's father, old Mungo Moorhouse, had been the farmer of the Laigh Farm in Ayrshire. His neighbour, old Tom Rennie, had worked the neighbouring farm of Greenhead. There were two daughters, and this was one of them. Lucy had gone to London against the wishes of her father, it was said, to become a singer. Many years ago she had appeared in Glasgow and sung in Bel's drawing-room.

"Yes! Lucy Rennie! That's to say I was Lucy Rennie. Then I married a man who could never quite make up his mind whether he was a Belgian or what. So after he died two years ago, I decided to become British again. Is this your belonging?"

Robin was standing beside Phœbe now. The train, having passed beyond the station, was moving backwards to allow the Garavan carriages to be attached.

The little woman detected a look of understandable impatience in Phœbe's face as she replied: "Yes, he is. He's staying here. I've just brought him out, and I'm going home now, Mrs.—?"

"Mrs. Hamont." Lucy Hamont held out her hand. "At least we caught a glimpse, didn't we?" She laughed, adding: "I'm looking for some people coming through from Italy in the

51

other part of the train. Goodbye!" and went off searching windows for her friends.

II

It was strange to feel alone. Strange, but not unpleasant. Robin had climbed a little way above the railway station.

His mother's train had gone, tunnelling its way beneath the Sardinian town of old Mentone, which, standing brown-red and piled-up on its hill above the harbour, divides the closed bay of Garavan from the opener, more extended West Bay with its fashionable villas and gardens.

In his mind he followed her. During the next hours the train would thread its way through many such tunnels, circle many lovely bays, would stop at many scented stations, until at length, with its full load of the rich, the adventurous and the fashionable, it would leave the shining coastline, turn north, and rush, a real express train now, through the darkness of the winter night towards Paris.

He stood looking about him. Self-aware, probing his own impressions. Things seemed unreal. Unreal and strangely beautiful. It was impossible for him to imagine that anyone could belong to these olive-yards, these sun-drenched mountains, in the same way as he, Robin Hayburn, belonged to Glasgow. The wet streets, the boom of the ships on the foggy Clyde, the smoke-blue outlines of far-off hills were, all of them, part of himself.

Robin folded his arms and turned to lean against the wall built to contain this narrow, hillside street. There beneath was the bay of Garavan, and on one side the little harbour with a white yacht or two and the fishing-boats tied to rings on the long, projecting jetty, or dragged halfway up on the little beach of sand. Safe enough, thus, for a sea that has no tides. More than one was already preparing to move out of the harbour, hoisting those red lateen sails that belong to all Mediterranean waters. On the Quai Bonaparte, under the low plane-trees, young fishermen were tending their nets and teasing the passing girls. Behind them was the old town, a warren of Italianate houses, built one against the other, and rising up in streets that were partly stairways to the plaster cathedral of St. Michel and the chapel of the Conception. Behind him, the sloping hillside, dotted with little white and pink houses, rose to the high wall of rock that keeps Mentone from the north wind and the winter. Farther over, the Italian coastline and Bordighera.

Robin felt puzzled. Were his senses muted? Wrapped in cotton wool? Should not he feel this beauty more intensely? Should not he feel a more real regret, that his mother had just left him? "Your father needs me at home, Robin."

For a moment Robin saw his father. "Sir Henry Hayburn," he said, smiling to himself, though he could not have told why.

And presently indifference allowed the image of his father to drop from Robin's mind.

He pulled a leaf from a geranium plant that had grown up from the little steep garden down there on the other side of the wall, crushed it between the palms of his hands and smelt it.

Yes. He supposed he was sorry to have his mother leave him. "Go straight back to the hotel, Robin. And don't catch cold."

And he had disobeyed her and come up here to look at the view, whenever the train was gone. Queer that he felt so detached. Would there be a reversal of this? Would he become unhappy, tense, desperately lonely?

He smiled mistily, and again looked about him. He didn't know. But he had better take his mother's advice and get back.

For another hour, perhaps, this unreal town would lie warm in the winter sunshine. But thereafter the sun would begin to dip towards the cliffs of the Tête de Chien above Monte Carlo, the coastline and the mountains would be flooded in operetta pinks and ambers; the sea, bright blue and silver now, would slowly change, through grey, through rose, through dove colour, through dying reds and purples, to a mere, murmuring blackness, reflecting the stars and the diamond lights, stringing the bays of the French and Italian Rivieras.

III

It was dinner-time on the same evening. Mrs. Hamont stood at the door of the hotel dining-room waiting to be escorted to a table. The head waiter saw her, hurried forward and bowed.

"Here I am again," she said in excellent French, giving her hand unconventionally, as though to an old friend. Handshakes, she had found, and other judicious unbendings, could help.

"So Madame has just come?" The smiling waiter was asking the obvious as he led the rustling little lady across the crackling parquet to her place.

"Yes. I was in Cannes. But Cannes has become so dull with the Queen's death. I thought I would come here to Mentone, where it's always quiet anyway."

The waiter understood utterly. Bowing once more, he conveyed to her the depth of his understanding. He was indeed sorry, he said, for the British people that they had lost their much-loved queen.

Mrs. Hamont raised her eyebrows, sighed, sat down, threw her furs from her shoulders, arranged the bunch of real, locally-grown violets on her corsage and looked at the menu.

The waiter, perfectly disguising his impatience to be gone and attend to others, strongly advised this and that. But Mrs. Hamont was a woman who knew her own mind. She saw what she wanted and, having requested that, allowed him to escape.

Now she could sit back and look about her. The room was familiar from one or two earlier visits. It was the

54

typical dining-room of a good Riviera hotel, a hotel that was comfortable without foolish luxury. A polished parquet floor. Large windows of plate glass to catch the winter sunshine. Crystal chandeliers. Gilded cane chairs. A couple of palms in tubs. And too much steam heating for the taste of most Britons.

Waiters were hurrying here and there with the inevitable tureens of steaming bouillon. People were coming in. Those who, like herself, intended to go to the entertainment in the Casino tonight wore evening clothes. Others, some of them invalids, had taken little trouble with their dress.

Now, for a moment, Mrs. Hamont's attention was taken by the wine waiter, who came to discuss her half-bottle of wine. When she was free to look about her once more, she found that the young man she had seen on the platform this afternoon had seated himself at the table next to her own.

He was handsome, this boy. Handsome, but strangely dark-eyed to be the son of Phœbe Moorhouse.

Here, among the elderly and delicate, Lucy Hamont was pleased to find herself within talking distance of anyone so attractive. "We met on the platform, didn't we?"

"Yes." His flushed smile of recognition was quick. It lit his face almost too brightly.

"Your mother said you were staying. Been ill?"

"Yes. Bad chest, I am afraid."

He did not need to tell her. "You've come to the right place." She seemed charmingly anxious to reassure him. "This place is wonderful for that sort of thing. Look. We'd better get our names right. My name is Mrs. Lucy Hamont, what's yours?"

"Hayburn. Robin Hayburn."

"How do you do, Robin?" She stretched across a hand. Robin stood up quickly to take it. "You see, I'm calling you Robin at once, because I knew your mother and all your mother's family when I was a girl. We lived in the next farm in Ayrshire." Then, answering a look of bewilderment in the boy's face: "I left home very early. I went to London. Turned

55

into something quite different from a farmer's daughter, if you know what I mean." Of course he knew what she meant. She could see he was not slow. "So your mother married a Mr. Hayburn, was it? And had you, Robin?" she went on, after a pause for plate-changing.

"My father's name is Sir Henry Hayburn." Robin, still unused to Henry's honour, smiled to avoid seeming pompous.

"Oh! I didn't know. I'm so out of touch with Scotland now. Then I should have called your mother Lady Hayburn. But, dear me, what does it matter? She's only Phœbe Moorhouse to me!"

Robin liked this woman. He liked her easy brightness, her way of taking him on an adult level. It flattered his young manhood.

"How do you spend your evenings?" she asked presently. "Do you go to the Casino?"

"This is my first evening alone. Mother has been with me until now. I've brought books."

"Study?"

"I suppose so."

"You don't happen to write, do you?" Then in a moment she laughed. But without mockery. His face was flooded with colour. "I see you do! Well, you're in the right town for it! So many of them came here, you know. Our own Robert Louis Stevenson. Aubrey Beardsley is lying up in the cemetery above the town. And of course endless Frenchmen. Have you published anything?"

"Oh, good heavens, no! Well, in a newspaper only."

"What? Articles?"

"No. A short poem."

Now she felt a real sympathy for him. Had not she, too, been an artist? This was a nice boy; a boy she could present to her acquaintance. And as the son of her old friend, Lady Hayburn.

"You must show me your poetry sometime, Robin," she said later, finishing her meal and preparing to go. "You see,

I was—still am, a little—a singer. I know what it is to be— what shall I say?—on that side of the fence. Will you?"

Robin felt shy, but flattered. "If I ever have anything that I think—"

"Oh! Here's an American friend of mine! Denise St. Roch!" Lucy Hamont half rose, holding out her hand to a young woman who had come into the dining-room and, having heard her name spoken, was coming to greet her.

"Why, Mrs. Hamont! You here! Isn't that wonderful? I've just arrived this minute!"

The boy sitting by himself at the next table had never before seen anyone like the newcomer. He watched her with gaping admiration, as she stood talking with his neighbour. The effect she made upon his quick sensibility was immediate.

Miss St. Roch was unconventionally dressed in what appeared to be one long garment of grey stuff, full, girdled and falling to the ground, with a triangular hood hanging from the shoulders. It might have been a monk's robe or an Arab's burnous. Her head, proudly held, was covered with close-cut blonde curls, and her features had a classic straightness, giving her the look of a Greek boy. Her skin was warm, almost tawny, suggesting the Latin woman who happens, by exception, to be fair. She made Robin think of a young saint in a church window; except that young saints did not also have feminine elegance.

"Are you staying here?" Mrs. Hamont was asking.

"Only until I find somewhere. I've got a book to write. A man I met in Paris told me there were studios where I could work up in the old town. Old houses converted, I suppose. Anyway, somewhere I can get peace." Her voice was slow, American and to Robin entirely charming; although he did not know it belonged to the Deep South. "Well, I suppose I must eat something." She was turning away.

But Lucy Hamont detained her. "Oh, Denise. This young man is the son of Lady Hayburn, a very old friend of mine. Mr. Robin Hayburn—Miss St. Roch."

57

The American now took notice of Robin for the first time. As she held out her hand, it seemed to him that a shadow passed across her face and was gone.

"Mr. Hayburn comes from Scotland, like myself," Mrs. Hamont said.

"Oh." It was almost, Robin could not think why, as though this information reassured her. "It's nice to meet you, Mr. Hayburn."

"Miss St. Roch writes, Robin. You had better get to know her."

"Please, Mrs. Hamont! I've come down here to work, not to make friends. Look, he's waiting for me." She indicated a waiter who stood signing to her and, turning without ceremony, she went.

As she crossed to her allotted place, many eyes turned to follow the progress of this young woman with her strange elegance and her vivid looks.

IV

Whether Lucy Hamont's life had been a success or a failure, depended entirely on how you liked to look at it.

If taking flight without sanction from her father's farm—if spending several years of poverty and study and thereafter enjoying a good working career in music with all its anxieties and interests—if making a late marriage with a wealthy and elderly cosmopolitan banker, and soon thereafter experiencing a prosperous, but rather lonely widowhood lived mostly in continental pleasure resorts, spells success, then Lucy Hamont had been successful.

If cutting herself off from her own people and closing the door to all prospects of becoming a settled and diligent Ayrshire farmer's wife, as her only sister had done—if becoming a rather rootless citizen of the world, comfort-loving and possessing few illusions, spells failure, then Lucy Hamont had failed.

She had few friends, although she had many acquaintances. Her first overbold escape to London had perhaps left its marks upon her spirit. And even now, at the age of fifty-three, rich, and with the struggle comfortably behind her, Lucy was still almost too fit to look after herself, almost too well able to appear what she chose to appear, almost too quick to discover motives in others.

She was not a passionate woman, and thus her life had not been a series of foolish, time-wasting mistakes. She was well aware of this, and was a little proud of it; failing to see that her art, which for so many years she had served faithfully and with diligence, might have been finer if she had possessed more fire and sensibility to give it.

This morning she was thinking of many things as she sat on her sunny balcony, a rug about her knees, taking coffee. The meeting with Phœbe Moorhouse—Lady Hayburn, she must now remember—and that attractive boy, had been stirring up all kinds of memories and self-examinations. No. She had not, on the whole, been plagued by strong feelings. She had liked her elderly husband well enough and respected him. Yet, strangely, it had been a Moorhouse, an uncle of that boy she supposed, who had come nearest to being—who most certainly could have been the love of her life.

This morning the strong February sunshine, streaming down on white villas and high protecting cliffs, was beating back the alpine winter from this hothouse made by nature. Date-palms that had no right to be in Europe, stood basking just beyond her balcony in the morning stillness. A gardener in a green apron was watering pots of cactus and prickly pear set along the wall of the front garden.

Yes. She must ask Robin about his Uncle David Moorhouse. It had happened on one of the few visits she had paid to Scotland after it had ceased to be her home. But it had all come to nothing. David had already engaged himself to marry money and she, Lucy, had been determined not to force an elopement. She was not, after all, without a conscience. Besides

59

it had been a test of David's strength. And David had failed. He had played for safety. He was a Moorhouse.

She bent forward, put her elbows on the little table, held her cup in both hands and stared before her. The strong light made her frown, but there was, too, perhaps, another reason. Moorhouses. She ought never to have let herself be hurt by David Moorhouse. To Lucy Hamont the artist they were everything that was smug, self-important, provincial and philistine. Indeed, now that she thought of it, why on earth had she bothered to speak to Phœbe Moorhouse yesterday?

The sunshine was making a rim of diamonds on the absurdly blue sea. Over there, the long breakwater with its little beacon tower at the end stood back against the sun. A white steam yacht had just weighed anchor and, turning out of the harbour, was making in the direction of Monte Carlo. Sailors in white duck were polishing the deck brasses. Someone's cook, coming from the market, was walking along the promenade there beyond the garden, borne down by a great basket containing early vegetables, yellow mimosa and a live hen.

Lucy set down her coffee-cup and smiled to herself. Why should she bother with these old memories? What had that more than twenty-year-old story to do with her now?

Chapter Six

ROBIN came downstairs that morning in high feather. He did not quite know why. There was no particular reason for it except that his age was twenty, that, unaccountably, he was feeling better than he had done for many weeks, that he had made two charming friends at dinner last night, and that here, in this beautiful place, he was free, with no one to say him nay, whatever he might choose to do.

Robin's curiosity was lively. His perceptions were quick. Thus on this, his first sojourn abroad, it was not surprising that his response to what he found around him, so much of it beautiful, should be continual and stimulating.

The sense of being alone, of being his own master, of being somehow at one with this crisp, dazzling brightness, of being a young gentleman staying in a Riviera hotel—a character in a fashionable novel—lifted up his spirits.

The hotel cat, a black Persian, was sitting polishing his ears on one of the little garden tables laid ready with coffee-cups for those who cared to have their breakfast out here in the sunshine.

"Good morning, Grimaldi," Robin said, running his hand over the velvet head. "Did you ask permission to sit up there?"

But the cat, interrupting its toilet, merely sat blinking yellow slits in the strong light and waving its black, feathery tail.

"I beg your pardon." Robin shook it by one fore-paw. "I forgot you were a French cat."

At this the cat, whose days of kittenhood were not yet in the far distance, leapt from the table, scrabbled halfway up the trunk of a palm-tree and turned to look down at him mischievously.

"No, Grimaldi! Don't ask me to play with you this morning.

I've got other things to think about." Robin turned, and, quitting the hotel garden, stood at its entrance for a moment, deciding which way to take.

He looked across at the piled-up houses of the old town. He could see windows and balconies that seemed as inaccessible from here as caves high up on the face of a precipice. Yet heads appeared at these windows, and whole families could be seen out on these balconies. How did they get there? He must find out.

Now he was walking up a back road looking into steep hillside gardens or down upon the roofs of buildings he already knew. Presently he had passed under the remains of an old town gateway and was in the Rue Longue, the main street of the little mediæval town of Mentone. Here, as he had hoped, was the access to these houses he had been looking at from shore level. Dark stairs led up from the narrow street to rooms that must be lit by these high windows, that must have access to these hanging balconies. On the other side, stone staircases, some of them named streets, led steeply up through arches to yet more stairs and yet higher houses. The place was a warren, a hillside labyrinth, built at a time when the peoples of this coast must crowd together for safety.

Robin's curiosity had eyes for everything. The shafts of morning sunshine, striking narrowly down between high buildings, and through chance openings, robbed these old conglomerate buildings of any feeling of slumdom or menace. He had seen the overcrowded quarters of his own Glasgow. And he sensed the difference. Here, the native population had long since learnt the art of living close-packed together.

The narrow street was cheerful with the noise and motion of any southern town. On a stool placed at random on the cobblestones a woman sat cutting up vegetables for the pot, while she gossiped with her neighbours. Young children crawled near her. In a doorway a young man, dark and aquiline as the god Pan, squatted on his haunches plaiting a basket. He wore a coarse linen cap pushed to an angle on his

62

black, thick curls. An old woman sat on the first steps of an ascending street, making up little bunches from the violets she had bought early this morning in the market, and was now getting ready to re-sell to visitors down in the modern town. A peasant went by leading a mule. In one of its panniers was a wooden chair while in the other crouched a tiny brown boy. A carnation and a twig of mimosa decorated the animal's halter. In a little den of a shop Robin could see garlic heads, wine, oil, long, strange sausages and ropes of macaroni. In another an old man sat fashioning rope soles.

All these sights, common enough to those who know the Middle Sea, were new to Robin. He took them in and savoured them.

II

Presently coming to a staircase, he glanced upwards. He could see a window at the top of the first flight. Curiosity got the better of him. If he went up there, would he not have a view over the whole of the Bay of Garavan? Would he not, indeed, be looking from one of these very windows that seemed so inaccessible from below? Turning, he climbed the stairs. He had guessed rightly. He stood now looking down upon the little harbour, the bay with its promenade and, in the middle distance, the garden of his own hotel.

He was busy picking out familiar landmarks, pleased at having got himself there, when he heard steps descending, then was surprised to hear himself addressed.

"You're not the young man I saw in the hotel, are you?"

He turned. The American of last night was coming down towards him. She was the last person he would have expected to find on this old staircase. Then a scrap of her talk with Mrs. Hamont came back to him. She hoped to find a place in the old town to work, she had said. This was a pleasant encounter.

63

"Good morning!" he called to her. "Looking for your studio?"

"How do you know I'm looking for a studio?"

"Because I heard you say so."

"Oh, well, I am. And there's one up there I want to have a look at. But I can't get in. I think they've given me the wrong key."

"Let's see it."

She held out a key, so large and old that it might have belonged to the gates of an ancient city. "Oh, it's a handsome key, all right. There's no mistake about its handsomeness," she said drily. "But it doesn't seem to do what keys are meant to do. I'll have to go back down town, I suppose, and see the agent," she added ruefully. "You're not looking for a studio, too, are you?"

"No. I came up here just to look out of this window."

"It's a grand view, if you feel like looking at it."

The head with its short curls and its Greek profile was now beside him on the landing. For the first time in his life, Robin felt sharply the nearness of a beautiful woman. "Look here. Let me go up and try," he said.

"That's very nice of you. But I haven't much hope. Still, a man's always a man when it comes to things like locks and bicycles and sewing-machines. It's right at the top, if you don't mind." She followed Robin.

At the top there was an open landing. The walls here had been newly coated with whitewash, and a door, old and solid, was newly painted bright blue.

"Well, there it is!" she said, looking at her companion.

"I'll try in a moment, when I get my breath."

"Of course." There was an alarmed, questioning look.

And then, quite suddenly, a smile of understanding sympathy broke over her face.

To Robin, to whom it was directed for the first time, Denise's smile conveyed a world of tenderness. It was, in its way, quite breathtaking. Friends of longer standing and less

64

impressionable, perhaps, knowing it well, had been heard to say that, yes, Denise St. Roch's smile was, of course, quite a smile, but that she was born lucky, that her face just did that. But to the young man it was a mystery and a wonder. And this time, indeed, the friends' implications would have been wrong; for the impulse behind this smile had the kindness it implied.

"I'll see what can be done," Robin said, glad now to bend down and hide his boyish confusion. For a time he wrestled. But presently it struck him that if he did not try to thrust the key as far as it would go, but drew it back a little, seeking to turn it as he withdrew it, then it might find its groove. He was right. Almost at once the key found its place, and the old lock, recently oiled, turned easily.

"Good! Didn't I say it took a man to do these things?" She followed him into the empty room he had just thrown open.

It was a large room, bare and whitewashed, with a stove in one corner. It had been several rooms in earlier days. But now that good rents were to be had from foreign artists, someone had thrown these smaller rooms together to make a large studio. Lesser rooms, deep cupboards almost, led from it. And there was running water. But the glory of the place was the long window at one end, a window that could be thrown open to give access to a long balcony.

"Oh! Come and look at this!" She had thrown the glass door open and was out on the balcony, hanging over and looking at the harbour and the bay below them. "Isn't it wonderful?"

Down there, the Quai Bonaparte with its crowded life of fisher-folk, artisans and visitors. The plane trees that bordered it on the seaward side waved in the sunlight. An open carriage was passing. From here they could see the glossy backs of the horses, the top of the driver's silk hat and two coloured parasols. They could look down upon the decks of the yachts and the fishing-boats in the harbour. And farther over, the magnificence of the green mountain slopes and the high, grey cliffs that stand between France and Italy.

Robin was uplifted by his adventure. He had eyes for everything. "And now," he asked, "what about your neighbours?"

Tall houses stood encrusted irregularly against the hill, even as this one was. They could look down on jutting roofs and other balconies. One or two of these balconies had shrubs and garden chairs; used, perhaps, by unconventional foreigners or artists. But most of them had clothes hanging out to dry, crawling children, and kitchen tables.

"Fun, isn't it?" Denise turned to him.

"Renting this?"

"Oh, I think so! Wouldn't you? It won't need much furnishing."

Robin's enthusiasm was certain it would not.

III

As they went from the balcony to look once more at the studio room, a sudden draught of wind slammed the main door shut.

Denise turned to Robin. "Hullo! Got our key, I hope?"

"No. I left it on the outside. But the door won't have locked itself." He crossed to examine it. "It has! We're locked in!" he said, with a sheepish grin. "What can we do now?"

"I really don't know."

It was a new experience for Robin to find himself shut into an empty house—if this eyrie of a place could be called a house—with a young woman. And by no means did he dislike it. She had said last night that she had come to Mentone to work, not to meet people. But now, until they could devise a way of escape, she would have to go on meeting him!

"Well? Can't you think of anything? A clever boy like you!" There was a ring of annoyance in her laughter.

"Think of what?"

"I'm asking *you*." She went to the door and banged upon it noisily, hoping that someone lower down on the staircase might hear them. But presently, as this brought no one, she came back to Robin. "They'll find our whitened skeletons in about a month, I reckon," she said. She was hoping this young man would stop merely gaping at her and do something.

Robin took hold of himself. The situation had put him on his mettle. They had got in by his ingenuity, now they must get out. It was a real hanging balcony, he saw, supported by a bracket on the wall. "We might pitch something down," he said.

He turned back, searching everywhere. But there was nothing that could be thrown to attract the attention of those beneath them. The place had been swept bare and clean.

"There's too much noise in the street for shouting to be heard up here," he said presently. "But what about pitching down some water? We might hit one of these balconies. I'll see if there's water in the tap." Finding this was so, Robin cupped his hands, and thus, by going to and fro quickly, he was able to bring it and throw it down.

This device worked, for presently an angry woman came out upon a flat roof far below them. Signs, calls, and the glint of money in the sun, at last brought the plight of these gesticulating foreigners to her understanding.

In turn she signed that she would come up and try to release them.

"Well, that's that," Denise said. "Now I guess we'll have to wait quite a while until she finds us. What can we do? Tell each other the story of our lives?"

IV

Now, since there were no chairs, they had settled down at either end of the high balcony, sitting facing each other.

"Well?" There was a smile of amused inquiry on Robin's face.

"Well what?"

"What are we going to talk about?"

But Denise said nothing. Her mood, it seemed, had changed. Her head, shining in the sunlight, was turned now, looking down through the patterned iron balustrade at the movement on the street and in the harbour. After a time she turned back and took to examining Robin, detached and abstracted. "You look very like a young man I used to know. It gave me quite a shock when I saw you last night." She was speaking almost to herself.

To the young man at the other end of the balcony, these words held all kinds of implications. To be like a friend of Miss St. Roch! And had he merely been a friend? Or had she loved him? What was he like? Robin wished she wouldn't turn away again, but would go on talking. "Was he a great friend?" he asked.

She turned back slowly. "What? Well, I guess I thought so, anyway."

This was maddening to Robin's curiosity. His mind was full of a hundred questions. Yet he only dared to say: "And where is he now?"

But she only shrugged her shoulders and continued in her reverie, leaving Robin to watch her gloomily, assuring himself the while, that even as he felt now, so also must Tantalus have felt.

Denise was far away. Her eyes saw what was going on down there before her, but her thoughts were busy with memory.

Like many another daughter of Louisiana, Denise St Roch had been sent to finish her education in Paris. At the end of the nineteenth century it was still a point of rank among French Creoles that their children should not, when they chose to speak their ancestral language, speak it with an accent that was impure.

France had gone to the young girl's head. It was there she felt she belonged. She was clever and high-spirited; and if her New Orleans upbringing had been, in most respects,

68

traditionally French, her sense of independence, of personal freedom, had become very American; particularly after meeting other young people of her own nation in the pleasant liberty of the large American circle in Paris.

After two years in France she had gone home to New Orleans—half with reluctance, half with pleasure. Reluctance to leave Paris. Pleasure at the thought of seeing once more the handsome cousin who had been chosen by her parents as her husband. At the sight of him, after the long separation, her maturing affection had blossomed into love; the sky seemed clear and the future promised settlement and happiness. But presently she began to find out things. His ways were said to be dissipated, even in this uncensorious town. He was spending borrowed money. He was supporting a coloured girl. Down here, as Denise knew, generations of Creole girls before her had been forced to accept this treatment; but her new-found independence would not let her do so. Yet she had taken it sorely and become, in some ways, hardened.

Sitting nursing her knees on the floor of the balcony, Denise St. Roch sighed and turned again to look at this strange young man whose strong chance resemblance to the cousin she had once loved and almost married had at first startled her and even now was re-awakening disturbing memories. Yes, absurdly like. The same young handsomeness. The same dark eyes. The same hair perpetually falling over his brow. Her cousin would be different now, she supposed. He would be older, fatter perhaps. Indulgence would have had time to leave its marks upon him.

"I wonder how much longer she's going to be?" Robin said, meeting her gaze.

But Denise only smiled dreamily, shrugged once more and closed her eyes. "This sunshine makes me sleepy," she said.

Yes. It had been a life-and-death struggle to get away again. But after a sharp family battle she had been allowed to return to Paris for yet another year, to study music and to heal her wounded spirit. Her short allowance, her father hoped, would put an end to Parisian glamour. Whether it did or not, he never quite found out. For Denise refused to return home. She had found her profession, she wrote, and was able to keep herself.

Music had been merely an excuse to get away. But she was well-educated, had a sense of words and could string together situations. A meeting with an English writer of serials living in Paris gave her the answer to her problem. During their attachment he had taught her what the fiction market wanted.

And now, at the age of thirty, Denise St. Roch was a finished product. Her strange good looks made her popular, and she knew how to turn them to account, together with that soft gaiety inherited from generations of well-bred, plantation Frenchwomen, women brought up, it would seem, only to please. Yet she was a modern, living independently, industriously and well; receiving profitable sums for stories sold to America and Britain—and sometimes even to France, for she was bilingual—stories that had as high a polish and were as well-made and glossy as the paper upon which they were coming, just at that time, to be printed.

And her life had given her the materials for her purpose. If she wanted sultry backgrounds, then she was at home among the swamps and bayous, the magnolias, the live oaks and the mockingbirds of her native State. In these days the French quarter of New Orleans was under a cloud, and as a young woman of good family she had not been allowed to see much of it. But she knew it by hearsay and could use it now and then as a condiment in her literary cooking. She was familiar with the Paris of studio life, and, whatever she knew of its reality, could give it the air of gaiety her kind of stories demanded. Monte Carlo was, of course, an open book, and from the people she saw there, it was not difficult for her to imagine a brightly coloured Mayfair, although she had not, so far, bothered to cross the Channel.

The young man opposite to her was rising to his feet. "I think I hear someone at the door now," he said.

70

Half an hour later, Robin met Mrs. Hamont as, by chance, he crossed the public gardens which then only partially covered the mountain river running down to the sea through the town on the west bay. Now, as he walked with her back to lunch, his spirits had given themselves to the flowers and the sunshine. The still somewhat artificial magic of this, the least artificial of Riviera towns, had taken hold of him. His senses, quickened by this morning's adventure, were no longer muted. They were wide open. Now he felt, as, indeed, so many people from the North have felt when first they find themselves in Mediterranean lands—that, in coming here, he had, in some manner unexplained, found his way home. It was a change from the apathy of yesterday; a change he welcomed.

He was watching the construction of wooden stands in the centre of the gardens when Lucy called to him. "Hullo, Robin!"

"Good morning, Mrs. Hamont."

"What are you looking at?"

"I was wondering what they were doing."

"They're putting up these stands for the orange and lemon festival, I suppose. The peasants down here have always had some kind of festival at the lemon harvest, I'm told. The town encourages them now to amuse the visitors, of course. But it's traditional enough."

"A harvest in February, Mrs. Hamont?"

"Yes. It's difficult for a Scot to realise, isn't it?"

"I can't believe you *are* Scotch. You don't sound—"

"I'm very Scotch indeed, Robin! Quite as Scotch as you and all your Moorhouse relatives! Come back to lunch with me and I'll tell you all about myself."

Which of course Mrs. Hamont did not do. Still, it was pleasant for him to walk beside this elegant woman; to know she was a family friend, yet without any of the stuffiness of

71

such a relationship; pleasant to be encouraged to talk freely and with all a young man's artless selfishness about himself; pleasant to tell her the foolish story of Miss St. Roch and her studio.

At the door of their hotel she turned. "Robin. I've arranged to drive to Monte Carlo this afternoon. If you like to have a seat in the carriage—? I know you've been unwell, so you must be the judge. But really, it's such a beautiful day, and we can be back before sundown. I'll ask Denise to come too. She can't have settled down to work yet."

When, later, Robin tried to look back on this first drive to Monte Carlo—tried to fix detail—the memory eluded him, dissolved into sunlight and the laughter of a young woman.

In their carriage, with its trotting horses and its fringed linen sun-awning, they drove under great cliffs, through woods of low pine, passed olive-yards and orange and lemon gardens where the vivid, ripening fruit hung burning in the sunshine. Through a village where the children threw spring flowers into the carriage hoping for sous thrown back in return.

Lucy was amused to note the quick friendship that had sprung up between Robin and Denise. For her American friend was, she knew, very often cool with strangers. And amused, a little, at the effect a young man seemed to have upon her. Denise seemed above herself—oddly excited, somehow.

Hearing he was new to all this, it pleased Denise to assume his extreme innocence. They were driving, she told him, through a set scene cunningly contrived to trap new-comers like himself. When they came to Monte Carlo she maintained that its triumphant vulgarity was run by the devil in person. Its unnatural tidiness. Its new paint. Shops that told of foolish spending. Perfumes. Furs. Clothing. Jewellery. They had all been put there by the Lord of Darkness himself. The arsenic green of young grass, grown overnight on the lawns of the Casino gardens. The patterned beds of forced flowers, ready, at the first sign of wilting, to be taken up and replaced by others. The fountains, that were, she said, spraying real diamonds.

To the young man it was a strange afternoon of nonsense, of laughter, of—he did not yet know what else.

This friend of Mrs. Hamont's bewitched him. Now she was pointing out the mob parading in front of the Casino. Men and women of fashion from every country: French, Russian, British, Austrian, American. All of them come to pour money into this place of absurd luxury. And their hangers-on. Persuasive creatures with furtive eyes, who were ready to procure for you, legally or illegally, anything you paid for: diamonds, shady evidence, commercial beauty. Threadbare dressmakers. Prim ladies' maids. Gentlemen's servants. Young women hanging on the arms of old men. Opera-singers. Prostitutes. Placid French provincials who had come to see what this wicked Monte Carlo looked like.

The great Casino, Denise said, was the High Temple of the Fiend himself. Robin walked up the steps to have a look at him. But all he could see was the crowd milling about those who were already seated at the tables. Yet, he could almost believe that the devil was here somewhere among these tense faces; somewhere in these gilded halls, shuttered against the day, and lit, inexplicably, by oil-burning lamps.

It was cooler as they drove back after tea to the pine-woods of Cap Martin. Cooler and more peaceful, with glimpses of a green, glassy sea breathing down there among the rocks.

The others in the carriage, as it seemed to Lucy, had taken their mood from the waning afternoon.

Now Denise St. Roch talked quietly sometimes with Robin, sometimes with Lucy herself, speaking, as it seemed with longing, of her own native Louisiana, of those low, warm lands across the sea where the white people had once been as French as those here in France.

She was a moody creature, Mrs. Hamont knew. Quick in her changes. But she had never seen Denise St. Roch in this, almost homesick mood before.

Chapter Seven

BEL MOORHOUSE had always done her best to maintain a nimbus of superiority around the person of her only daughter Isabel. And this was easier, now that Isabel was safely married and in London. The distance helped. In her house in South Kensington, Bel would say, Isabel dare never for a moment think of putting up with this, that or the other, as she, her mother, had to do in Glasgow. Or, Isabel had scarcely been settled in London before she found that the costs of entertainment would have to be immense. Or again, in London people took far more care over what they wore, and thus Isabel had found herself obliged to do her utmost not to shame her husband.

All of which was another way of saying that Isabel was a perfect housekeeper, that she was triumphantly in the swim, and that she was always exquisitely dressed. Which, perhaps, did Isabel's good sense less than justice, though her mother's pride did not see it thus.

Bel's only daughter had married a young Englishman named James Ellerdale some five years ago. He had come to Glasgow in the early 'nineties to the head office of Dermott Ships in the hope of making a career for himself. Now, after nine years, he was doing so. He was in charge of the firm's London office. Jim was a young man of character, and good family—much better family than the Moorhouses. These two things delighted Jim's mother-in-law. It helped to keep the nimbus snugly tucked about Jim's wife. That he had no money behind him worried Bel very little. Isabel's husband was an Englishman, and had an Englishman's speech and manner. These were qualifications that ranked very high in the eyes of such as Bel.

To those who saw them with less bias—Jim's own friends,

for instance, or neighbours in South Kensington—young Mr. and Mrs. James Ellerdale seemed a nice, unimportant couple. He, very much like every other young Englishman of his kind; she, fair, good to look at, and possessing a not unattractive Scots voice.

But the nimbus was scarcely to be perceived on this February afternoon, as Isabel stood in her mother's drawing-room in Glasgow. Bel had persuaded her to come north for a fortnight with her three-year-old son, Lewis, writing: "Everything is so appallingly dull, with the war dragging on and with the Queen's death. Try to persuade Jim to allow you. And, of course, bring the baby with you. His grandfather wants to see him."

"Who are coming this afternoon, Mother?" Isabel asked, looking down on the fine lace, the glittering silver and the eggshell china on her mother's tea-table.

Bel hesitated. She had known very well that Isabel's twenty-seven years would find no excitement in a tea-party of middle-aged aunts. But Bel had told these aunts of their niece's arrival and had assured them that Isabel was insisting upon seeing them. A statement, let it be said, which was disbelieved by each aunt in turn.

"Oh, some of your aunts thought they might drop in," Bel said off-handedly.

"Thought, Mother? How can you read their thoughts?"

"Don't be ridiculous, dear. They *said* they thought."

"Did you invite them?"

"Well, what if I did, Isabel?"

"Oh, nothing. Only you might have said so at once."

For a moment Bel could not restrain a feeling that it was, perhaps, the idealised Isabel, safe in distant London, who was the most lovable, after all. But she continued in a voice that was sweet and full of reason. "Besides, I think you ought to see them, dear. And of course they are all dying to see Lewis."

"I wonder." Isabel gave herself a justifiable look of approval in the great drawing-room mirror, patted her fair hair and

75

smoothed her thin waist; then, turning to sniff a bowl of Roman hyacinths on a side table, looked about the handsome Victorian room. "If they are," she said at last, "it will only be to compare Lewis with their own grandchildren."

"I don't think it's very kind of you to say that, Isabel."

Isabel moved over to the window, looked across at the bare trees of the Botanic Gardens, the dull wintry lawns and the dusty shrubberies. Why did her mother so often manage to goad her into sharp words? She looked up and down the terrace, regretting her rudeness. Two figures, fat and familiar, were approaching. "There's Aunt Sophia and Aunt Mary, just getting out of a tram," she said, turning round.

Was it possible there were tears in her mother's eyes? A knife of contrition ran itself into Isabel. She must remember that Tom was in South Africa, that her mother was on edge. She went to Bel quickly. "Oh, Mother! I'm a beast!" she said, putting her arms about her. "I don't know why I talk like that! I forget you have things to worry you!"

Isabel pulled out her handkerchief and wiped the tears that now threatened to become abundant, adding: "There now. You can show off Lewis and me as much as ever you like!"

II

Mary and Sophia did not, indeed, particularly want to see Isabel and her son. They had children of their own with growing families, and they had seen Isabel often enough. But each of them, different in most ways, belonged to those who would rather be visiting than staying at home. Thus each had expressed much interest in Isabel's coming and declared that she was longing to see Bel's London grandchild.

If their hostess had been on the verge of losing her composure, neither of her sisters-in-law was aware of it, as they crossed the room to greet her.

"Bel, dear!" Sophia was saying. "And Isabel! How nice to

see you, dear! And I hear you've brought that wonderful son of yours with you! We must see him. Where is he?"

Isabel greeted her aunts and was preparing to reply that Lewis was, as one might expect, in charge of Sarah, the right-hand woman of Grosvenor Terrace, who had brought up herself and her brothers, but Sophia was going on:

"And how on earth did you manage to bring him all this way from London, poor wee man? I would have been terrified!"

"I would never have risked it," Mary said, looking at the cakes on Bel's tea-table. "We never took the children farther than Arran when they were as young as that."

Like every young woman who finds her ways with her child criticised by elderly aunts, Isabel stiffened a little. But she had promised to behave. "Oh, he was very good," she said lightly. "He slept most of the way."

"And did you keep him in bed all next day?" Mary asked.

Isabel laughed. "Oh, no! He wouldn't have stayed. He was far too excited at seeing everybody, and he was perfectly well!"

"Well, dear, you know your own child best, of course; but I know that when my children were young—"

"Did you hear that Phœbe stayed for a night with Isabel in London, then came north with her?" Bel said, coming to her daughter's rescue, while she helped Sophia out of an old and shabby sealskin jacket. An action that Sophia regretted, as the worn lining had been torn badly some days since and she had neglected to mend it.

"Phœbe? Has Phœbe come home? I didn't know," Sophia said a little flustered. And then, looking at the jacket, still dangling unnecessarily in Bel's hand. "Dear me! Is that a tear? I must mend it whenever I get home!"

"I wouldn't be too sure about leaving a young boy like Robin in a place like Mentone," Mary said. "Anne looked it up on the map for me after church on Sunday, and we found it was very near Monte Carlo."

"Well, and what about that, Aunt Mary?" Isabel asked.

"We had had a wonderful sermon on the evils of gambling, dear," Mary went on. "That's why I told Anne to look it up for me. Robin would never be in Mentone if he was my boy."

"But because he's in Mentone, that doesn't mean he spends all day at Monte Carlo gambling, Aunt Mary."

But Mary McNairn, who did not like her pronouncements to be questioned by one of the younger generation, merely drew off her gloves, pulled out the fingers sulkily and said: "That's all very well, Isabel. We just don't know."

"But how was Robin? Didn't your Aunt Phœbe tell you?" Sophia asked, pushing a strand of hair beneath her hat, folding her jacket to conceal the lining, laying it aside and sitting down.

"Here's Phœbe to tell you herself," Bel said, turning to greet her youngest sister-in-law.

"Robin's all right." Phœbe had overheard Sophia. She submitted to be kissed by Bel, nodded to her sisters and her niece, then, crossing to the fire, bared her hands, and, slumping down on the rug with the suppleness of a young girl, held them to the blaze to warm them.

"Does he like Mentone, Phœbe dear?" Sophia asked conversationally.

"It's not a question of *like*, Sophia. It's a question of his health."

"And what does he do with his time?" Mary asked. There was meaning in her voice.

Phœbe, her face turned to the fire, shrugged her shoulders. "He's got to rest a good deal, of course. And he promised to try to find someone who would teach him French."

"Aunt Mary's terrified he gambles away all his money at Monte Carlo," Isabel couldn't help saying.

"He's got no money to gamble," Phœbe said, without turning. Then suddenly she swung round, her face glowing from the heat, and sat looking at her sisters. "By the way, just as I was leaving Mentone, do you know who spoke to me? Do you remember Lucy Rennie?"

"Of course, Phœbe dear," Sophia said.

78

"That's the girl from Greenhead that ran away with a man and turned into a platform singer," Mary said evenly.

"Oh, we never knew it *was* a man she ran away with, Mary," Sophia interposed generously.

"Yes, it was a man. What else would it be?" Mary's voice was final and complacent.

"You remember her, Bel, don't you?"

Bel remembered Lucy Rennie very well. She could have told them things about Lucy Rennie that none of them knew. How their brother, David Moorhouse, had been dangerously attracted to her on the eve of his marriage to Grace Dermott. But all Bel now said was: "Yes, Phœbe, she sang in this room once, for some charity. You must all remember that too."

"What is she doing now, Phœbe dear?" Sophie asked.

"She's a widow."

"Wealthy?" Mary asked.

"She looked wealthy."

"Is she staying down there?"

"I think so, Mary."

"Did she meet Robin?"

"Yes. Why?"

"Aunt Mary's frightened a woman like that may take him to gamble at Monte Carlo," Isabel said, laughing.

"It's all very well to laugh. But I never thought much of Lucy Rennie," Mary said, now settling back in placid anticipation as Sarah arrived bearing a teapot of glittering silver.

"Oh, by the way, Phœbe dear," Sophia said, as she took a cup from Bel's hand and gave it to Phœbe, who still sat on the bearskin rug, "just this morning, while William was reading his paper at breakfast, he saw that Henry's mother's—that's old Mrs. Hayburn's—house in Dowanhill is being advertised for sale again by the people who bought it from the Hayburn boys after she died."

Phœbe said nothing. Sophia's words had called up memories. At that time the world had seemed to crumble all about the raw young man who now was Sir Henry Hayburn. Henry

and she had come a long way since then; and some of the
coming had been painful.

"Why don't you get Uncle Henry to buy it back, Aunt
Phœbe?" Isabel asked.

Phœbe came out of her reverie. "We're all right where we
are. We don't want to make any change."

"But it's a beautiful house, Phœbe dear! And Henry must
surely have some feeling for it," Sophia said. "Besides, now
that you are Sir Henry and Lady Hayburn, don't you think it
would be just—?"

"No, I don't, Sophia."

"But in Henry's position, Phœbe dear! Oh, I know you're
always just the same old sixpences! That's what's so nice! But
all the same, you'll have more entertaining to do, and it's
such a lovely big house! And besides, as I was just saying to
William this morning—"

III

Phœbe walked back to Partickhill muffled in her furs and
ruminating gloomily. She went by Dowanhill to have a look
at the house Sophia had been chattering about. She stood at
the entrance gate looking at it for a moment. It was a great,
spreading Victorian villa, with a large garden. She remembered
how once, as a young girl, she had paid a formal call with Bel
upon the old dragon who was Henry's mother. That was the
only time she had been inside. This house had no place in her
affections. She had seldom heard Henry mention it. But still—

In the early twilight, Phœbe pushed on, head down against
the chill, dusty wind.

If she had been the mother of a family, as now, at forty,
she might have been—a family that could have filled this house
and made it cheerful. Then, perhaps. She thought of the only
child she had borne: a child that had not come into the world
alive. Her own son would have been twenty-one now.

A man was lighting the street-lamps, thrusting his long lighter expertly at one gas-jet after the other, igniting each quickly and hurrying on. It was not yet dark enough for these lights to be effective. Their burning points seemed only to increase the greyness of the waning day.

There was Robin, of course. Henry had many plans for Robin. But who, in these days, would dare to look into Robin's future, except Robin's father?

Now Phœbe wondered what it was that had thrown her into this mood of gloom. She knew better, she told herself, than let herself be annoyed by Sophia's talk; or Mary's smug and ridiculous notion that Robin must be going to the bad on the Riviera. Was it a stray pang of jealousy over Isabel's successful maternity? Was it a sudden, unnamed anxiety for the young man she had left waving to her as the train moved from the Garavan Station?

But here at last she was home. She hurried up the gravel walk towards her front door, bent forward in a final battle with the wind, then took her key from her muff and let herself in.

Her husband had come back before her. He had just taken off his tweed cape, and stood warming himself by his study fire.

"Hullo, Phœbe. It's bitter outside."

"Yes."

"Where have you been?"

"Bel's."

"What were you doing there?"

"Seeing Isabel and her baby."

It was a trivial enough conversation, but during it he had taken off her outdoor coat, helped her to throw aside her hat, and now she stood, her husband's arm about her waist, dishevelled but warm, looking into the yellow flames.

Phœbe felt her mood soften. Here, beside Henry, was where she belonged. As she looked up at him, her strange eyes caught the firelight. He bent down and kissed her. She was pleased, yet something in her forced her to say: "Feeling sentimental?"

81

"Why not?"

"Oh. No reason."

"Were you in a bad temper when you came in?" Henry asked.

"I was."

"I thought so." Then, without pursuing this: "There's a letter from Robin. He seems all right. He's been for a drive to Monte Carlo with a woman who says she's an old friend of your family. Rennie, or something, her name was. What are you laughing at?"

"Nothing much. I had better tell Mary, that's all."

"I don't see what Mary has to do with it. Does she think he'll take to gambling?"

"Exactly. And Sophia thinks we should buy your mother's old house. That it's 'more like our position'." Here Phœbe mimicked, a little, her sister's chattering eagerness.

She was surprised to find that Henry did not reply to this at once. They continued to stand together looking into the fire. At last he spoke.

"So the old house is for sale?"

"Sophia says so."

"Well, you can tell Sophia from me that when I do move I'll go to a better house than that. Why should your brothers be in fine country places and not me—if I have the money to take me? And haven't I got a son to come after me?"

Phœbe could only turn towards her husband in amazement. This was a new Henry.

"Henry, do you mean that?"

"Why shouldn't I mean it?"

"I don't know. It's just not like you. We've been very happy here."

He disengaged his arm and flung himself into a chair.

"And what's to keep us from being happy in a new place too?" he asked.

Chapter Eight

ROBIN was dressing at his leisure, having drunk his morning coffee in his room. It was just after ten, and another silver morning. Outside, almost touching the iron rail of his balcony, a palm-tree stood motionless, its young fronds made luminous by the morning sun shining through them. Beyond, where leafy gaps allowed, he could see the absurdly blue sea.

Bred as he had been in a land of mists and sombre, if perhaps more subtle colours, Robin's eyes took quick delight in this, the brilliance of the south. It was all so new, so uplifting. And this morning the world seemed particularly bright. He moved about his room humming snatches of a tune the band had played at tea yesterday in Monte Carlo.

Yes. She was wonderful, Miss St. Roch. The most wonderful person he had ever met! And her wit was tremendous! Of course, it would have to be. She was a writer; and writers had to be witty.

Mrs. Hamont was charming too. Like a pleasant aunt or something. And how lucky she had known Miss St. Roch!

He was standing, brushes in hand, giving a final lick to his lank, dark hair, when there was a burst of loud barking, accompanied by wild snarls.

Robin went to his balcony. Over there, safe from harm on the branch of an umbrella pine, was his friend Grimaldi, the black cat, mocking at a giant wolfhound that was leaping and snapping in an ecstasy of fury. Worn out by this, the great beast at last gave up and sat back silently on his haunches, his tongue out and his body quivering, now contenting himself with staring up at his tormentor, hoping, perhaps, that Grimaldi's nerve might, in the end, fail him and that he might be hypnotised into coming down to be torn to pieces.

"Grimaldi, I'm ashamed of you!" Robin shouted.

At this Grimaldi got up, shook his full coat and, arching his tail, walked with care along the branch in Robin's direction. "No," Robin went on. "Don't you try to jump from there to here. It's too far. And if you fall, well!"

But Grimaldi had no idea of doing anything of the sort. He had achieved his purpose, since, once again, the handsome animal beneath, maddened by seeing him move, was leaping and gnashing his teeth in a useless attempt to reach him. This Grimaldi appeared to find amusing.

"Paul Morphy, what's all this about? Hold your tongue!" Robin was surprised to see Miss St. Roch come out into the garden, fearlessly seize hold of the great creature's collar, attach a chain to it, and drag him away from the tree. "What do you see up there, anyway?" Looking up herself, she saw Robin.

"Good morning!" he called. "It's only the hotel cat. Aren't you frightened of being swallowed whole by that beast?"

"Don't be silly! Paul Morphy's a grand boy! I bought him last year—just a grey, woolly baby he was—from an old shepherd up there in Alsace. I'm taking him to the studio to show him where he's got to live now."

"I'll come with you."

"I've got to go to the agency first and say I'm taking the place."

"All right. I'm going into town."

She had not meant to make this quick friendship, Denise reflected, as, a few minutes later, she found herself walking with Robin. She had left Paris, indeed, to escape her friends. And now, within a day of her arrival almost, here was a young man who had attached himself to her and seemed to think he had every right to do so. And what was worse, he knew her hiding-place up there among the old houses.

And yet for some reason she did not resent him. Why? He was quick, gentle and gay. Was it that? Or was it because of his close likeness to the man she had once hoped to marry? Was he stirring her memory pleasantly?

"I say, is this awfully pushing of me?" Robin was saying, as though in answer to her thinking.

"Is what pushing?"

"Forcing myself on you like this."

"You won't force yourself on me, young man, if I don't want you."

Robin laughed. "How do you know?"

"You'll find out if you try."

Robin thought about this for a time, looking about him as he went. A steam yacht in the harbour. A couple of English girls on mules. A new-fangled French automobile. A horse char-a-banc full of trippers, driving towards Italy. "Do you want me today, then?" he asked at length.

"Well, I don't seem to have sent you away. Do I, Robin?"

"That's the first time you've called me Robin, Denise!"

She was surprised at his pleasure.

II

About a week later, Robin was hanging over his balcony once more. He was sucking the end of the pen he had taken up to write a letter home. Had he been told that he was waiting to shout goodbye to Denise, who was going to Nice for the day, he would have denied it. But this was just what he was doing. She had shopping to do, she had told him, and a friend to visit. Now, boyishly, he was hating the thought of her absence even for so short a time.

He had just passed a week of enchantment, helping her to put her studio into order. He was filled with amazement at Denise's cleverness. She had managed to rent chairs, tables, and Heaven knew what else. It had been great fun; for whatever Denise did had, somehow, the cheerful, improvised air of a picnic.

Now all was ready, and Denise, after her day in Nice, would leave the hotel, move into her new quarters and settle to work. It was pure romance for Robin to think of her writing up there alone, hour after hour, in those queer, high surroundings. He would have given the world to be able to do the same. And yet, so far, he had been reluctant to tell her of his own ambition to write. He did not know why. Especially as he hadn't much minded telling Mrs. Hamont about it. But his reluctance was to be dispersed.

As he had expected, Denise now came out through the garden on her way to the railway station.

He called: "Good morning!"

"Oh, hullo! Is that you up there, Robin? Good morning!"

"I only wanted to tell you that I would fetch Paul Morphy today, and take him for a walk."

"Oh, thanks." Denise found difficulty in restraining a laugh. He looked so like the little boy who is left at home. "You look very—well what? Thoughtful, this morning. What are you doing with that pen? Going to write a novel?"

"Would you like me to write you a short story?" he asked, grinning.

"I don't believe you could."

"I've tried before, you know."

"Have you? You never told me."

"What will you give me if I do?"

"I don't know. Tell you if it's any good, maybe."

"All right, then. You'll see."

"Good. Well, goodbye." She went away. And presently, in her hurry, she had forgotten all about it.

But Robin had not. He had turned back into his room and was pacing up and down in a sudden frenzy of plot hunting.

Now he had an idea. Yesterday, Denise and he had gone to the Casino for tea. He had watched an odd couple sitting near them: a richly dressed woman having tea with a threadbare, faded little creature. And yet the rich woman had allowed the poor one to pay; scarcely thanking her.

86

And the poor one had seemed to expect to do it. He had drawn Denise's attention. But she had not been particularly interested. Yet here, surely, must lie an interesting tangle of motives.

Now Robin worked out the situation as he guessed it, invented an ending and sat down in triumph to write. But it was not easy. He was unpractised and, despite his excitement, words refused to obey him.

But he continued the fight all day. Writing and rewriting. Trying it this way and that. He was exhilarated, exhausted and engrossed. So engrossed, indeed, that for most of the time he had forgotten Denise and why he had undertaken to do this.

She reappeared at dinner. "Well, Robin," she said, "you're looking wild a bit. What have you been doing?"

He was surprised at her question. Didn't she remember? "Writing that story I promised you, of course."

"Oh? You wrote it? Have you got it?"

"No. I'm going to re-write it this evening."

"My, my! That sounds very, very serious to me!" was her comment.

III

It was some days before Robin brought Denise what he had written. Bold and cheerfully confident in most things, he was shy about this.

Denise was now in her studio in the Rue Longue. She had begun her serial story. On sunny mornings Robin could see her on her balcony high up there above the street, her fair head bent to her task, her great dog crouched beside her. Seen thus, the American woman personified the very world, the very way of life about which Robin dreamed. Young, beautiful, successful, following a trade that he himself now burned to follow. If other feelings towards her were growing out of this, his inexperience had not yet made them precise.

"How am I to know when I can come to see you?" he had asked her. "You'll always be working now—or out."

"You had better just come up and try the door."

"Why not hang out something as a sign when you *are* free?"

Denise laughed. "What? Signal to my gentlemen callers to come up and call?" But she saw this had displeased Robin, was out of key with his idea of their friendship.

And she noticed the faint flush as he replied: "That's all very well. It's quite a long way up for me, you know."

She remembered his breathlessness on that first day when they had climbed up together and he had helped her with the key. She smiled, the same irresistible smile as then. "All right, then, Robin. There's a ledge on the balcony. I'll put a pot of flowers there if I feel conversational. And I'll tell any other friends that turn up. Yes. It's quite a climb."

He saw that she did not want to appear to do this for himself only. But he was pleased and thanked her.

It was after that she said: "You still have your story to show me."

"It's finished. When shall I bring it?"

And now he was sitting out here on her balcony, nervously fidgeting with Paul Morphy's ears, leaning over to study the street beneath him with an interest he did not feel, forever putting back his lank dark hair, and now and then casting furtive eyes at Denise, guessing where she had got to, as she turned a page.

And Denise, in turn, wondered what to say about this. It was strange to her and outside her line of sympathy. And doubly strange that a young man should be writing anything of the sort, setting down thus the feelings of two women and making a story of it. And yet, in his way, he had caught their hopes, their fears, and their hidden resentments perfectly; too cruelly, indeed. But she wished he were not there, self-conscious as a schoolboy, awaiting some kind of verdict from her.

At length she set the few sheets straight on her lap and looked at him. "Now, what put a story like that into

88

your head, Robin?" she asked.

"Why not?"

"Well, not many young men would see a subject in just two old women."

"Perhaps not. But does that matter?"

"No. Not quite. Well—not if it's interesting."

"And is it?"

Denise coloured a little. "Oh, it's well written; nothing we couldn't put straight," she said slowly. "But it's all too—I don't know—well, to me, not exciting enough. I'm being honest, you see."

"Of course."

She wished he would not be so intense. Not hang so eagerly upon her words. "Have you tried to write before? Surely this is not the first thing you've—"

"Oh, I've scribbled this and that."

"You're taking this more seriously than I thought."

"Yes."

They both fell silent for a time. The noises of the street came up to them. The cries of children. Somewhere, at an unseen window, a woman was singing a strange tuneless song, a song that had been left behind in her blood by the Saracen raiders of long ago. Presently the tune changed to one that was popular just now on the boulevards of Paris.

"Suppose you try again. Would you like to, Robin?"

"Of course, Denise."

"We'll work out a better plot for you this time."

She spoke to him as one writer to another. She took this situation and that, showing him how they might be developed, might be used with effect.

And if, sometimes, Robin found her ideas too sensational, her discussion surprisingly frank for a woman, yet it was all part of a new excitement, a new enchantment.

Down there, in the bay, the sea sparkled. White yachts moved in the harbour. A breeze ruffled the olive yards on the far off hillsides.

Flattered and engrossed, Robin Hayburn told himself that now, surely, he was in touch with the life for which he was intended.

IV

The sun was shining, but it was a day that called forth effort. Lucy Hamont, wrapped in a long coat of white tweed, was forcing herself, head down, against a sharp breeze that might almost be called a gale. She was on the promenade of the west bay of Mentone, taking her morning walk.

Little painted, argonaut waves of blue and green that broke into neat curls of foam covered the sea. Palms in nearby gardens and here on the Promenade Du Midi itself danced hither and thither, tossing up their silver undersides to the wind. The white February sunshine, hard and unrelenting, held no warmth.

Presently Lucy became aware that someone was calling to her. She looked up to find Denise St. Roch, dragged along by her wolfhound, coming towards her.

"Hullo, Denise! Where have you come from? I thought you worked at this time of day." Clutching the skip of her white pancake hat—which threatened to come adrift despite yards of veil—Lucy held out the other hand.

"I felt wooden-headed this morning, so I thought I had better come down and have a walk." Denise wore a scarf about her curled head, her honey-coloured skin was glowing and her smile showed a mouth full of dazzling teeth. Today there seemed nothing of the Frenchwoman about her. Her bearing was radiantly, triumphantly American.

Lucy found herself envying Denise her youth, her vitality and her looks, as she said: "You must have given our young friend a wonderful time yesterday, Denise! He was full of his visit to you at dinner. Were your ears burning?"

For a moment Denise looked at Lucy earnestly—strangely

earnestly, Lucy thought—before she said: "Was he? What did he say?"

"Oh, that there was no one like you! He's written something for you, I hear."

For reply, Denise took Lucy's arm and turned her round towards the town. "Come on in somewhere out of this wind. To Rumpelmayer's or anywhere where we can get a cup of chocolate."

"*Can* he write?" Lucy asked as, with the wind at her back, Denise's arm through her own and the great dog dragging on the lead, they were, all of them, scarves and veils flying, propelled towards the town.

"I don't know. Yes, I think so. He's going to do some more for me. Then I may get a better idea."

"You see, I'm specially interested," Lucy said.

"Why?"

"I'll tell you when we get inside."

Rumpelmayer's was full, noisy and redolent of French coffee beans, French perfume and French cigarettes. All the town, it seemed, felt cold and had come in to drink an eleven o'clock cup of something hot. British residents abounded; for in those days Mentone was more than half British. English cathedral town spinsters in cotton gloves. Rich provincial dowagers with villas for the winter. Italians, the women heavy with furs, the men gold-ringed and possessive. Parisian women, stiffly corseted, heavy-featured, and fashionable. A family of Middle West Americans, the parents rich and homely, beaming on their young people, and all of them enjoying the lark of being in this Europe that was so sure of itself. A few cosmo-politans, well dressed, distinguished, and of a nationality it was impossible to determine. Overindulged children, running out of control, and threatening to entangle themselves with the waitresses wheeling cake-trolleys or balancing steaming trays.

At last they had found a place, given their order, tied the great dog to the iron centre leg of the marble table, and now they could settle down.

91

"Do you like Robin Hayburn?" Lucy asked, as it seemed irrelevantly, looking at her friend.

"Yes. Very much. Why?" Denise smiled a little as she returned the intent look.

"You see, in a way, I belong to the same solemn Scotch background as he does," Lucy said. "Not a type that breeds artists."

"No, I daresay not."

"And yet I ran away from home to become a singer."

Why was Mrs. Hamont saying this, Denise wondered? "Well, I didn't run away," she said. "But I stayed away, which came to much the same thing."

Her companion pulled off her gloves, looking abstractedly at the people about her as she did so. "I paid for it, in a way. But I did what I wanted to do."

Her friend smiled. She said: "Sometimes paying is worth it."

After a time Lucy came back to earth. "Denise, I'll tell you something," she said. "I nearly married that boy's uncle! Queer to think, isn't it?"

"Well, why didn't you?"

Lucy shrugged. "The Moorhouses—his name was Moorhouse—all made money. And turned so appallingly respectable and self-important that they would never have put up with a gipsy like me."

"So you liked him, but couldn't stand his people? Was that it?"

"Well, that's—I don't know—yes, that's about as real a reason as any. Shall I pour out this, Denise?"

"Yes, please. But you still feel sore about it sometimes?"

Again Lucy shrugged. "I'm a fool to feel anything."

"But maybe you wouldn't mind seeing that boy getting a little education just to annoy them? Is that what you're getting at, Mrs. Hamont?"

Lucy Hamont looked up from the cup she was tasting. "Well, shaped to another pattern in spite of them, shall we say? How delicious hot chocolate can be on a cold morning!" she added smiling.

Chapter Nine

PHŒBE HAYBURN had been bewildered by her husband. That Henry should, as it now seemed to her, suddenly want to blossom before the world, giving himself the importance of a country house; that he should want to become a social somebody, was incomprehensible to her. The Henry she knew wore old clothes, had the habit of wanting meals at any odd moment, and thought of nothing but his work.

Yet, had Phœbe been a different kind of woman, she would have understood that her husband, like many another brilliant man, moved along the single track of his brilliance.

And for Henry, the track of his brilliance had run straight, ever since he had refounded his father's firm of Hayburn and Company, and given to it all the forces he possessed. Hayburn and Company had grown steadily, and Henry's sense of achievement had grown with it. For years it had been quite enough that he should count more and more in the world of Glasgow engineering, to which his every fibre belonged.

But now the track had run farther. It had borne him out into the wider world of recognition, where men of achievement were given honours, irrespective of what that achievement might be. He had become Sir Henry Hayburn, and he felt that he must live according to his label. Social advancement, for its own sake, or the wish for a more distinguished way of life, had, for Henry, almost nothing to do with it.

Like most one-track people, Henry had no difficulty in believing what he wanted to believe. He was one of those who are accustomed to getting their own way. And such people are seldom inconvenienced by imaginations that illumine the points of view of others.

Thus, to Henry's thinking, a frame for the importance to

which he had just climbed was not only right, but quite necessary. And if Phœbe did not, at first, see this, she would, of course, quickly come to see it.

And now, practical in all things, he had begun to consider what steps he should take. The two people closest to him, after his wife and son, were his brother Stephen and his brother-in-law David Moorhouse. Again he determined to consult them. Stephen, as Henry saw him, went everywhere and knew everything. And David lived in surroundings such as Henry now sought for himself, and must, surely, have much to tell him that would be useful.

So it came about that, on a bright Saturday morning of early March, Henry asked his telephone clerk to get him Mr. David Moorhouse at Dermott Ships. Presently word came back that Mr. Moorhouse did not usually come into work on Saturday mornings. Well, then, Sir Henry's brother, Mr. Stephen Hayburn? No. Mr. Stephen Hayburn had not found it necessary to come in this morning either.

It was a part of Henry's simplicity that he found nothing to criticise in this. He had always looked up to Stephen and David, and what they did must, automatically, be right. "Well, get Mr. Moorhouse at Aucheneame House."

David received Henry's telephone call in his dressing-room, where he was having a late breakfast. "What? Coming down in that motor-car of yours with Phœbe for tea? Yes. We will be delighted to see you both. Yes. And you can look in on Stephen and bring him with you. No. I haven't been at the office for a day or two. Influenza. But it's very cold weather for that open shandrydan of yours. What? Oh, all right. Have it your own way. We'll be glad to see you however you like to come."

At lunch-time Henry told his wife of his intention. "I want to ask David about this house business."

Again Phœbe showed surprise, for he had said nothing more of houses after his one outburst that evening. "House, Henry?" she asked. "What house?"

94

"I told you I wanted a country house two or three weeks since," he said, a note of impatience in his voice—impatience born of the knowledge that he might in the end have to be firm about this.

Phœbe did not reply. She sat looking before her, eating her chop mechanically and pondering. "What we want before a house or anything else," she said at last, her eyes fixed on vacancy, "is to have Robin home and well again."

"I don't see what that has got to do with it."

"It has everything to do with it for me. And for you, too."

"Robin's going to be all right," Henry said sulkily.

And now, for reasons he could not himself define, Henry became possessed of a smouldering determination to force this. Force the buying of a country property. Force fate. Force himself to expel the fear from his mind that Robin might not live to inherit it. Force Robin, once returned, to follow the track that he, his father, had laid down for him. Force him to take his place as the son of Sir Henry Hayburn.

In the dark places of his mind—less confident places—these things had somehow become entangled each with the other.

II

Mrs. Robert Dermott, taking advantage of an unusual burst of March sunshine, sat in front of Aucheneame House, Dumbartonshire, a large, still somewhat raw-looking mansion, that her dead husband, Robert Dermott, the founder of Dermott Ships, had built forty years ago.

Judging that here it would be sheltered, the strong-minded old woman had marched out from the lunch-table before her daughter, Grace Dermott-Moorhouse, could stop her.

Fumbling in her black velvet handbag for her long-distance spectacles, she found them, put them on, shaded her eyes with one hand and sat looking about her. She was still a large woman, still firm of face and purpose. She was glad to be out here alone for a moment, glad to have the sunshine of the early year penetrate her bones, glad to sit and remember.

From Aucheneame the ground sloped gently to the River Clyde less than a quarter of a mile away. Immediately in front of her was a wide lawn terminating at a wall and dotted here and there with low, trimmed shrubbery. Below that, a long field, at the foot of which were the main road and the railway track running close together. And beyond these came the sand-flats or the shallow waters of the river itself, depending upon whether the tide was out or in.

It was in now, and the great steamers that had been lying waiting in deep water at the Tail of the Bank farther down were now moving upstream towards Glasgow.

"Granny, what are you doing out here? You'll catch cold. Come in at once!" Her grand-daughter, Meg Dermott-Moorhouse, a long-legged girl of fifteen, stood in front of her.

Mrs. Dermott did not remove the hand that was shading her eyes; she merely said: "Meg, come and sit down beside me, and tell me if any of these boats belong to us."

"What? To Dermott Ships?"

"Of course. What else do you think I meant?"

Meg sat down as she was told and examined the markings of a vessel as it moved down there in front of them. "No, that's not ours," she said. "But, wait—there's something coming down. Yes, that's a Dermott boat."

"I wonder where it's going."

"China, probably. I was in the office for a minute yesterday, and I heard someone say on the telephone that there would be a sailing for China at the weekend."

Mrs. Dermott smiled approval, her eyes still on the great cargo-steamer as it churned its way down the muddy channel. Yes. Meg was Robert Dermott's grand-daughter. Pity she wasn't a boy. She was alert, and would have done well in business.

Sparrows were noisy in the shrubbery. In the field beyond the wall the farmer, anxious to push on, Saturday afternoon or no Saturday afternoon, was diligently guiding his plough behind two great brown horses. White, complaining seagulls skimmed the clear March air behind him, watching the new-turned furrows. Black rooks, settling at a greater distance, pranced importantly on the fresh earth, croaking and quarrelling over the worms they found there.

"Granny, do you think Father would let me go into Dermott Ships?" Meg said, as though she had guessed something of what her grandmother was thinking.

Mrs. Dermott took off her spectacles, turned to her grand-daughter, looked at her seriously and said: "No, I do not! What makes you ask such a thing?"

"I don't know. I wish I had been the boy, instead of Dave."

Her grandmother put on her spectacles again, looked ahead of her, and fell to considering this. Meg was right, of course. Her twenty-one-year-old brother, Robert David Dermott-Moorhouse, was a handsome, misty, indefinite creature. "Well," she said at length, "we can't change that, can we?"

"I don't want to be polished and finished and dressed-up and married off to some stupid young man!"

"My dear child!" the old woman exclaimed, turning once more. "Who's been talking to you? What on earth have you been reading? And who's going to force you to marry anybody, stupid or clever?"

"You can say what you like, but that's what happens among our kind of people. And I don't see much fun in it." Meg kicked the gravel beneath her gloomily.

"Nonsense! You'll have great fun! I had a splendid life of it running committees and helping your grandfather, and watching him building up Dermott Ships step by step." But still, the old woman was pleased with her grand-daughter.

"That's all very well, Granny. Times are changing."

"They're not going to be any more difficult. They're going to be easier."

"How do you know?"

97

Old Mrs. Dermott took to looking about her yet again. Yes. The child was right. Times were changing. The pace kept on getting quicker. Even the face of this quiet valley kept changing. Down there, beyond the road, they were building a row of workmen's cottages. Her husband had always been sympathetic about workers' conditions. But in his time there would have been ways and means of stopping what must inevitably become a blemish on the view from Aucheneame House here. And farther down the road, but still within sight, someone was building a shed where, they said, you would be able to get your motor-car mended and buy the oil or whatever it was that made it go.

She was deep in memories, thinking of the time when, long years since, she and Robert Dermott had driven down thus far and chosen the site of this house as a place that could never possibly be desecrated, where the city would never reach them, when she was roused by her grand-daughter saying: "What I really need is a college education."

But there was no time to pursue this, for there was the tooting of a horn, a cloud of dust in the drive, and Sir Henry Hayburn, with his wife and his brother, had come to a standstill in front of Aucheneame.

III

A motor run was an elaborate business. Most people felt compelled to dress for it. Even for the short distance of ten miles or thereabouts, Stephen wore sporting clothes consisting of knickerbockers and a Norfolk jacket, and over these a long and heavy leather overcoat. On his head was a leather cap, and he wore goggles. Phœbe, too, was clothed to the ground in leather, and wore a leather pancake on her head, which was held in position by a thick veil, tied beneath her chin and so fixed that her face and hair were covered, thus protecting her entire head from the dust and the March winds. She could safely have opened a hive of bees in this headdress. Henry alone of the three remained much as usual: clad in his old Inverness and his tweed helmet. He had omitted to wear goggles, and, as a result, there were traces of dusty tears upon his cheeks.

The noise of their arrival brought Grace Dermott-Moorhouse out to meet them. "Hullo!" she called, waving and laughing. People still laughed, a little, at the idea of their friends arriving in a motor-car. "Here you are, all you brave people! You must be perished with cold! Come in and get warm at once." And while the party began to disentangle itself from the rugs and to climb down: "Mother, what are you doing out here? Do you want to get pneumonia?"

Old Mrs. Dermott made no reply to this. But she got up and prepared herself to greet the guests and go inside with them.

"David has had a shocking cold. Influenza, really. I don't know what to do with him," Grace continued, apologising thus for the fact that her husband was not here on the doorstep like herself. She kissed Phœbe as best she could through the veil, and led the party indoors.

"You'll find David in his smoke-room," she said to the men. "He asked me to send you to him."

Henry and Stephen found themselves with David in his snuggery. Like most of the rooms in Aucheneame, it was in the worst possible taste. White pine, stuffy, tasselled hangings, and in the one window a palm in a brass pot standing on a cane table. The room of a Victorian Glasgow grandee. Old Robert Dermott had built a large house to add cubits to his dignity, then, seeing the walls up, had, it seemed, let it go at that, handing the interior over to commercial decorators. And neither his daughter nor his son-in-law possessed urge or knowledge to improve upon what had been done.

But though most of the Aucheneame rooms were large and cold, this one was small and stuffy. The master of the house rose from a green plush chair. David wore a black velvet smoking-jacket with quilted facings. His visitors guessed he had been asleep.

"Hullo," he said, looking for once a little dishevelled. "Come and sit down. There's time for a smoke before tea. Cigar?"

Stephen chose the deep chair opposite to the one David had sunk back into, leaving Sir Henry Hayburn bolt upright on a small chair between them. It was nothing to either of them that Henry's dignity had grown in the eyes of the world. Thus they were surprised when presently he said:

"I want to buy a house. I mean, a place like this with some style to it. And I thought I would like to get your opinion."

David sat nodding wisely. He felt that this activity would give him time to think over Henry's words. Well, of course, there was no reason why Henry should not get himself a country house. He could afford it, David supposed. But what good would it do him? Henry and his family weren't the people for this kind of thing. Their lives seemed, somehow, one continual picnic, a continual improvisation. Henry thought about nothing but his work. He had never held a gun, never sat a horse—so far as David knew—and would never bother to take his proper social place in whatever surroundings he found himself. Phœbe was all impulse, and Robin bookish and arty.

"What does Phœbe think?" he asked, thus to avoid, still longer, the bother of giving his opinion.

"Oh, Phœbe—I don't know. She'll get used to the idea." Henry looked at Stephen.

Stephen's thoughts had been much like David's. There was, of course, nothing against Henry getting himself into more imposing surroundings. Still, he too could not help feeling how unsuitable the notion was. Could it be possible that Henry was becoming ambitious? Stephen was as much surprised as Phœbe had been. And really, how much better he, Stephen, could have managed everything. He could have filled a large house with people who were at the same time the right ones

100

and amusing, given pleasant weekend parties and been adored by his gardeners.

But like David, Stephen also temporised. "I would think about it, Henry, before I did anything rash," he said. "Have you got anywhere in mind?"

"No. Nowhere special. I thought David could tell me something about upkeep and that sort of thing."

"Hullo, Uncle David! I've come down to see how your cold is! And to get your signature on one or two papers. Polly's next door with the ladies." Wil Butter had burst in upon him, virile, uncomfortable and full to excess of boisterous good humour.

David coughed a little to show his younger partner that he must really expect nothing of his frail condition. "Come and sit down, Wil," he said feebly. "Glad to see you. How did you get here?"

"Train, of course. We walked up from the station."

IV

"And how have things been at the office?" David asked. Not because he wanted, or, indeed needed to know, since both of them were well aware that the affairs of Dermott Ships went forward upon their prosperous way whether David was sitting in the Chairman's room or whether he was not. It was of much more moment that Wil Butter should be on the spot to keep all the whips cracking. Still, David felt the question was expected of him.

"Oh, all right. Business a bit slow, but that'll mend. I'll show you this week's figures. I've brought them. And by the way, I've been reading the riot act among some of these young clerks at the office, you will be glad to hear. Too much monkeying and not enough work!"

David smothered a sigh. Must he look at figures on a Saturday afternoon? And with this cold hanging about him?

101

But he must not be so foolish as to discourage Wil's zeal. For he well knew that the more his nephew worked the less he, himself, need trouble. Wil was, indeed, David's sure shield against personal effort. The enduring of a pinprick or two was a low price to pay for his nephew's assiduity. "I'll be glad to go through these figures with you after tea, Wil," he said, assuming what he felt to be the right expression of seriousness; and adding: "And I'm glad you've been pulling up the clerks. I must say I did feel there was a certain slackness. I had meant to speak myself."

Wil smiled, taking David's comments for exactly what they were worth. He turned to his other uncle. "And how is Sir Henry?" he asked genially.

"All right, thanks."

"Lady Hayburn with you?"

"Yes. Your Aunt Phœbe is here."

The three older men, each in his separate way, felt the vulgarity of Wil's questions.

"Your Uncle Henry is thinking of a country place," David said, as coldly as he dared.

"Good, Uncle Henry! Where?"

"I haven't thought yet."

"But you just feel you should be cutting a dash somewhere, is that it?"

"It's not a question of cutting dashes," Henry began uncomfortably. "It's just that—"

"Your Uncle Henry is thinking about his position," David interposed.

"Time he had a dignified home." Stephen spoke for the first time since Wil's arrival. Wil paid no attention to him.

"Well, you know, there comes a time—" David was beginning unctuously, but just then there was a welcome tinkle outside the door. David jumped up. "Hullo! Tea! Come along, everybody." He was delighted to seek refuge from Wil's gaucheness, even in a drawing-room full of women relatives.

"Wil! Wil, come here, dear." Polly Butter, a plump, chattering little thing of twenty-six, sought to make herself heard above the general noise of teacups, greetings and invitations to sit here and there. "Wil," she said when at length he stood beside her. "Here's Aunt Phœbe. She's just been telling me about Mentone."

"Hullo, Aunt Phœbe. Back safe? How's Robin?"

"And she says, Wil, that it's just like midsummer. Fancy! Blue sea and sunshine and flowers and everything! We must go some time."

Wil received his wife's enthusiasm with a husband's calmness. "I don't know how you're going to do that, old lady, with a boy of six and a girl of four."

"Oh, I don't mean now. I mean—"

"Talking about the Riviera, Grace," Mrs. Dermott said, turning to her daughter at the tea-table. "Why don't you and David take a run down there this Spring? It would do David all the good in the world."

Grace, having poured tea for everyone, sat back and looked at her mother. "But how can I? What about Easter? I've promised Dave he can bring some young men from Cambridge."

"Nonsense. You can put them off."

Grace looked round the company of relatives seated in her large, ugly drawing-room, made sure that everyone was supplied, and smiled an indulgent, apologetic smile at her mother's ageing foolishness. "Darling," she said, "I can't break promises. But you're right about David. I wish he would go somewhere for a change! He hasn't really been well since Christmas."

Much to the surprise of everybody, Wil Butter picked up the thread. "Yes, Uncle David. Why don't you go off for a month and take someone with you?"

"But how—?"

"Oh, the office will struggle along without you. I'll be there."

David did not quite like this. He knew very well how faint the struggle at the office would be.

"Go on!" Wil was insisting. "Go on; and if Aunt Grace can't go, take Stephen Hayburn."

"What? Both of us away from the office at once?" Stephen asked. The idea, nevertheless, enchanted him.

Wil did not even bother to notice this. He turned to his hostess. "Well? What do you say, Aunt Grace?"

"If it could be managed—" Grace said, smiling.

"Of course it could be managed!"

"I believe you just want to get rid of two old fogies!" David's smile began to widen at the thought of himself and his crony Stephen on a bachelor holiday.

Wil grinned genially, thinking how very right his uncle was, gulped down his tea and held out his cup for more. "Why not fix it here and now?"

"You had better choose Mentone, then, and see how the boy is doing," Henry said.

"Mentone, then?" Wil asked. "Is that fixed?"

David turned to his wife. "What do you say, Grace?"

"Of course, dear. It was my suggestion."

"And you'll come, Stephen, as my guest?"

"Well, it's very kind, if—"

It pleased Wil, to be giving this exhibition of decisiveness. This was how he managed Uncle David at the office. "That's that, then. And there's no more to be said."

Chapter Ten

"LOOK, Denise!"

"Wonderful, isn't it?"

Denise and Robin were sitting on mule-back high above Mentone. They had come up by the cobbled track that leads to the old hill town of Castellar, then continues over a gap in the lofty mountain wall down into the first valley of Italy. A track which, though it looks nothing, has played some part in European history.

They had stopped on the hill above the cemetery to allow their animals to breathe. Here the way runs level, giving sweeping views of the bay of Garavan and the mountains.

And on this afternoon of March it was indeed beautiful. Far down there beneath them, the bay, placid and blue, lay, closely ringed about by white villas. Other houses, more scattered, stood embedded in the woods of the lower hillside. Higher, the silver-green of the olive tree, the richer greens of the orange and the lemon; next came the steeply ascending terraces of vines, of vegetables, of spring flowers. Still higher, the weathered limestone rocks sparsely covered with heath and thorn; and above all of these, the massive precipices, grey and towering, their edges hard and broken cutting into the blue of the clear springtime sky.

"Glad I dragged you away for the afternoon?"

Denise smiled in reply. She had come to a halt in her work, and was glad to fall in with Robin's proposal that they should hire mules and ride to Castellar for tea. Yes. It was pleasant up here with the perfume of narcissi heavy in her nostrils and all the glory of the Riviera spring about her. "Ready to go on?" she asked after a moment, turning her mule's head and letting Robin follow along the stony path.

Why had this excitable young Scotsman attached himself to her? Denise found herself wondering, as her animal ambled along, taking its own time. Robin's enthusiasm for herself was so young, so callow, so unselfconscious and, if you really thought about it, so silly. The enthusiasm of a spoilt boy. But not of a stupid boy. Nor yet of a dull boy. Yes. Bright was the word for him; bright and quick. He would snatch your thoughts from you and throw them back embroidered with his own kind of fantasy. That was it. Robin amused her, kept her alert and stimulated.

Swaying easily to the sure-footed steps of her grey mount as it picked its way by the side of vineyards and through groves of gnarled olive-trees, Denise, with her monk's cassock and close-curled head, was looking more like a young saint in a church window than ever. A shining, mediæval boy who had, in his high spirits, jumped up on this dull, docile beast, and was riding it sideways because he could not be bothered to turn and sit properly astride.

Was Robin in love with her? It was hard to believe that this unbridled gaiety was love. Robin was more likely to be in love with what she stood for—or what he imagined she stood for. He wanted to be a writer like herself. To know such people as she knew. To live what seemed to him a life of easy freedom. Well, perhaps he might, although Denise could scarcely think so. Unless, of course, he had enough money to publish his own books and wait. Then, in time maybe, those light, oddly original stories that, somehow, he always managed to write no matter what they had first decided upon together, might find him admirers and earn him some repute.

Now once more the track went upwards. Now they were leaving behind them the young vines and the terraced beds of flowers. Now, up here in the wild thickets of the hillside, violets and anemones grew as they best could among the tangle of heath and arbutus, of dwarf juniper, of rosemary and myrtle. Now, for a time, they must give all their thought to guiding their mules among these steep ascending rocks, to

106

clinging to the creatures' backs, to avoiding the low branches that overhung their way. But presently the track was running level once again upon a high, forgotten terrace overgrown with little twisted mountain pines.

"They climb like cats, these beasts!" Robin called to her.

She stopped and looked back at him. His thin, handsome face was flushed by the hazards of the climb. His collar was open, and the loose black bow he now wore as a neck-tie had become undone. The inevitable strand of hair hung over one eye.

The picture Robin made for her troubled Denise's senses. Did it stir memory? Provoke old feelings? Was she touched, maternally perhaps, by the young man's aspect, youthful and gallant, and yet at the same time frail?

"Are you all right?" she asked.

"Yes. Of course. Why? Do I look queer?"

"No. Tie your tie." The famous smile was sympathetic and quizzical.

Was she, then, on her side, in love with Robin? Denise wondered. Well—? But not in a way that need worry either of them. Just enough to heighten her pleasure in this odd and sudden friendship; to give her patience when Robin burst in upon her while she was hard at work—a thing she would not tolerate from others—burst in, disregarding the agreed sign of the flowerpot on the balcony, to jabber excitedly about a new idea of his own. She had lectured him about this. Yet she did not really mind.

"You know, Denise, I think it would be better if I made Maurice a clerk in, say, some office, instead of a fiddler in an orchestra," he said now, as he came to a halt beside her.

"Can you think of nothing but your stories? Even up here?"

"Well? Why not?" Robin had the one track mind of his father. "But don't you see? It would make Maurice much dimmer. More true to life. Less arty and picturesque."

"Well, try him that way if you feel like it. But not too *dim*, please! We'd better go on." As she went, Denise sat brooding over Robin and this obsession of his. Now, why did he, so vivid, so vibrant himself, continually choose the half-tones in his work, always seek to avoid what was exciting and immediately effective? If he were going to do anything he must change this odd bias. The public bought bright colours and strong situations. "I'm going to show one of your stories to a man I know in Paris," she called back moodily. "He'll put you and your dim stories in their proper place! He's been reared in the business."

"Right. I can stand it. Which story do you think?" But just then they had rounded a bend and Robin shouted: "Look! There's Castellar now! What a wonderful place!"

There, across a deep valley perched stark and remote upon its hill of ancient olive trees, the little town stood high and aloof, its brown crumbling walls and red roofs weathered by the years.

"There are plenty of hill towns like that around here," Denise answered.

"Still, you can't say that one doesn't look like a bit of history!"

"Oh, it's romantic enough, Robin. Captive Saracen maidens, and all the rest of it. Now it looks as if we've got to go round this way," she added, moving forward once more.

II

Lucy Hamont sat finishing her meal. She felt at a loose end tonight. The professional teacher from whom she and two more were to have learnt some of the finer points in the new game of Bridge had sent word he could not come. The message had arrived too late to allow Lucy to arrange other distraction for herself.

"What has happened to Mr. Hayburn?" she asked of her friend the head waiter as he passed her table. "He doesn't usually go out for dinner. Is he ill?"

108

The waiter replied that he had heard nothing, and that there had been no order to send anything to Mr. Hayburn's room.

Lucy sat back looking about her idly. She rotated the stem of her wine-glass, ruminating. Robin was in her mind. And Denise St. Roch. Their friendship seemed to be growing fast. And Lucy did not now quite like it. She was not sure why.

But there he was, crossing the emptying dining-room, hurrying in as others were leaving, embarrassed at being so late for the *table d'hôte*.

Lucy was surprised at her own feelings of relief. Why, after all, should she worry about Robin Hayburn? "Hullo! There you are! I was just wondering what had happened to you!"

The young man sat down and accepted with apologetic thanks the plate of soup that was set before him with more speed than ceremony. "I've been with Denise to Castellar for tea."

"To Castellar? And how did you get up there?"

"We hired mules."

"I thought you had been out in the sun."

He put a hand to a tingling cheek. "Yes. I was. It was wonderful! Like midsummer. What a strange old place it is!"

"Don't overdo!"

"Don't you worry, Mrs. Hamont. I'm having a tremendous time!"

And indeed he seemed to be. His eyes were bright, and all of him seemed to have become much more alive in the last weeks. Lucy sat watching him. A vague smile remained on her face, a friendly mask behind which she could think. "I'll drink coffee here at the table," she said to the waiter, who had come to remove Robin's plate. "I want to talk to Mr. Hayburn." Then turning to Robin she went on: "Well, I must say you don't look particularly homesick." She spoke the words lightly, but they were sent up as a kite.

The kite took the wind as she intended. "Well? Would you be?"

"What do you mean, Robin?"

109

"I've always wanted to have artists as my friends. I've wanted to create something. I've always wanted to—I don't know— Oh, you must see what I mean, Mrs. Hamont."

Lucy saw perfectly. But she decided to say: "Yes, I think perhaps I do."

"Oh, but you *must*! We both come from much the same stuffy background! You must have felt the same thing!"

"Yes, I do understand, I suppose." Lucy sat pondering. She did not bother to cast her mind back into her own past. She was done with that. And for some reason, this boy's present engrossed her. But what, particularly, was he finding in Denise that seemed to him so exhilarating?

"And now I'm getting so much from Denise St. Roch; and from you!" Robin went on.

"Oh! My dear boy!" Lucy laughed. But she was touched. "And what on earth can *I* have to give you?"

"Sympathy. Freedom to speak about what really interests me! Understanding!"

Lucy determined to be crisp. "Rubbish, Robin! Didn't you have every freedom to talk at home? Surely you did! An only son!"

Robin's face darkened. "No! Of course, Mother—no. She doesn't really understand me, either."

From which Lucy gathered that in the boy's opinion, at least, Father's understanding fell far short even of Mother's. But Robin had better learn to understand others. Not to count on others understanding him. She would continue to be crisp. "And what wonderful things are you learning from Denise?"

"Oh, quite practical things! At the moment, as you know, it's the short story. She thinks I'm doing better. Now she's making me read Maupassant to study the shape and so on. And it's very good for my French."

"I'm sure it is!" Lucy might have laughed, openly and mockingly this time. But she only smiled, anxious neither to appear to despise his new-found interest, nor to turn his

110

confidences from herself. She took a sip of coffee, then went on: "It may surprise you to know," she said, "that I'm worrying about you, a little, young man. Promise me you won't exhaust yourself."

"With what?"

"Well—long excursions like today's. Exciting new friendships. New discoveries, perhaps. Too much mental stimulation, shall we say?"

"My dear Mrs. Hamont! I'm feeling splendid. And I'm awfully happy. In fact I don't think I've ever been so happy before."

III

Her talk with Robin had left Lucy restless. And now, the night being fine, she had put on her furs, looped up her long dress, come out of doors and was walking on the promenade by Garavan Bay.

It was a night of strong moonshine. Out there she could see every elegant curve of a great white yacht as it lay in the trembling black and silver of the harbour. The light blinked steadily at the end of the breakwater, and she could now see townspeople moving here and there along it, dark shapes, darkly discernible against the deep, luminous blue of the sky. At times, when there was quiet for a moment, a girl's laughter crossed the water to her.

Lucy folded her arms beneath the furs that wrapped her, and strolled along thinking. What was Robin Hayburn to herself, or she to Robin? And yet he filled her mind tonight. Denise St. Roch had, she could see, captivated the young man. Whether by intent or not, Lucy did not know. Standing still for a moment, she bent over the railings of the promenade, looked at the dark water running in and out among the stones down there beneath her, and fell to considering this. But wasn't that just what she had wanted? Hadn't she caused these two

111

to meet? And hadn't she done so in the best of good faith, because she had thought Denise would amuse him, and give his exile some interest? What was wrong with that? And further, hadn't she suggested to the American that Robin Hayburn might need some educating, some shaking out of the Moorhouse pattern?

Lucy turned from the railing and continued to walk along slowly. One or two people passed her. A squat, middle-aged French couple. A young fisherman and his girl. Two Englishmen in evening clothes, elderly and fat, discussing the London Stock Market under a Mediterranean moon and leaving behind them the scent of fine cigars. Lights streamed from long windows, outlining stucco balustrades crowned with pots of aloes and cactus.

But now it looked as though something had happened to Robin. Lucy understood very well all young enthusiasm's new-discovered passion for an art. She had once felt all this herself. But with Robin there were other considerations. Was it driving him into a condition of over-sensibility? Driving him to a frenzy of effort to please his charming teacher? An effort that might defeat the purpose of his stay down here in the south? What if the boy were really falling in love with this not inexperienced woman? Moving towards an affair with her?

But why should she, Lucy Hamont, trouble about Robin Hayburn? Once again Lucy asked herself this question. She supposed she had come to like him. She understood his background, as he himself had said just now, and this, perhaps, made her feel protective towards him. But protective from what?

Somewhere far away a dog was barking. From a little wine-shop just beyond her, near where the road branches upwards from the Hanbury fountain towards the Italian frontier post, she could hear the notes of a melodeon and the voices of young men singing. Lucy stood still to listen, to let her thoughts run free for a moment, then she went slowly on.

Protect him? Why indeed should she bother? Had she not

broken away from the old conventions herself? Taken her existence into her own hands and come through, on the whole, not badly? Was she jealous of Denise? Yet how could she be? She, Lucy, was a middle-aged woman more than twice Robin's age. Or was an instinctive loyalty rearing its head? A loyalty to the people they had—or so Lucy imagined—both of them sprung from? To old ties? The old stricter ways?

She reached the fountain, decided this was far enough, and turned back. Now the ancient town was in front of her. The huddled buildings rising up on their hill and making squares, oblongs and angles of black shadow in the white moonshine, were pierced here and there by lighted windows. On the quay beneath them a chestnut-seller's brazier was burning.

She had met Denise in Paris, accepted her for what she was, and liked her very well. Denise was a free woman. Gallant in her way. Seeking support from no one, and in no need of it. Taking life as she found it; bestowing her affections as it pleased her. A hard-working craftswoman, but, it was said, no great artist. Yet she mixed freely with the species, was popular, and talked their jargon.

Was Robin worth more than that? Was there, beneath his callowness, some real spark of talent? And had he mistaken Denise's easy, sophisticated friendship for something better?

Walking faster now, Lucy Hamont told herself not to be a fool. What if he had? And really, if Denise St. Roch had decided to seduce him, what could she do about it? He was a young man, and why should a young man run away from experience? Still—

In her hotel garden she stood for a moment looking up at Robin's balcony. The glass doors were shut and the net hangings were drawn across, but a desk lamp was lit, and she could just discern a young man's head as it bent over a work-table.

IV

As she came into lunch next day, she found he was not in his usual place. He was sitting with two others. When he saw her, Robin stood up.

"Mrs. Hamont, you must remember my uncles David Moorhouse and Stephen Hayburn."

The men got to their feet.

Lucy felt her cheek flush a little as she held out her hand. "Of course I remember your Uncle David! I ought to! We were at school together. And I think perhaps I *have* met Mr. Hayburn." She saw that David's colour had risen too. "But I didn't know you were coming," she exclaimed. "Robin didn't tell me."

"They came down on a night train," he explained. "They wanted to surprise me."

His uncles smiled rather foolishly.

"But I'm keeping you from lunch," she said. "We'll see each other afterwards." She left them and crossed to her own place.

So that was David Moorhouse! After more than twenty years! She sat crumbling her bread and watching him. He was half turned away from her, thus making it possible for her to examine him.

The David Moorhouse who had, just before his marriage to Grace Dermott, told her he loved her. But David had, in the end, married Grace and the solid prosperity she brought with her. Who was she, Lucy Hamont, to say that David had been wrong—or even dishonourable? Dishonourable to herself, perhaps. Though in her own world Lucy had seen worse. Yet he had hurt her. He had touched her affections as no one else ever had. After the David incident she had become more detached, more for herself, less easily stirred.

Well, there he was, sitting across the room from her, with his years of prosperous marriage written all over him. The chestnut hair that she remembered had turned sandy, and there

114

was a thinness on the top. The old good looks were there, but he had grown thick and important.

This meeting had fussed her. But now that she was given time to look at him, Lucy was pleased to find that the sight of the middle-aged David Moorhouse left her unmoved. It would be amusing to talk to an old friend. That would be all.

He found her in the garden after lunch.

She looked up at him smiling. "Well, David? How many years is it?" She saw that he, on his side, was still somewhat embarrassed.

"Years since what?" he asked, a little foolishly.

"Since we last saw each other, of course," she said gaily.

"It must be—let me see—I have a son of nearly twenty-one. It must be over twenty-two years. A long time, Lucy."

"Is your son like you?"

"No. He's like Grace—like his mother."

"How is your wife? I saw her once. A sweet expression, I remember. Why didn't you bring her with you?"

"She couldn't get away. Busy with the family."

"What a pity!"

"She sent me off with Stephen because I had been run down."

"How unselfish of her!"

"Oh, she doesn't care much about travelling."

They had wandered down to the front and were watching the movement in the harbour.

"You don't look different, Lucy," David said, seeking, it would seem, to lift the conversation to a more personal level.

Lucy laughed. "Nonsense, David! I am an old widow woman. An old Riviera hack. Of course I look quite different!"

"You don't look different to me."

Lucy lost patience a little. "Well, you look different to me, you know. You look—what shall I say—more prosperous."

"Please! Not just that!"

She resented his foolish earnestness. "You must forgive me,

115

David," she said, "but for a long time now I've found the greatest difficulty in feeling sentimental about anyone. Even old friends."

He turned from her for a moment. His eyes followed the movement of a little sailing boat. "I was unfair to you once, Lucy," he said at last.

"Were you, David? When? I had quite forgotten."

She would have excused herself and left him; for now she was angry with this foolish emotion-mongering. But as, by chance, she looked towards the old town, she saw Robin hurrying towards it, looking very much as though he were trying to escape notice. So he was going to Denise this afternoon, too?

Now, in the face of this sticky, middle-aged sentimentality, Lucy suffered a revulsion from her feelings of last night. Let the boy go and burn himself up if he must! Anything rather than this unmanly fingering of the fringes. She turned to Robin's uncle. "But I'm delighted to see an old friend, you know, David. Shall we walk up the front for ten minutes? I don't think the sun is too hot. Look. I'll put up my parasol."

And thus they went, turning their backs on Robin, as Lucy had intended.

V

"So you know Robin?" David said as they walked together.

"Oh yes. He's an old friend of mine now."

"His lungs are threatened."

"Yes. I guessed that, David. How do you think he's looking?"

"I don't know, Lucy. Sunburnt, of course. But he looks thinner to me. Resting in his room this afternoon, he told me."

Lucy did not reply to this. She was not sure if she liked it. She wished Robin had not lied quite so flatly to his uncles and gone to Denise as to a secret assignation.

116

They walked along beneath the parasol, silent. Now, perversely, her feeling of a moment ago swung in the opposite direction. She had deliberately invited David to walk this way that Robin might escape him, and now she found herself regretting it. She almost wished his uncle had seen him.

"He's learning French, he tells me," David was saying.

"French? Oh yes. I hear he is."

"It will give him something to do."

"Yes." Then, after a moment, Lucy's change of mood prompted her to say: "He's been doing some writing, too, you know."

"Writing?"

"Yes. Short stories."

"He didn't say anything to us about that."

"I'm surprised he didn't, David. He's been working quite hard."

"Well, I suppose if it keeps him interested— He'll have better things to do when he gets home."

The artist in Lucy rose against this. "A friend of mine who is helping him tells me his work is quite good. Shall we go back? It's getting hot."

David, as he turned, wondered for a moment at the abruptness of her tone. But he continued: "Robin won't get much sympathy from Henry Hayburn about scribbling, Lucy, I do assure you."

Lucy was glad to leave him and go upstairs. Her mind was in a state of sharp irritation and confusion. She could not fix her judgments between Denise St. Roch and Robin's smug, Moorhouse uncle.

In her own room, cool behind its slatted shutters, she flung herself down on her long chair, stared at the ceiling, and called herself a vacillating fool. She wished she had never bothered to be kind to Robin Hayburn, never got to know him.

Chapter Eleven

PHŒBE folded Stephen's letter, laid it down on the lunch table, and poured herself more coffee. Having done so, she sat with the cup in both hands, elbows on the table, staring out of her dining-room window.

This year the Scottish March was mild. The buds on the trees outside were already swelling. A bush of forsythia in full bloom made a glory of yellow. Birds were noisy.

But Phœbe did not notice. Her mind was on the letter. Before he had left for Mentone, she had made Stephen promise to write of Robin's condition at once on his arrival. Now he had done so. The news of Robin was not bad. He seemed bright and in high spirits, but he looked, Stephen wrote, thinner and a little keyed-up. Two ladies, as Robin himself had probably told her, had been very kind to him, taking an interest in him and befriending him. And one of them, an American and a writer of some sort whom Stephen had not yet met, was amusing Robin by encouraging him to write. But Stephen was going to lecture him about going slow.

Stephen closed his letter with exclamations at the beauty of the French Riviera, the flowers, and the sunshine; wrote that David was much improved already, and that as for Robin, Phœbe had no reason to worry. Which, of course, caused Phœbe to worry very much.

She wished now that she need not show this letter to Robin's father. And, indeed, had she been another kind of woman, she might have burnt it, and pretended it had never come. Robin's dabbling in poetry, or whatever it was, would be a red rag to Henry. But tactful deceit was not in Phœbe's make-up. It did not for a moment occur to her that Henry need not see what his brother had written.

And yet she wished he need not. For Henry was in a remote, rather angry mood these days. Phœbe knew these moods. Of late, when her husband had something he was determined to do, he had developed a way of saying nothing whatever about it until he could announce the accomplished fact. Now she knew from his defensive silences that something was afoot. Henry had acted furtively over accepting his knighthood. She suspected he was now doing the same over the buying of a house.

She was sitting pondering the letter, drinking her coffee, and wishing that their lives might go back a year or two—that Robin was still a schoolboy, well and happy, and that Henry was merely a busy engineer—when presently she heard the sound of a motor-car coming to a standstill at the gate. A moment later her husband passed the window. It was very unusual for him to appear at this time on a weekday. She jumped to her feet and ran to meet him.

"Henry, is anything wrong?"

"Nothing."

"Well, then, what are you doing here?"

"Get your things on, Phœbe, and come with me to look at a house."

"House? What kind of house? Don't tell me you've *bought* a house, Henry, without asking me!"

"Very nearly, anyway. You'd better come and see it."

"*Have* you bought it?"

"Come and see."

"Seeing it won't tell me if you've bought it! Where is it?"

He told her it was in the Buchanan country, some miles from Loch Lomond.

Phœbe turned from her husband and walked back into her dining-room. Worry over Robin had set her temper on edge. This high-handedness had roused within her a quick fury. Now, standing in the window, she turned to face him, her colour high, her strange eyes blazing.

119

Henry followed her. She had given in so easily over the knighthood, that he had not expected this.

"Sometimes I think I've married a madman!"

"What's wrong, Phœbe?" As he watched her, his face took on a look of—what was it? Pleasure? Interest?

Whatever it was it fanned her annoyance. For she was quite unaware that standing thus with her eyes alight and her skin glowing, she had turned herself back into the beautiful, desirable young woman that Henry had married, the young woman who, all too often now, was hidden behind a mask of everyday living.

She took up his word. "Wrong? Am I never to be consulted about anything now? Moved about like a bit of furniture?"

He actually smiled.

Goaded, she thrust Stephen's letter at him. "You should be thinking about your son's health! Not about your own ridiculous ambitions!"

"I'm ambitious for him as well as for ourselves. And surely Robin is going to be all right? He won't be in France for ever, Phœbe."

She watched the cloud of doubt pass across her husband's face. Was Henry pleading with her? Now his eyes were on the words of Stephen's letter, but she saw they did not take them in. Now, looking up again, they held the old hurt look she knew so well. And now suddenly, his trouble kindled her senses, even as her anger kindled his.

Here before her was the man she would never be able to withstand, and Phœbe knew it.

"Oh, Henry!" She threw herself at him. There was so much she wanted to say; to protect him from himself; to teach him not to be so sure about this boy who meant so much to him; to show him, however dimly, that he, Robin's father, might one day have to be strong. Or had Henry already become fearful? And was he arguing with his fears? Passionately, Phœbe blamed herself for being tongue-tied. Now she could seek only to show him by the fierceness of her hold how

120

close she felt to both of them—how much they mattered to her.

He kissed her and put her slowly from him. Stephen's letter had fallen down unheeded.

"Are you coming with me, then?" he asked.

"Yes, I'll come."

II

And then, in just such time as it took for a lady to get herself into a leather dust-coat, a leather hat, and a veil; such time as it took for a man to turn the starting-handle of a motor-car, assure himself that the engine was running, jump up and take the steering-bar, Sir Henry and Lady Hayburn were off.

Quickly they made their way out of Partickhill, along Hyndland Drive, and thus into the farther, rural part of Great Western Road, passing Balgray Farm and the boating pond, and heading for Anniesland, where the long, straight road then terminated, splitting up into country lanes. They followed the narrow road to the humpbacked Canal Bridge at Temple, made for the toll-house of Canniesburn, ran through Bearsden, and were out into the glory of open country that lies to the west of Glasgow.

It was a sunlit day, of white, piled-up clouds floating high in a sky of clear blue: clouds that cast patches of shadow on rolling upland fields, pasture or purple-brown where they had been fresh-turned by the plough. To the left against the sun, the dark slopes of the Kilpatrick Hills. To the right, open country and woodlands, and beyond these, and mottled by the clouds, the long line of Campsie Fells, the first of the northern ranges, covered by the rough grass that makes them look, on such a laughing day of the early year, as though their flanks were clothed in rich green velvet.

They ran along the winding, narrow road, raising the dust behind them. Farm-boys, drowsing in carts, came to life, jumped from their seats, went to the heads of their horses, then looked back angrily at this new-fangled thing that passed them by. A high-stepping young pony from a nearby mansion-house reared up on its hind legs, threatening to break the slender shafts of the governess cart to which it was harnessed.

Larks were singing. Everywhere by the roadsides, on the moors, by little streams, against the grey stone dykes, the flowering gorse was a triumph of yellow. Over there the birch-woods were still bare, but now there was a purple haze over them, purple from the buds full of rising sap that would presently burst and put forth the young green. Here and there, as they passed under high trees, nesting rooks flapped and squabbled in the branches.

Phœbe could not have told why she had thus suddenly given way to Henry, suddenly allowed her anger to be drained out of her. On every count he had been unreasonable over this matter of a house. Was she not to be its mistress? Would she not spend more of her time there than he would? And yet now, as she sat beside him, she did not seek to press the question he had left unanswered.

She was instinctive rather than reasonable towards her own. And she became bewildered when her two men, her husband and the young man who was to all intents her son, pulled in opposite directions. But today Henry had pulled her towards himself, and for the time, at least, she felt content that it should be so.

"Have you seen this house, Henry?" she asked him as the car ran on.

"Of course."

"When?"

"Yesterday."

Now the road was rising, now passing among trees, now running up through a cutting. Suddenly they were on the hilltop.

"Henry, stop! You *must* stop!"

"Stop? Why?"

"We must look at this!"

And indeed there was much to look at. Loch Lomond, Ben Lomond—the Ben, as Glasgow people call their mountain—and beyond these the mountains of the Western Highlands lay before them, sharply cut from the bright March air. The upper cone of the Ben and the summits of more distant mountains were still white with snow. Lower slopes were brown with dead heather or yellow with the winter bracken. And nearer, beyond these moors from which the winding road would presently take them, was the fertile Buchanan country, with its white farmsteads, a mansion house or two standing among the trees, then, at a greater distance, the young woodlands stretching down to the shores of Loch Lomond itself, a sheet of bright water scattered with shaggy islands.

"It's beautiful!" she said.

"You've seen it before."

"Of course. But never quite like this."

Henry let the car run forward on the incline.

"The house is just there, near the bottom of the hill," he said.

III

A day of colour and emotion. And so Phœbe was to remember it. The blue of the sky. The gleaming whiteness of the high clouds. The yellow gorse. And this sudden, renewed uprush of feeling for the impetuous, difficult man who was her husband. An uprush that had nothing of reason about it—was it not, indeed, born of Phœbe's anger and Henry's wilfulness?—unless it were the reason that these two were still, after many years, of one flesh; still able, on such rare days as this, to strike the fire of passion, each from the other.

Phœbe sat in the window of her drawing-room in Partickhill

watching the early spring evening die over there in the distance beyond the river, beyond the high cranes of the shipyard, beyond the Renfrew hills.

Henry's long legs were stretched out before him as he lolled by the fireside. The reading lamp on a side-table was already lit. Some journal, arrived by post that evening, lay across his knee. He had not yet, however, broken the wrapper. It was unusual for him thus to sit relaxed and desultory of an evening. But for Henry, too, this day had not been as other days. He must remain near Phœbe.

They were a strange couple, this. Both of them quick; neither of them stupid in the things of every day; passionate, but still, in the language of passion, strangely inarticulate. And yet, stirred by today's happenings, they felt compelled to grope, each towards the other.

"So you're to have a new house, Phœbe?" He held the journal in its wrapper between his face and the fire.

"Well, you've arranged that, haven't you?" But her voice was gentle and warm.

"You liked it?"

"I thought the country out there was beautiful this afternoon."

"But you liked the house, too?"

"Yes. I liked it very well. You can afford to keep it up, can't you? And Bel and everybody else keeps dinning into me that we must live up to our position now. I suppose living at Whins of Endrick would be doing that?"

Her husband did not reply to this at once.

She looked across to the distant hills and the cold, dying sunset. Yes. The property of Whins of Endrick was a pleasant place. Again to herself, she pictured the mid-Victorian, merchant Gothic house standing among green lawns and birch-trees. It was a place of little distinction, perhaps, but the picture pleased Phœbe very well. Yet it seemed a large, lonely place, for herself and Henry. Could she, a woman, ever learn to drive a motor-car? she wondered.

124

"Of course we can keep it up. I wouldn't be such a fool as to take it if we couldn't do that."

"And your work?"

"The car. It means breakfast sooner, that's all."

Phœbe turned from the window and looked about her. Here was her home. Leaving this house would cost her something. It was her young marriage. Robin's boyhood. But now, in her gentler mood, she chid herself for wasting feeling over bricks and mortar.

"When Robin comes home and is back in the yard he can stay in lodgings if it's too much for him to travel," her husband said.

She came over to him. "Oh, Henry, do you think Robin will ever be able to stand your kind of work now?"

For a moment, Henry seemed to harden. "He's got to. He can't throw away everything I'm building up for him."

"Building up for *him*? Aren't you building it up for yourself?—No, dear! I didn't mean that!" Tonight she could not bear to let the different, softer Henry escape her. "I know exactly what you mean. But surely you see that Robin may never be—well, just very strong."

"Other young men have been ill and got better, Phœbe."

She knelt down on the hearthrug before him, putting her hands on his knees. "Oh, of course, he's going to get better. We mustn't expect anything else, must we?"

"No." He was looking gloomily past her into the fire. "He'll have to. He's all we've got."

Phœbe leant forward looking up into her husband's face. Its trouble was lit up by the firelight. What was he thinking? He looked almost angry now, defensive. It seemed to her as though he were inwardly arguing with himself, arguing with his fears. He had conquered so much in his life. Was it impossible for him to grasp the chance of defeat now? What if Robin became well enough only to remain abroad? How would Henry take that? But she would not look into the future. If she must be torn between the two of them, father and son, it must not be tonight. Tonight she belonged to Robin's father.

Still kneeling, she straightened herself in front of him. "Everything's going to be all right, Henry," she said.

He bent forward, drew her to him, and hid his face in her breast.

Chapter Twelve

THE day following these happenings was to be Isabel
Ellerdale's last day in Grosvenor Terrace. Tomorrow
morning's train was to take her, together with her son Lewis,
home to South Kensington.

Bel's feelings were mixed. She had, of course, told everyone
how wonderful it had been to have her daughter with her
again, even for a short two weeks; and little Lewis was a
cherub. But cherubs, Bel found, especially when they had
missed the benefit of faultless training at the hands of their
grandmothers, tended to be noisy and destructive, and could
make their grandparents feel the weight of those advancing
years. And so, perhaps, it was better that Lewis and Isabel
should withdraw once more into the golden distance; thus
allowing Bel to boast of the high mettle of her grandson and
the distinction of his young mother, without exhaustion and
at peace.

And yet on this last day the drag upon Bel's affection was
real enough. For still, her daughter, crisp and critical, and her
grandson, young and barbarian, were of her own flesh, and
the sight of their preparations for the return journey to London
somehow depressed her.

She was not particularly pleased, therefore, to have Sarah
come to her as she sat watching Isabel pack, and to be told
that Mrs. Butter, young Mrs. Butter and young Mrs. Butter's
little boy awaited their pleasure in the parlour downstairs.
The ladies descended with reluctance to be met by a gust of
greeting from Sophia.

"Bel, dear! We just flew in for a minute to say goodbye to
Isabel! It's tomorrow you go, isn't it, Isabel dear? And here's
wee Billy." She indicated her grandson, an open-mouthed child

127

rendered expressionless by a threat of adenoids. "His Granny promised to take him to see the plant that eats flies in the big hothouses in the Botanic Gardens. Didn't she, dearie?"

The expressionless child said nothing.

"And do you know, Auntie Bel, we were busy tickling it with a bit of grass, just to see if it would snap shut, and we thought maybe it was going to, but a gardener came and told us not to touch the exhibits. Wasn't it a shame? Well, we'll just have to try another day, won't we, dearie? So then Billy said he would like to visit wee Lewis before he went back to London, and we just ran across to see if you were in!"

Bel could not believe that this emotionless child had expressed a desire to see either the fly-eating plant or his little second cousin, whom he had never seen before; but she pulled the bell to summon Sarah, and upon her appearing asked her to bring Lewis down.

"And d'you think Billy could have a wee biscuit, Bel dear?" Sophia went on before Sarah had time to go "No, thanks. We don't want tea or anything, dear."—Bel had not offered it— "But it's just that I'm sure he's hungry, with his walk in the garden. Aren't you, Billy?"

The expressionless child standing at his mother, Polly Butter's knee, answered with a firm "yes".

"And how is your husband, Polly?" Bel said, sitting down and assuming a manner that was, she hoped, just sufficiently gracious and yet regal enough to impose decorum upon this altogether too familiar gathering.

"Wil's just the same old sixpence, isn't he, Polly dear?" Sophia interposed, but Bel determinedly kept her head turned towards Wil's wife, paying a disciplinary inattention to Wil's mother. Polly, grasping her intent, blushed apologetically all over her round, plump face, and hastened to make conversation demurely. "Well, yes, he is very busy, Auntie Bel, thank you."

Bel, confused now by her determination to be dignified,

128

was not quite clear why she should be thanked for Wil's busyness; but Polly was going on.

"You see, with Uncle David in France, and everything."

"Of course."

"He had a letter from Uncle David yesterday. He's feeling much better. Isn't it nice?"

This was so guilelessly said, that Bel, in whose mind less amiable thoughts were perhaps hovering, could only—avoiding her daughter Isabel's eye—indicate that a weight had indeed been lifted from her mind.

At this moment Sarah reappeared with Lewis and a plate of biscuits. The little boy, having himself paid no attention to an offer of a biscuit, planted himself without saying a word in front of his elder cousin and remained thus, his small hands behind his back, watching Billy's untidily open mouth as it chewed; only now and then withdrawing his stare to follow the descent of the crumbs that kept falling on the carpet.

"Aren't they just lovely together!" Sophia exclaimed.

Bel and Isabel smiled mistily. Each of them thinking how much superior in every way little Lewis Ellerdale was to little William Butter.

"Mentone must be a lovely place," Polly resumed, guessing perhaps that the beauty of Mentone was a safer topic than the beauty of grandsons. "Uncle David enclosed a postcard in his letter just to show us."

"I have always heard it was, Polly," Isabel hastened to say, since she saw that her mother did not just then look like responding.

"Wil is missing his Uncle David terribly at the office, isn't he, Polly dear?" Sophia said.

"I've never really heard him say so, Aunt Sophia. And after all, it was Wil who thought Uncle David should go."

"Well, Polly dear, he said he was missing him to me!"

As nobody believed this, there was a pause.

"Has he seen Lucy Rennie, I wonder?" Sophia tried again.

"I've no idea," Bel said.

Sophia said no more. Now she gave herself over to watching the children with foolishness and fondness.

Bel watched them, too, but without bringing much of either of these qualities to her watching.

Billy had finished his biscuit, and as nothing more looked like happening, Polly rose to put an end to a call which she had felt from the moment of Sophia's suggesting it, would prove cool and fruitless.

II

And, indeed, Sophia's visit, along with her grandson and his mother, had done little to decrease Bel's feelings of depression. Her mood seized on all of them, now that they were gone, and judged them more harshly than she would, in a brighter and more generous moment, have ever dreamt of doing. But today she hated the thought of Sophia's foolish good nature. She hated the thought of Polly's smug young wifehood. She hated the thought of Polly's husband, Wil Butter, with his cleverness and push. She hated that Wil was becoming more and more a force among the Moorhouses, and that he did not bother to hide his disregard for the opinions of the older family. And now Wil had actually taken upon himself to advise his Uncle David to have a holiday! Bel even hated the thought of little Billy Butter, for eating his biscuit untidily and dropping so many crumbs on the parlour carpet.

"Who on earth is this Lucy Rennie, you all keep talking about?" Isabel asked as they came back from bidding their unwanted guests goodbye at the front door.

Bel took up the parlour hearth shovel and the brush and began to sweep up Billy's crumbs from the carpet. "Oh, she's a woman your Uncle David was once in love with," she said crossly. "I dare say your Aunt Sophia would like to think he may fall in love with her again!"

"Uncle David!" Isabel went into a little peal of laughter.

130

Bel straightened herself from her sweeping and looked at her.

"How old is Uncle David, Mother?" Isabel asked.

"About my age."

"Well!"

"Well, what, Isabel?"

"How can he fall in love with anybody?"

"Why not?"

"It wouldn't be decent!"

Bel bent over her sweeping once more. She resented this, and yet she did not quite know how to reply to it. "People have married again in their early fifties," she said defensively.

"Oh, *married*. Yes. That's different. For convenience sake, perhaps. But surely not, well—swept off their feet!"

"How do you know?" Really, the presumption of young people, Bel reflected, as she took the crumbs, all of them now on the shovel, and put them into the fire. Did they think that at the age of, say, forty, all passion came to a standstill?

"But I always thought, Mother—" Isabel stopped, still looking amused. Her mother was right. Isabel had a young person's difficulty in imagining how her elders could have any such feelings.

Bel disliked this talk intensely. She was torn between two strong and opposing impulses. One, to tell her daughter roundly that she need not be so arrogant as to think that the blood of her parents was already congealing in their veins; the other, loyally to maintain a veil of decorum between her own generation and the younger one. The escape she chose from this impasse did her no particular credit. "I don't know how we ever got to talking about these things," she said stiffly, rearranging the fire-irons. "Is that someone out in the hall?"

And it was. To her relief, Phœbe Hayburn came in.

"Hullo. I'm not waiting. I only wanted to say goodbye to Isabel and tell you that Henry has bought a house."

"A house, Aunt Phœbe?"

"Whins of Endrick near Drymen."

131

"An estate?" Bel asked.

"I suppose you might call it that. Where's Lewis, Isabel? Upstairs? I want to say goodbye to him, too."

"But what about this house, Phœbe? Tell us about it. You *must* be pleased."

"Yes. Quite pleased, Bel. Henry is, anyway," Phœbe said. "Come on, Isabel."

Left to herself, Bel went to the window and looked out into her own back garden. She twisted the cord of the window-blind with impatient fingers. Green buds were showing on the black stems of a little smoke-begrimed lilac-bush. Couched to spring, a large marmalade cat was watching a sparrow hopping on the dingy grass.

How did it come about that Arthur and herself should, at their time of life, have so little to show for their importance? They seemed to be eternally rooted to this terrace house, while those they had helped at different times in the family's history went on and passed them by? Mungo and David had lived in country splendour for years. Now Phœbe and Henry. And Phœbe did not even bother to look pleased about it. It wasn't that Arthur was poor, Bel knew. He had established their elder son in a flat in Hillhead, and bought Isabel her house in London. It was a pity, Bel reflected. Arthur had always worked so hard. Indeed, it wasn't fair!

The marmalade cat, the lilac-bush, and the sparrow began to swim unsteadily before her. She took out her handkerchief and sought to control herself. Why was she so depressed? It was unlike her. She would follow the girls upstairs and see what they were up to.

III

Outside in the hall she saw Sarah's comfortable, middle-aged figure standing at the open front door. Bel was about to draw back again, when the sight of a telegram froze her where she stood, her discontent swallowed up in an ecstasy of dread.

She took the telegram from Sarah, who remained standing before her, making no move to go. The boy stood waiting.

"Nasty things, telegrams, these days, Sarah," Bel said, seeking thus to conquer the quick stab of alarm.

"Yes, mam." Sarah's voice was hoarse. She saw her mistress break the trembling envelope, saw her face turn grey and fixed, heard her say: "Thank you. There's no reply." And watched her as she moved to close the door.

"Oh, Mrs. Moorhouse, what is it?"

Bel's voice seemed infinitely tired. "Seriously wounded."

"Not our Mr. Tom?"

Bel nodded. There might be days of paralysing anxiety, now, until they knew more. And then? No, the ultimate fear must be pushed away.

"But is that all it says?"

Again Bel nodded. She stretched out a hand towards this old friend. "Come into the parlour and stay with me for a little, Sarah. I'll be all right if you do that. Just the two of us alone. Before I telephone his father or anything."

Chapter Thirteen

THE waiter came in as usual, left Robin's morning coffee tray by his bedside, threw open the long sun shutters, and went.

Now Robin lay, his hands behind his head, looking out at the brilliance of the sky, which, but for the top of a palm tree, was all he could see from his bed.

His feelings were flooded with pleasure at the thought of a new day. What a stroke of luck that he had met Denise St. Roch down here! That a writer so accomplished, so entirely charming, so sympathetic to himself, should give him her advice and friendship was a joy he could not have foreseen. He wished he could write home telling them what Denise was doing for him. But Sir Henry, he was afraid, would disapprove. Now, for a moment, as he lay thinking, resentment clouded Robin's face.

But with so much approval down here, why think of its lack elsewhere? To banish the picture of Sir Henry disapproving, he made for himself another that he liked better: the picture of his friend as she looked the other day sitting perched on her grey mule while it made its way up the dusty mountain track to Castellar. Her quick smile; her elegant boyishness; her tart, American gaiety.

Robin had, indeed, become much obsessed by the thought of Denise. But the obsession was still strangely unaware, strangely virginal.

At last he stirred, and drew the tray towards him. Now, as he did so, he saw a letter addressed to him in his father's hand. He cut it open with no expectation of interest. His father had written him several letters since he had come here: letters filled with enthusiasm over the happenings in Hayburn and

134

Company, enthusiasm he did not share. His mother's, he reflected as he unfolded the sheet, were better. She wrote of things he liked to hear about.

"My dear Robin," the letter ran, "this must be very short, but it has good news for you. I have bought the house and property of Whins of Endrick near Drymen. Your mother likes it and is very pleased. It is, as you know, a grand district. We can see the Ben from the windows. You will be coming home when the weather is warmer, which should not be long now. We will certainly try to be settled in time for your arrival. A summer out there should put you right on to your feet and let you get on with your studies. Your mother will be writing to tell you what the place looks like.

"We are both very well. Warm love from us both. Tell the uncles about this.

"Your affectionate father,

"HENRY HAYBURN."

For a time Robin lay back on his pillow. This letter had, somehow, fallen like a stone through the brittle surface of his happiness.

Now he threw back the bedclothes, put his bare feet to the floor, then, taking the letter into his hands, flung himself into a chair by the window. Here in the sunlight he re-read what Sir Henry had written. His father called this good news, but Robin could not see it so. "You will be coming home when the weather is warmer, which should not be long now."

But Robin wanted to stay where he was. This letter made him realise how much. Here, in these few weeks, his spirit had grown wings!

Thanks to Denise St. Roch. Robin folded the letter once more, and bent forward, his dark hair hanging, his elbows on his knees, contemplating the sunlight as it fell upon his veined feet. No. He did not want to leave her. If Mentone meant Denise, then in Mentone he must stay. Until now he had let himself drift in a dream without a future. That was finished.

135

His father expected him to come home soon and follow the old, dull ways. Robin hoped he would not be well enough to go. He felt, even, that a continued threat of illness would not be too high a price to pay for his liberty. And this new country house? He neither knew just where it was, nor cared. For him it would be prison.

There was a knock at his door. Robin stood up hurriedly. Before he had time to throw his dressing-gown about him, Stephen Hayburn entered, bathed and shaved, but not yet dressed.

"Morning, Robkin!" The name this uncle gave to Robin. "I was on my way from my bath. Hullo? Is everything all right? Let me have a look at you."

"I'm all right."

But Stephen took hold of Robin's shoulders and turned him to the light. To distract attention from himself, Robin held out the letter.

His uncle sat down in the chair he had just quitted, and, being without his eyeglass, held it at a pompous arm's length. "Oh! Your father has got *that* house, has he? I know it. Nice place. Of course! I did hear the old woman had died, and that she had no heirs. Well, that should be very nice for you." Stephen looked up. "My dear Robkin! What on earth is the trouble? Look here. You're too excitable; that's what's wrong with you!"

Robin's face was flushed, and he looked unhappy. "See. You haven't had your coffee yet. Have it quick and get dressed. And I'll come back and talk to you."

But the last thing Robin wanted was a searching talk with his uncle. What purpose could it serve? What was there to say? He must be dressed and away from here before Stephen returned.

He washed, flung on his clothes, gulped down a cup of coffee, and left the hotel by a back way in a shorter time than he would have believed possible.

He had told himself that he wanted to escape merely in

136

order to think. But now he found his feet taking him up in the direction of the Rue Longue. And why not? Why not go to Denise? It was still early. But it was her custom, he knew, to be early at work.

As he stood on her landing, panting, a shyness overcame him. What could he say to her? Why, indeed, had he come? Yet he could not bring himself to turn and go downstairs again.

Having regained some breath, he knocked. There was no answer. He knocked once more, and yet no one came. This was strange; strange that she should have left her studio at this hour. He put his ear to the door to hear if anyone moved inside, but the door was old and thick, and there were other noises on the staircase and from the street below.

Robin turned and went down slowly. He spent the rest of the morning aimless, unhappy and alone.

II

Philomene wondered what was wrong with Mademoiselle St. Roch. She could see her out there ranging up and down her balcony in a dressing-gown, unable, it would seem, to settle down to anything. Philomene was the Mentonese woman who came to clean the studio each morning. She knew, by this time, that Mademoiselle was a writer, and that she liked thus to wander back and forth, thinking out her work.

But today there was more annoyance than thought in Mademoiselle's face. Something had upset her. What was it? Why didn't she come in, have that shower-bath of hers, and get dressed?

For a time Philomene gave herself over to reflections about Mademoiselle's toilet. It was strange, speedy, and almost masculine. Standing there in her shallow tin bath, she allowed that shower she had somehow rigged for herself to play on her head, while she soaped down her firm, slim body. Philomene liked helping Mademoiselle dry herself; to watch her bend to rub her dripping hair with a thick towel; to see the close fair curls spring back into shape all over her head, crisply like a boy's. And Philomene had seen little evidence that Mademoiselle did much, or indeed anything, with her skin to get that look of brilliance. Indeed, she seemed to take all that for granted. Now, if Mademoiselle had been French—

But Philomene was right about Denise. She was restless and out of temper. As usual, she had risen early and begun to work. This morning, however, the going had been slow, ideas had refused themselves, and presently she had made up her mind to stop trying and have coffee, hoping thus to induce them to come.

But after breakfast things had gone no better. She had downed tools and come out here determined to look for reasons for this mental standstill. There had been a letter from New York yesterday telling her that a set of magazine stories had been rejected. That, of course, was annoying. She had written them by request. Still, these stories would sell elsewhere. Such things had happened before. No. That might keep certain hypersensitives from work for a day, but she could not afford to be so temperamental. Denise liked to see herself as a disciplined craftswoman, ever fit and ready to take up her pen.

Indeed, she had been talking to Robin Hayburn about this just yesterday. "If you must have moods," she had told him, "then you must learn to turn on the right mood at the right moment, or you'll never get anywhere."

Which brought her to Robin. Thoughtfully, Denise stopped to twist with mechanical affection the pointed ears of her great wolfhound as he lay out here in the sunshine. Down below in the harbour and beyond the morning sea lay calm and blue, except where a yacht, moving across its surface, left a fan of waves—broken waters that sparkled.

Now somehow the thought of Robin filled Denise with a

sharp sense of irritation. Was he beginning to take up too much of her time? Of her thought? Was his eagerness somehow taking possession of her—of her work?

Denise turned from her dog and continued to pace the balcony. Was Robin altogether too unaware? Was he too ready to accept that theirs was only a friendship? She wondered now what would happen if she decided otherwise. But today, at all events, work was no good. Perhaps in the evening. Now she might as well give herself a holiday.

III

As she came inside to dress, there was a knock at her door. "See who it is, Philomene," she said, "A message? For me?" She broke the hand-delivered letter open.

This was opportune. A friend she had believed to be on his way to New York had sent an early messenger from Monte Carlo with a note to say he was dropping over to Mentone to see her. And could she meet him at the railway station?

Denise was pleased. Had it been a day when ideas were coming, she would perhaps have welcomed the interruption less. But even then—well, Sam Carrick was the best of men and a good friend. She would have felt obliged to stop work for him.

As she hurried with her dressing, there was another knock. Again she was about to tell the woman to answer when she recognised it as Robin's. She laid a finger on her lips and motioned to Philomene not to stir. She did not want to see him this morning. She wanted to give the day to Sam Carrick, to enjoy his company and hear the Paris gossip.

The two women stood still for a time. The knock came again. They continued to stand. At last Denise crossed barefoot to the door. Through its thickness she caught the sound of footsteps descending. All was well. Presently she would go to meet her friend.

139

"Hullo, Denny, you old humbug! How are you? It's good to see you!"

"Humbug? You're the humbug, Sammy! I thought you were on your way home!" She was fond of this great, loose-built countryman of hers. His thirty-five years sat proudly on his large shoulders. When his hand took yours, you felt it crushing in the bones. "Sammy," she had once told him, "there's an awful lot of you!" To which he had replied: "Well? Can't have too much of a good thing. Can you, Denny?"

They had to disentangle themselves from the crowd at the railway station, and were making their way towards the public gardens before he had opportunity to say: "I am going home. But I was sent down here on a special assignment. Nothing much. Scandal among crowned heads, that I didn't particularly want to handle. But I got what I was told to get and sent it."

"Interesting?"

"No. Not at all."

He was comforting, somehow, this great creature. He radiated an easy strength, an abundance of masculinity, as he ambled along beside her. In times past, Denise had known pangs of jealousy over the neurotic wife he had left behind him somewhere in upstate New York. "How's Barbara and the boy?" she asked.

"Grand. Well, the boy is, anyway. I'll see them soon now. I sail in three days."

"I hope you didn't mind me sending you those stories of mine to take with you to New York?" Denise said, trying the while to think kindly of Barbara's nerves.

"Mind, Denny? Do I ever mind anything you want me to do for you? And what about that story you sent along with them? Who's this youngster Hayburn, anyway? I've got a letter about him for you. That's partly why I came to see you."

But now Denise had turned to greet some friends who were sitting in a café by the gardens taking mid-morning coffee.

140

IV

Lucy Hamont had been drinking a solitary cup, when all at once she had become aware that Stephen Hayburn was bearing down upon her.

Stephen's middle-aged distinction was enjoying the sunshine. The coat and trousers of pale grey, the checked waistcoat encasing his neat rotundity, the black stock with the large pearl pin, the grey top hat and gloves all suited their wearer admirably. He was coming up the street as though he owned the Riviera. Now and then he held his glass to his eye in order to take in some detail of the fashionable rabble. This elegant girl. That bedizened dowager in the wheeled chair. These roses and carnations in a flower-woman's basket. Those fluffy white puppy dogs, held out for sale in the rapacious brown hands of that fellah who looked like a bandit. A stranger would have guessed that here was some gentleman of consequence, who had, for half an hour, felt it his duty to remove his magnificence from the precincts of his stucco palace, for the purpose of bestowing lustre upon the morning promenade.

As he came up to Mrs. Hamont sitting there on the pavement beneath the striped awning, Stephen raised the grey top hat and allowed himself to smile.

Lucy's face lit up. "Hullo! What have you done with David?"

Stephen stopped, leant upon his cane, and looked down at her. "David? Oh, writing letters. Dutiful husband and all that sort of thing, you know."

"It's much too fine this morning for duty."

"That's what I said." Stephen's smile had become a little jaunty.

"Have you had coffee?" Lucy hazarded. She liked Robin's cheerful, rather dressy Hayburn uncle. Much better, indeed, than she now liked his Uncle David.

"Yes. But how can I refuse to have some more?" He replaced the grey hat and sat down beside her.

141

Stephen Hayburn looked about him with approval; at the palm-trees, drowsing over there in the public gardens, at the riot of flowers, at the colourful crowd. He smiled at Lucy with friendly intimacy. It was pleasant sitting here with this agreeable woman. He felt it was his right setting. He was glad David had refused to come out this morning. Now, with the sun's heat penetrating his bones, Stephen felt not unlike a sleek and well-fed tom-cat whose days of mousing and the tiles were, perhaps, not so active as they had been, but were not yet so very far behind.

"You haven't seen my nephew Robin anywhere, have you?" he asked conversationally.

"No. Why?"

"He was a little unreasonable this morning. He seemed absurdly upset by a letter from my brother. He showed it to me. No bad news or anything. It was just to tell him they had bought a house and property outside Glasgow."

"They?"

"Yes. His parents. Said something about expecting Robin home soon to see it, and that sort of thing. Robin doesn't appear to want to go or something. Which is a mystery to me. You would think—"

"But didn't Robin tell you why?"

"No. I looked into his room after my bath. Said I would go and dress, and then come back and talk to him. But the bird had flown. Looks as if he meant to give me the slip."

Lucy looked at Stephen seriously. "The boy is living under some strain, Mr. Hayburn. I like him, I know why he's been sent here and it worries me. I'm glad to be able to talk to you."

"Thank you, Mrs. Hamont." Stephen sat drinking his coffee, while his eye followed the come and go on the pavement. (Dam' smart-looking girl that with the grey poodle! French.) He decided he might now put a question to this woman beside him. "Then perhaps you'll forgive me for asking: but, after all, this boy belongs to my brother, and you're a friend of the family. Has Robin started some love affair down here?"

Stretching a glove over her knee, Lucy considered this. "I'm beginning to think it's quite possible."

Again Stephen took to watching the passers-by. Robin? Who would have thought it? No time since he was a little thing in a pram. Still, boys must keep growing up, he supposed. It made their uncles feel old, though. (Funny how foreigners never wore their clothes well. That man there, for instance. Expensively dressed and so on. But the hang of his coat was wrong.) He turned back to Lucy. "What about this American? He seems to be seeing a lot of her?"

"Have you met Miss St. Roch?"

"No, I haven't. You know her well, do you?"

"Miss St. Roch is a friend of mine."

"I'm sorry. I didn't mean—" Then after a pause: "Well, after all, what business is it of ours?"

But Lucy did not want to let it go at this. "That's not quite the answer," she said. "You know very well why Robin is here, Mr. Hayburn. And it's certainly not to be strung to breaking-point."

"Strung by what?"

"Well—all this new excitement. This writing mania, and—"

"Excitement about the girl who is teaching him to write?"

"Please! I know nothing about it. Still, I blame myself now for introducing them."

Stephen's eyes strayed once again to the passers-by before he turned back to say: "My brother Henry hates Robin's arty leanings, anyway. What kind of girl is this American?"

But Lucy was calling: "Denise! There she is! You'll see for yourself, Mr. Hayburn. Denise! Hullo! Oh, hullo, Mr. Carrick! What are you doing down here?"

Denise, followed by Sam Carrick, was crossing the pavement to their table.

V

With a keen interest, Stephen fixed his eye-glass and settled back to talk to the Americans, who, responding to Lucy's invitation, were sitting down for a moment's talk. He took in Carrick's large, good-natured person with approval, making the mental comment that they seemed to be able to breed outsizes over there, and was content to leave it at that. But this girl who was with him, this Miss St. Roch they had just been talking about? Quite a beauty in her way! And she had the courage to wear what suited her looks! It would be no surprise to him if that rascal Robin *had* lost his head a bit over her. Any young man would. But what about Miss St. Roch? Would someone so poised, so obviously fit for the world she lived in, bother with his callow, excitable nephew?

"Now where did we meet last, Mr. Carrick?" Lucy was asking Sam.

"I don't know, Mrs. Hamont. Could it be somewhere in Paris?"

Since these two had given themselves to this question of grave importance, Denise turned to Stephen. "You're one of the wicked uncles! Isn't that right?"

He must adjust his glass for this! His smile was now compounded of amusement, distinction, and, he hoped, a pinch of naughtiness. "I *am* the wicked uncle, Miss St. Roch. There's only one of me!" Handsome girl this. Some fellah ought to paint her. Perhaps some fellah had.

"But I thought there was two of you? Robin said—"

"Oh yes. There are two of us. But Robin's Uncle David Moorhouse is not wicked at all. He's nothing if not good!"

"I see." She laughed. Lively old boy this. Even if, like most old boys, he was being silly.

"So, you see, Miss St. Roch, I have to be wicked for two."

"I would be very, very interested to know just exactly how you manage to do that, Mr. Hayburn."

Stephen, foolishly enjoying himself, was about to say he

144

supposed wickedness was a gift like an ear for music, but Sam Carrick had turned at the sound of his name.

"Hayburn?" he asked. "I didn't get your name first time, sir." He looked at Denise. "Any relative of this youngster, Robin Hayburn?"

"Of course, Sam. He's Robin's uncle."

"Well. I think you'd better read him the letter I was going to show you, Denny. I know what's in it. It should have some family interest." He took it out of his pocket. "See who it's from?" he asked with a smile, as her fingers broke the seal.

Denise's brows arched with surprise as she turned to the signature. "From *him*! Now, how did *he* see Robin's story?"

"Happened to be in Paris. Heard I was going home, and came to ask me to do something for him. So I thought he had better look at your friend's stuff."

As she read the letter the others waited. Why should this writer of much distinction trouble with a boy's scribbles?

Denise turned a page.

"And so, my dear young lady, these are my feelings; if things so little definable may be called feelings; my intuitions let me rather say. I am amazed to be told that your young friend has written so little; that this short 'conte' is indeed among his first. For, even if it be possible, here and there, still to discover a certain 'gaucherie' in the setting-down, he strikes a note that is both delicate and sure. I have seldom found those fleeting half-thoughts that go to make up the greater part of our daily consciousness so skilfully netted, so dexterously pinned down— their wings still vibrating—to a mere three or four sheets of paper.

"And thus, if I judge rightly, it is in the direction of his quick delicacy that your interesting friend's talent must be led. As I see it, my dear colleague, it would be a great pity to allow him to become a glib and 'plotty' story-teller, to cultivate a hasty, thin veneer. There is a new and unusual sensibility in these few pages that calls for tender care in its development.

"Forgive me if I dare to intrude upon your time. But we

writers must, don't you think, hold out a pointing hand when young and undoubted talent knocks at our door to ask the way?

"In Paris I was told of your commendable and tireless industry, and I am pleased to think of the material reward it must so happily and gratifyingly bring to you."

"Well, Denny? Does he tell you all he told me?"

Denise gave Sam the letter. The others were surprised that she looked almost displeased.

"Have you met him?" Lucy asked, referring to the author whose august handwriting Denise had just been reading.

"Oh, yes," she said drily. "Once in Paris."

Carrick looked up. "Can the others see it, Denny?"

"Of course."

"And don't you think it's wonderful?" He was puzzled. Women were queer. What was wrong with Denny now?

"It depends what you mean by wonderful." She looked about her grimly.

Lucy and Stephen were reading it together. Sam waited.

Presently Denise spoke. "Well, I guess that's me put in my place," she said.

"Place, Denny? What place?"

"Oh, can't you see what that old Europeanised word-spinner means? Listen." She stood up to look over Lucy's shoulder. " 'In Paris I was told of your commendable and tireless industry, and I am pleased to think of the material reward it must so happily and gratifyingly bring to you.' In other words: 'You're nothing but a money-making pen-pusher, so don't think you can start helping a young man who can write. You just leave him alone!' "

"Oh, no! No, Denny!"

"It's true. That's why he bothered to write to me at all." Moodily, she sat down again and turned once more to look about her.

But Sam Carrick was not a fool. And neither, he knew,

146

was Denise. Although his kindliness refused to admit to her that she was right, he saw very well that she might be.

It did not much surprise Lucy Hamont that Denise should presently stand up, hold out her hand, and say abruptly: "Come on, Sam; we've got things to talk about." Nor yet was Lucy much surprised at Sam's bewildered look, and his exclaiming: "What things, Denny?"

They shook hands—Carrick with a smile that was mild and apologetic, as though he was asking their indulgence for his companion.

"Well? And what do you think of all that?" Lucy said, withdrawing her eyes from the couple as they lost themselves in the distance.

"What? The letter?"

"Yes."

Stephen tilted himself back on his bright painted chair, and looked up at the striped awning above him, dangling his eye-glass on its ribbon the while with an air of deep thought. Then, coming back at last to a four-square position, he looked at his companion. "I've just been wondering," he said momentously.

"Robin will be pleased!"

"Yes. But what good will it do him? It won't stop that keying-up you've been talking about. It won't help him with my brother. It won't make him anxious to go home."

Lucy sat watching a market-woman go by. She was balancing a monster basket of tulips, narcissi and mimosa on her head. "No, I suppose not. And yet if a great singer had shown as much interest in my voice when I was a student, I would have been in Heaven for weeks!"

Stephen made no immediate reply to this. But at length she heard him murmur: "Poor Robkin!" as though to himself, and saw him stand up. "Time is going on," he said. "Are you walking back too? We can talk as we go." He gave the waiter a coin, offered her his arm, and led her across the gardens.

Some minutes later, walking thus together, Lucy caught their reflection in the plate-glass window of a shop. What a gay and agreeable couple Mr. Hayburn and she looked, there in the sunshine! Her parasol and feathers. His carefully chosen grey. How well they went together! How cheerfully elegant! How alarmingly suitable!

Her mind was not altogether on the problem of Robin as they continued onwards towards lunch.

Chapter Fourteen

STEPHEN found Robin in his room. The young man was lounging in his chair by the window. His aspect was gloomy.

"Hullo, Robin! You're there, are you? Why did you run away from me this morning?"

Robin did not move. He merely looked up at Stephen and said: "Hullo." He had tramped about all morning, unhappy and restless. And now he was sorry for himself; ready to dramatise a little.

"Are you all right, Robkin?"

"Oh yes, I'm all right."

Stephen felt annoyed. "Then why did you run away?"

"Because I had to be by myself to think."

"Think? What about?"

Robin sat up and put back the rebel strand of hair. "Must we talk about that now, Uncle Stephen?"

"Not necessarily. I only wanted to help."

"I'm an emotional fool, I suppose."

"Oh, are you?" Impatience with this play-acting sharpened Stephen's voice. "Well, it's lunch-time, anyway. Coming down?"

Robin sighed, dragged himself from his chair, took up his hair-brushes, and stood before his mirror.

Now his uncle felt a little malicious. "If you were looking for your friend Miss St. Roch this morning"—and from the sudden rush of colour to Robin's face, Stephen saw at once that he had been—"you wouldn't find her. She's spending the day with a friend."

Forgetting the languors of self-pity, Robin turned quickly. "Friend? Who?"

"A Mr. Carrick. An American journalist from Paris. She must have told you about him."

"No. She hasn't." Robin turned back to the mirror.

"Well, Mr. Carrick asked if I belonged to you."

"Who is this man Carrick? How does he know anything about me?"

"Didn't you send him some of your writing?"

"No. But Denise may have done without telling me." Robin turned to look at Stephen once again.

"Well, Mr. Carrick has brought Miss St. Roch a letter about your work, Robkin. He showed it to us."

"My work? From whom?"

Stephen told him the letter-writer's name. "Mr. Carrick thought the great man ought to see it."

"Uncle Stephen! No!" Again the colour was in Robin's face. There was little of pose about him now. "What did the letter say? Good or bad?"

"Good. Now that's all I'm going to tell you. We're late. Your Uncle David will be waiting."

"But, Uncle Stephen! I must find Denise!"

"Don't be silly, Robkin. Come and have your lunch. Besides, you probably won't find her. I've told you she's spending the day with Mr. Carrick."

But the meal was a penance for Robin. His impatience would not let him eat. Now the discontent caused by his father's letter was swallowed up in this news his uncle had given him. He must see that letter from Paris. He must climb up to Denise's door, even if the chance of finding her was only faint.

But when, at last, he was able to escape from the lunch-table, come out in front of the hotel, and look towards her studio high up there in the old town, he was left in no doubt of her whereabouts. For there she was, out on her balcony, as he had so often seen her. At this distance he could not tell if anyone was with her. But whether or not he would go up now.

150

A little time later, Sam Carrick turned to Denise. "Is that somebody knocking at your door, Denny?"

He had taken her to lunch in town, and now she had brought him up here to get the view from her balcony, to see her strange quarters, and to spend some time in talk, before he must go back.

Although he did not know it, Sam's own presence, male and benign, together with the large, bass tones of his familiar voice, had soothed the ruffled spirit of his fellow country-woman. He saw that Denny was less jumpy, less unpredictable, than she had been this morning. Now she seemed more like the Denny he had expected to find; the Denny the newspaper boys up there in Paris were always glad to see around. Bright, sensible, as women went, and a real pleasure to the eye. Why she had been gloomy over that letter about the Hayburn boy, Sam just couldn't figure out. But, then, the girls were like that. Moods one minute. Smiles the next. But you left them to their moods and made the most of their smiles. He had learnt all about that from Barbara long ago.

"Knocking at the door? I don't think so."

"Yes. There it is again." She seemed reluctant to go. He heaved his large, relaxed body out of the wicker chair she had placed for him. "I'll go and see."

"No! Let me!"

But he had gone, and was opening the door to a tall, thin young man who stood there, hot and much out of breath. His hair was damp on his brow and there was a surprised look in his dark eyes. Sam Carrick smiled. "Come in, son," he said. "I'm a friend of Denny's. You're not the Hayburn boy, are you?"

"Yes, I am."

"Come right in, then! Denny's got something to show you."

"Yes. So I heard. My uncle told me."

"Yes, that's right; we saw him this morning." Interesting

151

youngster this. Well, of course he must be interesting, if the old man had bothered to write a letter like that about four pages of his work. But that wasn't quite all. There was a fine-drawn quality about young Hayburn; a flickering change of expression that seemed to render his thoughts transparent. But Sam was surprised to see him go unbidden to the satchel that served Denise as a handbag, search for the letter, and take it out.

"I knew it would be here," Robin said.

"Go right ahead. Don't mind me." Denise did not appear to be pleased, Sam thought. But yet she had allowed young Hayburn to do this.

Now Robin was sitting on the edge of Denise's sofa-bed, crouched over the letter, lost to everything else. Denise was walking back and forth in the room. Sam, hands in pockets, stood leaning one shoulder against a wall. His eyes moved between the falling mop of hair bent over the paper and the face of the handsome, restless girl.

At last Robin looked up.

"Well, son? How do you feel about that?"

With a quick, low "I don't know what to say!" Robin crushed the letter between clasped hands, pressed these between his knees, and turned his face away from them.

"Denny and I are very proud of you. Aren't we, Denny?"

"Yes, aren't we?"

What was wrong with the girl? Why must her voice be so cool? "Of course we are." Sam sought to cover up her strangeness.

Denise took another step or two, then she went to Robin. She laid a hand on his shoulder. "Robin, of course I'm glad. It was just—I don't know—well, the old man tells me to keep my hands off your work. He doesn't seem to think I'm fit to help you. But never mind. I'm glad, all right."

Robin looked up. What was she talking about? "But, Denise—?"

"It's all right, Robin. Forget about that. I'm delighted.

152

And come back and see me soon. Sam and I haven't seen each other for quite a while. We've got a lot to talk about together."

Robin stood up. Was he being dismissed? Treated like a schoolboy? His self-importance did not like this. He looked once more at Denise. She was standing, waiting for him to go.

"You've been very good to me." His tone was young and uncertain, almost pleading.

"Oh no, my dear boy, I've done nothing! But we'll talk about everything next time I see you."

"Why did you send him away like that, Denny?" Sam Carrick asked when, a moment later, the outside door had closed behind Robin.

"I don't know, Sam. I just can't tell you." She spoke the truth.

"You might have let the youngster stay and talk to me. I liked him."

"You should have told me, Sam."

He made a movement. "I could go and shout to him."

"Oh, no! Don't do that!"

Sam sat down in the chair again. No. Women were queer. That was all you could say about them. They didn't know what they wanted.

III

Slowly Robin descended the old, worn stairway, emerging presently into the cheerful afternoon rabble of the Rue Longue. A woman with a little cart of rough pottery, to which a large, patient dog was harnessed, passed him by. A group of swarthy, staring children. Two priests deep in conversation. A local dandy in trousers of black velvet, a white shirt, and a red cummerbund.

But Robin noticed nothing. Why had she sent him away like this? Why was she so eager to be rid of him? Was it

153

inconvenient in some way? Inconvenient not to be alone with that friend of hers?

He thrust his hands into his pockets, and shrugged angrily. He was hurt. And he felt he had every right to be. Oh, he would have gone, of course, if she had given him time! He wasn't the kind of person to stay where he was not wanted. She needn't have been so definite about it. Ordering him away in front of that large American, as if he were a child!

He found his fingers crushing a piece of paper in his pocket. He drew it out. He had taken Denise's letter without noticing. Now he stood still in the street to re-read it. Again it gave him a stab of pleasure. It was almost too much, this praise and confirmation of a talent which, until a few weeks ago, even he himself had not taken quite seriously. He had had urges, of course, undefined hopes. But this!

He walked on, his feelings pulled in many directions at once. Why hadn't he got this when he was happy and unconfused? When he had nothing to bother him? He would have been able to give himself up to the pleasure of it. But now there was this morning's letter from his father, expecting him home soon. A letter he had hoped to talk over with Denise. Talk over with that unfriendly Denise who, it seemed, didn't want him!

All at once, jealousy flared like a meteor across Robin's sky. He halted, hesitated for a moment, wondering if he should go back, then angrily he thrust his hands once again into his pockets, hunched his shoulders, and continued down the street. Was it possible that Denise was in love with this Sam Carrick? The idea was unbearable!

Robin had taken no account of where he went. Now he had come down behind his own hotel and was on the promenade by the sea. Confused, he stood for an instant. A man on a bicycle swerved to avoid him. An elegant French automobile tooted its horn stridently, then powdered him with dust, as, grazing him, it rushed by. The ladies in their fluttering veils looked back to make quite sure he was

154

unhurt. The driver in his linen dust-coat took one hand from the steering-wheel to shake an angry, leather fist. Scarcely noticing, Robin crossed the road, and continued to walk by the sea.

Unbearable! But why should he care so much? Why should he feel this misery? Had he fallen in love with Denise St. Roch himself, then? It seemed so. And he had always been told that love, when it came, would make him happy! But she didn't want him. Didn't, even after this letter, seem interested in his work. Didn't want to see anybody but that man Carrick.

The Mistral, blowing along the Riviera today, had evaded the mountain defences of Mentone. Papers and dust followed Robin as he strode along in the direction of Italy. Little waves slapped the rocks.

He had better go home, after all. Better get back to where he belonged, whenever health allowed it. And yet, no. Now he had been told he could do something. Told he had a gift. If only he knew how to find a market for it! But he would find out somehow. He would stay here and work. He would earn something and lead his own life. And Denise could—

But he had better go and see her again. Just to be quite certain how he stood with her. The more he thought of this, the more it became a compulsion. But not now. Not while that man was there. Carrick would be gone tomorrow. Or hadn't there been something about a tram-car back to Monte Carlo just after dinner? Well, tonight, then. If he felt he had enough command of himself to behave with proper dignity.

Robin turned to go back. He put up the collar of his jacket. He was feeling cold.

IV

Denise, having seen Carrick mount a tram-car for Monte Carlo, was returning through the lighted town to her studio.

She had been sorry to let her friend go. He had brought

155

with him a breath of the cheerful tolerance, the pleasant bohemianism that went to make up what had come to be her normal life here in France. She thought of Paris now, and felt homesick for it. In Mentone the atmosphere had somehow become emotionally sultry. Robin's friendship, casually begun, had become too intense.

She had climbed up from the West Town into the older streets and now, for a moment, she was leaning on the balustrade of the stone terrace commanding the little paved cathedral square. Here she stopped to regain her breath, look about her, and allow herself to think. Down there, across the square and beyond the wide steps by which she would presently descend into the Rue Longue, she could see the lights of the villas encircling Garavan Bay, the lights of craft in the harbour and, far away, the diamond pinpoints ringing the bay of Bordighera.

Now as she came down to cross over she could hear church music. Now there was a breath of incense. Now, for a moment, she was a child at home again in New Orleans, kneeling in the great cathedral of St. Louis, fronting Jackson Square.

But an evening breeze blew away the memory, along with the incense that evoked it. No. She stood alone now, doing as she pleased, following her star.

As she turned into her own entrance, she heard footsteps descending, and prepared herself to give good evening to a neighbour as he passed her on his way down. But in a moment she found herself looking up at the shape of Robin Hayburn, dimly outlined against a feeble staircase light.

"Hullo, Denise. I've just been at your door."

"Have you?" In her present mood she was not particularly glad to see him. "I've just been seeing Sam off. We had dinner in town together. I'm tired now, Robin." But he seemed determined to ignore this. She had passed him on the stairs as she spoke, but he was coming up behind her. At the top he held out his hand.

"Give me the key. I know best how it works."

When he had opened, she went in before him and struck a match in the darkness to find the lamp.

"Look. I'll light it. Give me the matches."

She let him do that, too, although this boyish possessiveness did nothing to soothe her feelings.

"Tell me about Mr. Samuel Carrick." Robin's superior tones were full of jealousy. But whatever they were full of, Denise had little patience for them.

"What do you want to know about Mr. Samuel Carrick?"

"Oh. Everything."

"That's a great deal, Mr. Hayburn."

"Well, perhaps not everything, Miss St. Roch. But is he a great friend of yours, for instance?"

"A great friend." Denise took off her long cloak and threw it across the sofa. Now, leaning against her table, she stood watching him, her exasperation mounting. "Well?" she said. "Anything else you would like to know about Sam Carrick?"

His voice was aggressive, as he turned to ask the next question. "How long have you known him?"

"A few years."

Robin took to walking gloomily about the lamp-lit room. At length, however, he stopped to say: "You don't happen to be in love with him, do you?"

Denise had no intention of standing this. "Look here! You had better go home! If it's my life-story you want you won't get it tonight!" And seeing him hesitate: "Go on! Go away!"

"Denise! I didn't mean—!"

"Go away! Now!"

"All right. I'm going."

But as he went to the door he heard her say: "All the same, you may as well know that Sam has a wife he adores. In three days' time he's sailing for home."

"I don't care what he's doing!" Robin slammed the door behind him.

Denise felt her pulses beating, as she set about making herself some coffee. Had she been too harsh with him? Well.

tonight she didn't care. And he was badly needing to grow up. That Robin Hayburn—a man, after all—should show such childish jealousy was utterly absurd. But she did not really want to lose him. She would make it up soon by sending round a note or something. She liked him too much. And there was no need to worry. Of course she could whistle him back whenever she felt like it.

But was there knocking on her door? Was that Robin? Hadn't he gone away? She went to it, calling loudly through its thickness: "Who's there?"

"It's me, Denise! Let me come in and speak to you."

Her laughter was a little out of control as she turned the handle from inside.

As he came back into the room he, too, seemed overwrought. "Denise, I'm very sorry! I had no right to talk to you like that. Please forgive me!"

His foolish look of repentance as he stood there awkward before her, touched, suddenly, the hot quick of her sympathy. Thus surprised in her feelings, Denise clutched at the first words that came. "Are those the kind of manners you keep in Scotland, Robin? I've always heard that your people—"

"They're not my people!" Robin burst in. "I haven't a drop of Scotch blood in me! I've never told you! They picked me up in Vienna!" And as she had nothing to reply, he went on: "Denise, I don't want to go back! My real parents were artists! I want to stay here working beside you, earning my own living!"

What was wrong with the boy? What was he talking about? Was this nonsense or the truth? And why at this moment? But now, somehow, she could not bear his unhappiness. She went to him, put her arms about him, and kissed his cheek. "Robin," she said, "what is it?"

"Denise!" In his turn he clung to her. "I tell you, I don't belong to him at all!"

Him? Who was him? "Well, it doesn't matter tonight, surely?"

158

"Yes, it does! I tell you it does matter!"

He was shouting, and she could feel his body trembling in her arms. How could she bring comfort to him? Resolve for him this unexplained crisis? Loosen these fiercely stretched strings? "Quiet, Robin. Quiet." She put her lips against his mouth.

Now she felt his grasp tighten, his own lips press harshly in return. Now his body did not tremble. It had become importunate and male. "Robin! No!" But as he held her thus, refusing to let her go, this very refusal turned sweet to her feelings.

She would go to meet his inexperience.

V

When Robin got back, he went to his room, threw himself fully clad upon his bed, and lay there staring at the ceiling. He sought to recall those moments of trembling excitement: those moments of emotion, dazzled and seeking, then utterly resolved. How had this come about? And what would happen to him, now that he knew what it was to be a man? Would this knowledge change him fundamentally?

His vibrant senses remembered everything and nothing. Was he glad or sorry? He did not think of this. He felt bewildered and released. That was all. The world of adult awareness had opened to him; a world of fulfilment towards which, so far, his fledgling instincts had only groped and stumbled.

Chapter Fifteen

AS he came outside, Robin found Mrs. Hamont and his uncles sitting round a table in the garden. "Good morning, everybody," he said. "Good morning, Mrs. Hamont."

Lucy looked up at him. "Good morning, Robin. Had a good night?"

"At any rate, he didn't hear me when I looked into his room about eleven," his Uncle David said.

Robin shook his head. As he did so, his eye caught Lucy's, and at once he looked away again, turning to address the black Persian cat that had just then jumped up on the table. "*Bonjour*, Grimaldi," he said, making a ring of his fingers and running them down the creature's waving tail. "I'm going into town for a scribbling-pad, Uncle Stephen," he added. "Would you like to come with me?"

"Must I come at once?" Stephen asked.

"Yes. This minute."

Good-naturedly, his uncle got up to go with him.

Lucy sat watching the two retreating figures. The more she saw of Stephen Hayburn, the more she was coming to like him. He took life, she found, very much on her own level. He liked clothes to be smart, manners to be good, the corners of life to be round and polished. They had begun to establish an intimacy, too, over Robin and the problem of Robin. Stephen's attitude of tolerance suited Lucy's ideas exactly. "I like your friend Mr. Hayburn, David," she said presently.

"Stephen? But you've met him before, surely?"

"You forget how little I've been in Scotland, David. Sir Henry and Stephen Hayburn come from an established Glasgow family, don't they?"

"Well, it depends what you mean by established. The

160

Hayburns lost their money in the City Bank failure, you know. Henry, of course, has made his again. But well—" here David became confidential—"between ourselves, Lucy, I've had to keep Stephen ever since."

"Keep him?"

"He was my greatest friend. And I'm the chairman of Dermott Ships. You knew that, didn't you?"

Lucy inclined her head.

"Well"—David puffed his cigar for a moment—"there it was. Poor Stephen had to have some kind of life arranged for him. So I made a place in the firm." David looked about him with conscious benignity, then added: "He's my guest here, of course."

Lucy did not like this. She thought it ill taste that David should thus crudely demonstrate his own goodness by exposing his friend's lack of worldly gear. Now David was looking as though he were awaiting her praise, but instead of giving it she merely asked: "Did Mr. Hayburn never marry?"

"No money, poor chap."

She smiled. "He might have married it, you know."

"Not so easy for a man who has none of his own."

Lucy stood up. She had almost to bite her tongue to keep from saying: "What about yourself?" This smugness in the Moorhouse family had always displeased her. But again she only smiled. "I really must go. I've promised to meet someone. Goodbye, David."

She put up her parasol, caught her skirts from the dust and went.

II

"I'm glad to get you by yourself, this morning, Uncle Stephen," Robin said as together they walked towards the old town.

"Why this morning, particularly, Robkin?"

161

By most standards, Stephen Hayburn's life had been ineffective. He had made a cult of leisure, of taking the easy way. The current of his purpose, if ever he had a purpose, had not run deep; it had tended to disperse itself, running over the side-shallows, many of them sunlit and pleasant. Stephen had not been a striver. And the lack of this very quality had, perhaps, allowed him to taste life, to develop the tolerant sympathy that Lucy Rennie admired.

"I've been doing a lot of thinking, Uncle Stephen, and I want you to help me," Robin said.

Stephen turned to look at him. "Of course, Robkin. Well?"

As they passed under the plane-trees of the Quai Bonaparte, the half-sprouted leaves on the branches above them spotted the cobbles with shadow. A fisherman sat on the ground. Part of his net was dragged over his knees as he mended a rent in it. His thick fingers worked quickly, joining and knotting; muscle and sinew stood out on his spare brown arms. Across the Quai, the little eating-houses were getting ready for the day's business. Chairs were piled out of doors, water was thrown down, tables were scrubbed and floors sanded.

"Would you like to walk along the jetty, Robin? Or do you want to get to the shops?" Stephen asked. The boy, it seemed, had something on his mind, something he was finding difficult to say.

"Yes. We might."

As they climbed up the stone stairs to the high walk along the wall, a light south breeze met them. Lazy waters rose and fell, green and frothing a little, among the broken rocks placed there to protect the jetty on the seaward side. Looking down, they could see the dark shapes of fish moving hither and thither in the swell.

They sat down together by the lighthouse. There was something incongruous in the sight of Stephen dangling his immaculate legs over the end of the wall. But here they were undisturbed in a world of light and water.

"I'm glad you saw that letter, Uncle Stephen," Robin began.

162

"It would certainly be encouraging, if that was what you were setting out to do."

"But that's what I *am* setting out to do!"

His uncle turned to look at him. "I want to understand this, Robkin. Are you trying to tell me that you want to be a full-time writer?"

"Yes." Robin looked at Stephen intently. "I've found my vocation in life. Can you doubt it now? And I want you to help me."

"Help? In what way? How can *I* help?"

"You're my father's brother, aren't you? You could explain to him."

"Explain?"

"That I can never go into Hayburn and Company now, of course! Oh, that letter has made me so happy! I can't tell you!"

But Stephen was by no means sure about this. Or rather he *was* sure. Very sure. He knew exactly how his brother Henry would take this decision of Robin's. Besides, it was a rule of Stephen's life never to mix himself into others' quarrels, to avoid taking sides. For a time he sat looking about him. At the moving sea. At a steam yacht there close in front of him, rounding the jetty and coming in. At a tiny David, still by himself in the garden, yonder in the distance across the calm waters of the harbour.

"Please, Uncle Stephen!"

"It's asking a great deal of me, Robkin. We both know very well what your father will say."

"You've got a great influence with Father. More than anybody else."

Stephen could not deny this. He knew it was true. Though why, he could hardly tell. "But, Robkin, you'll soon be going home yourself."

"I'm staying where I am!"

"What do you mean? How—? See here! If you want me to help you, you had better tell me what you have been doing since you came to this place."

"Things have happened, Uncle Stephen. Everything is changed for me."

Stephen turned to look at him. "Changed, Robkin?"

Robin appeared to be struggling with embarrassment. For a time he did nothing but stare down into the green waters there beneath them. But at last he clasped his hands between his knees, turned to his uncle, and blurted: "I'm terribly in love, Uncle Stephen!" He spoke in tones that might have been extorted on the rack.

"In love, Robkin? That's no unusual thing at your age. I was—well, it doesn't matter about me. But of course that explains all kinds of things. Why you want to stay here and all the rest of it."

"No. Only partly. Or rather, it's all mixed up together."

"I don't know what you mean."

"But don't you see? It's Denise St. Roch who has changed everything for me!"

"You mean you're in love with Miss St. Roch?"

"Of course!"

Stephen did not see any 'of course' about it. It could easily—more conveniently—have been some pert little baggage of Robin's own age. A little Mentonese girl in a cake-shop. Or perhaps the pretty daughter of a British resident. But Miss St. Roch! A woman of the world who might be some ten, some twelve years older than the boy beside him!

Now his yesterday's talk with Lucy Hamont came back to him. Had Miss St. Roch allowed Robin to make calf love to her? But the boy's eyes were upon him, waiting. "Well? What do you want me to do about it?" Stephen asked.

"I don't know yet. I must talk it over with Denise."

"My dear Robkin! How do you even know she's in love with you?"

"If there's one thing I do know, Uncle Stephen, I think I know that!"

"Why?"

164

Robin did not answer. He merely bent, his dark hair falling forward, looking down once more into the sea.

"Robkin, I want to help you. And I don't see how I can without knowing how things stand. Are you in the middle of—well—an affair?"

"In the middle?"

"Robkin, has it happened?"

"Yes. Last night."

"I see." Stephen's eyes looked away from Robin this way and that. They saw the sea moving in the sunshine. They saw, in the distance, a four-horse brake going slowly up the hill towards the frontier customs post. They looked up to the grey, broken edges of the surrounding mountains. Presently they came back to earth. "But you've discussed nothing so far?"

"No. But I did a lot of thinking on my own during the night. I don't see why I can't just marry Denise, and stay on here without any fuss."

"Marry!"

"Yes. After that letter, I'm certain to get my work sold."

"Certain?"

"Well? Why not? So, you see, I— You're not angry, are you, Uncle Stephen? You see, if two people really love each other—"

Stephen Hayburn was struggling to his feet. "No, Robkin. I'm not angry. But you must give me time to think."

"Strict confidence, Uncle Stephen?"

"What do you take me for? We'll talk about this later."

He followed Robin silently back along the wall. Married? Had the boy's wits left him?

III

As Lucy crossed the gardens in front of the Casino, she became aware of Stephen Hayburn sitting by himself on a park seat. It would have been easy to pass him by, for he was leaning

165

forward, idly tracing circles with his stick in the freshly sanded walk, deep, it appeared, in thought.

Silently she stood before him for a time, waiting, amused, to see how long it would be until he noticed her. Something must indeed have taken hold of him, for he continued to be quite unconscious of her, scraping with his stick and staring at the ground in front of him.

Now, as she stood over him, Lucy felt a subtle change in her feelings towards Stephen. She had always liked him, recognised in him a bird of her own feather. But she had taken it for granted that, as a friend of David Moorhouse, he must be—if not rich—at least settled and prosperous. Now she knew that Stephen, for all his airs, was nothing of the kind. And this knowledge did nothing to decrease her liking for him; rather the reverse. Although, unreasonably, she still disliked David's indelicacy at having told her.

But she could not yet define this different feeling for Stephen. A new right to intimacy? A quickening of emotion? A rich woman's urge to befriend a poor man who attracts her? But Lucy was too much of a bohemian, too well aware of life's chances to feel patronising. The spin of the wheel had favoured this man less than herself; that was all.

At last, tired of waiting, she allowed the shadow of her parasol to fall across his scribblings in the sand.

"Mrs. Hamont!" He stood up, taking off his hat.

Lucy laughed. "Shall I tell you how long I've been standing here?"

He looked bewildered. "Standing here? Why?"

"You've been thinking about something very hard. Are we walking or sitting?"

They began to move slowly down the gardens in the direction of the sea, Lucy catching up her tussore skirts from the sanded walk, her head and shoulders glowing in the shadow cast by her red parasol; Stephen a model of immaculate middle-age.

"Do you ever wish," he began presently, "that you knew

absolutely nothing about anybody, and never had to mix in other people's business?"

Again Lucy laughed. "Often! And what is more, I usually manage to do it. I learned the art when I was earning my living in music!" But now, remembering Stephen's preoccupation of a moment ago, she regretted this bright reply. Did he want to tell her something? Had she hindered some confidence? "You were looking worried as I came into the gardens," she said earnestly. "Nothing serious, I hope?"

"I don't know what to think. Or rather I do know what to think, but I don't know how to act. Or if I ought to act at all!"

"Robin?"

As he said nothing more, she judged it best to allow him to continue beside her in silence. But, indeed, she would have been less than a woman had she not been filled with curiosity. At the lower end of the gardens she turned to him. "Would you think it very—what shall I say?—forward of me if I invited you to lunch, Mr. Hayburn? We could drive along the shore to Cap Martin. We still have time. It's only twelve."

For an instant he looked doubtful, then he reset his eyeglass. "I say! That's awfully kind!"

Yesterday she might not have given this invitation; but now, having given it, she was glad he looked so pleased.

And thus, presently, they were making a leisurely progress round the west bay, sitting side by side on the linen-covered seats of an old fiacre. Up in front the driver drowsily flicked his whip at the flies that hung above the straw hats on the heads of the horses. The sun shone. The sea sparkled. And Lucy was content to leave it at that. Stephen, she hoped, would presently feed her curiosity.

The dining-room of the Cap Martin Hotel was filled with lunch-time brilliance. Foreign royalty, it was known, was having its august meal in a private suite upstairs. Aware of this hidden consequence, hangers-on and those who hoped to hang thronged the great room where Lucy and Stephen found themselves. Flowers. Pails of ice. Cohorts of waiters. Baskets of fruit. Perfumes. Furs. Jewels. Polyglot chatter. It was better here, Stephen told himself, than drawing squares and triangles on his blotting-paper in his little room in Dermott Ships.

At a table nearby, Lucy recognised a Parisian actress, pointing her out to Stephen. He thought the actress ugly. But ether her wit or her influence must be prodigious. For her table hung upon her talk. They caught snatches of her broken English through gusts of laughter. Although she had the agelessness of the painted and bedizened, her guests were young, lively, and, as Lucy guessed, American. Among them was the son of a railway Crœsus come to study painting in France. She had met this boy in Paris. As she watched, the woman beside him raised her hand in greeting. "Good gracious! There's Denise! I've only just seen her!"

And Denise it was. Her colour, her shining head, her flashing teeth and her warm skin found a perfect foil in the dye and artifice of her hostess. Denise was listening now, smiling her well-known smile and turning her handsome eyes upon those about her. Happy, if looks meant anything, happy in her own world.

They turned back to their table.

"What a lovely creature Denise St. Roch is!" Lucy could not help exclaiming.

"Oh, yes."

"You said that doubtfully."

"No."

"Well, then?"

"Can you see her marrying my nephew, Robin?"

"See what, Mr. Hayburn?"

IV

Lucy Hamont lay long awake that night.

The sight of Denise St. Roch in Cap Martin had opened up

the way to an earnest talk with Stephen about his nephew. Determinedly, she had created the right climate of intimacy, and he had told her of Robin's confession this morning.

It was strange, Lucy reflected, as she lay wide-eyed in her darkened bedroom, watching the breeze gently blowing the net curtains back and forth before her window, watching the pattern made by the rays of a street lamp on her ceiling—strange that she had for so long suspected something between Robin and Denise; or told herself she suspected it. Yet now that she was sure, the certainty somehow shocked her.

Lucy was not a child. Here in France, as indeed everywhere, people fell into and out of such intimacies, and appeared, if they knew the rules, to emerge none the worse.

"The trouble is," she had said, "Robin's background is so—what shall I say?—uncontinental."

Stephen had pondered for a moment. "I know what you mean," he had said. "Robin's, indeed our own Scotch background, can be so innocent."

"He's probably head over heels in love with her."

"Of course! It's not only 'honour' that makes him talk about marriage."

"It's very sweet, don't you think?"

"I'm not sure if 'sweet' is the word. What do you think Miss St. Roch will do?"

Lucy had merely shrugged.

A late party was returning; probably from Monte Carlo. She heard the hooves of the horses, the noise of wheels, laughter, talk, the banging of a carriage door, then the sounds of the cab receding. Now the night wind made a rustling sound outside in the palm-trees.

And then, when they had come back, David had told them of a letter just received from Lady Hayburn, hoping, since David and Stephen would be leaving for home soon, that the doctor under whose care Robin was would allow them to bring the boy, too.

Propping herself high on her pillows, Lucy put her hands

behind her head and, abandoning every attempt to sleep, stared into the shadows of her room.

Presently then—in a week or two, perhaps—they would all of them be gone from here. Denise wherever and whenever the mood suggested. David and Stephen back to Scotland. Robin would most likely have gone with them, or perhaps—who knew?—with Denise.

And herself? It was too early for Homburg or Aix-les-Bains. To Paris or London. The sister of her dead husband lived in Brussels, but she was an old woman, a grandmother, and the cherished matriarch of a large family of solid, self-important Flemings; a family for whom she, Lucy, scarcely existed. But for whom, indeed, *did* she exist? Where did she belong? Lucy sighed. She had described herself to David Moorhouse as a Riviera hack. It was painfully near to the truth.

Now, as she lay thinking, she saw the rolling green fields of Ayrshire, the white farmsteads with their high trees, the brown-and-white cows, their udders heavy, coming in for the summer's evening milking. The sturdy figure of her sister as she drove them. The wheeling, barking collies. That, Lucy supposed, was her real background. But she had cut herself off from it years ago. And now Greenhead Farm had a new tenant, her father was dead, and her sister's children must almost be grown men and women. What would she, their aunt, have for these young country people? Or they for her?

And yet—? Was she going to be a lonely old woman? A demanding harridan with a bullied paid companion? There were plenty of them to serve as warnings here on the Riviera.

Lucy lay considering. Her thoughts turned to David Moorhouse. If, after all, she had married David? Well, she hadn't. But his friend? The man who was with her today?

She pulled up her coverlet, rearranged her pillow, and, not for the first time, gave herself up to the assessment of Stephen Hayburn. David had told her this morning of Stephen's lack of money. But she had money enough for two, she imagined. Stephen was amusing, genial, kindly; he dressed with a pleasant eccentricity, hated rough edges, and his judgments were easy and uncensorious like her own. In his heart Stephen, too, must be lonely.

She was beginning to see the way before her. Almost at once, it seemed, she would have to come to a decision. But first she must quickly and finally search her own feelings.

Lucy found this search so engrossing, that it was well into the early morning before sleep could drag her from it.

Chapter Sixteen

IT was not often that Stephen Hayburn found himself at a loss. For so long it had pleased him to make a picture of cheerful poise before the world, that practice had made perfect, or very nearly so. Against the troubles of his not particularly difficult existence, Stephen had found this adequate defence.

But in the days that followed his visit with Lucy Hamont to Cap Martin, Stephen felt disturbed and uncertain. Robin's confession bothered him. If Robin's doings had been told him by someone else, it is probable that Stephen would merely have shrugged his shoulders, told himself it was none of his business and let things be. But the boy himself had told him; speaking, too, of marriage and of earning his own living; hopes which, Stephen knew, were as likely to be realised as that his nephew should, one day, be voted president of the French Republic.

Now Robin seemed determined to say nothing more meantime. Stephen, therefore, after much thought, decided not to seek him out; decided to force neither talk nor advice upon him until he felt sure he had the right advice to give. Heaven knew, he had been no plaster saint himself. But he was man enough to be troubled by Robin's predicament, by Robin's health, by Robin's foolishness.

There was yet another more personal reason for Stephen's uneasiness. He was becoming aware that he was drifting into closer intimacy with Lucy Hamont. In these days he seemed to be forever finding himself alone in her company. He did not quite know how this came about. There was, of course, Robin to talk about; and Lucy was, so far, the only person he could talk to. But however it happened, they were always meeting at odd moments in the hotel, or running into each other in the little town.

Stephen did not dislike this closer intimacy. His dispeace came from liking it too much. Mrs. Hamont's company was, he found, very agreeable. But he felt that his hands were tied. Had he been rich, he now told himself, he would have pushed the friendship farther; to the point, indeed, of a proposal of marriage. But it was one thing to cultivate a façade of opulent bachelorhood, and another to deceive a wealthy widow into marrying you as a result of that deception. Old Robert Hayburn's elder son was not, when all was said, an unscrupulous rascal.

It seemed to him at times as though Mrs. Hamont were almost inviting a declaration. And this distressed him. He liked her too much, appreciated her qualities, valued her sympathy for himself too much to be indifferent to any embarrassment or pain he might cause her.

One evening after dinner Stephen found himself sitting alone, thinking of these problems and cupping in his hands a second globe of fine brandy. He had had the first with David before David had disappeared to write a letter.

Presently, he saw Mrs. Hamont, who had dined late, come from the dining-room. His eye took in her charming and expensive aspect, her plump elegance, and his eye approved.

She saw he was alone, and came towards him. He stood up.

"No. Don't disturb yourself." He was placing a chair for her. "No. I mustn't interrupt. David will be coming back."

"Not for a long time. He's gone to write a letter to his wife. He writes every day, you know."

He had expected Lucy to comment frivolously on David's sense of duty. But she merely said: "Then perhaps you will allow me to have coffee with you."

"Of course."

Lucy sat down and signed to the waiter. "Where's Robin?" she asked presently.

173

"I don't know. I wish I knew what to do about him, Mrs. Hamont."

He had hoped by these words to reopen, yet again, this difficult topic. But as he turned to her, he found her looking at him, earnest and abstracted. At once her gaze left him and her eyes took to following a party that was new to her. "Now, wouldn't you say these people were South Americans?" she asked. "Argentines, perhaps? Look at these diamonds! They probably have miles and miles of pampas or whatever you have there, with thousands and thousands of cattle ranging about on it!" She turned back to him, smiling. She was not disposed, it appeared, to discuss Robin tonight.

Coffee was set before her. "You know," she went on, as she poured it out for herself, "I think it's nice of David to write to his wife every day. Does she write every day to him?"

"I think so."

"They must be devoted."

"I think so."

"Think? Isn't that proof enough?"

"Oh yes. I daresay." Why was she talking like this? Why did she seem determined to remain in earnest?

"I was fond of my husband, but I didn't write to him every day," Lucy said.

"You've never told me about your husband."

"I shall some day. He was a fine man in his way. A clever banker, people said." She stopped for a moment, then continued: "We were married too late, and for too short a time. If he had left me with children, then I should have them now to belong to; have them to make life worth going on with."

Stephen found nothing to say to this. He had never heard her speak thus before. He could only look at her sympathetically, dangle his glass on its ribbon and wait.

"Don't you ever feel terribly alone?"

"Wish I were married?" The words sounded crude as he said them.

174

She coloured. "Well, yes. That's what I do mean, I suppose." She looked away from him, as he sat deciding what next to say.

"I've never been able to marry a woman of my own kind," he said at length. "I was brought up rich, and then, when I was a young man, all the family money went. I was too stupid or too lazy to make it again for myself. David keeps me going, if you want to know the truth. I'm surprised that David, being David, hasn't told you. Well, now you know what kind of a person I am!" That had been an effort! What had forced him to this honesty?

Mrs. Hamont looked embarrassed. But at the same time she seemed oddly pleased. "It was nice of you to tell me." Her voice was low.

He tried to answer lightly. "I may not be worth much. But to you, at least, I won't be an impostor."

"No. You're not an impostor."

Lucy swallowed down her coffee and got up, held out her hand, and said: "Good-night." Now she was gone, leaving him quite bewildered.

Why had she left him thus abruptly, and with what looked like emotion? He sat down again, drew out one of the cigars with which David's hospitality kept him supplied, lit it and gave himself up to a series of long, meditative puffs.

II

Upon his eight o'clock coffee-tray he found the following letter:

"Dear Stephen Hayburn,

"I have been sitting up most of the night trying to write this.

"It would have been much easier for me never to write it at all, much easier, in one way at least, just to say goodbye when your stay here was ended and let you go. But I have taken

175

more than one blind step in my life, and now, risking your good opinion of me, I am taking another. What you said to me tonight has at last decided me, unusual as it most certainly must appear to you.

"You seemed surprised that David Moorhouse had not told me of your circumstances. I did not answer you directly, because David had, indeed, done so. But it was one thing for David to tell me, and quite another thing for you to tell me on your own account.

"I wonder why you did it? Was it because you felt, as I myself have felt, perhaps wrongly, that a certain kind of sympathy was growing up between us? And did you feel it must not grow farther without my knowing how you stood in the world? That is what I should like to think—what, indeed, I did think, tonight—what touched me—what forced me to get up quickly and leave you.

"I am a lonely woman, Stephen Hayburn, who married, as I told you, late in life, mainly for companionship. My husband's death has left me with a fortune which is free, well-secured, and quite in my own hands. It is large enough to provide a comfortable home for more than one person. My reason for not having had such a home is that I have felt unsettled and without roots in these last years.

"That, then, is what I have taken the risk of telling you, however awkward the telling; though such a letter from a woman to a man must always surely be awkward. And yet why should I, at my age, finding myself in a position to stretch out a hand towards a chance of happiness, not, indeed, do so? If, however, this letter seems to you a mere impertinence, then I must beg you as a gentleman to destroy it at once, saying nothing to anybody.

"I shall be on my way to Monte Carlo when you get this with your coffee. If you want to see me, then you will find me walking in the casino gardens at eleven this morning. If you do not come, I shall understand very well, and you will never see me again.

"God bless you.

"LUCY HAMONT."

176

Shortly afterwards David looked in upon his friend. He found him standing in front of his dressing-table.

"Hullo, Stephen; up and about early?"

"Well, yes, I am, David."

What was wrong with the man? He looked pink, troubled, and fussy. "Feeling all right, Stephen?"

"Of course!"

"What are we doing today? We arranged nothing last night."

Stephen's face turned lobster red at this and it took on a look of guilt. "Oh—do you mind, David? I find I have to meet a friend in Monte Carlo."

"Friend? I didn't know you knew—"

"Well, as a matter of fact, yes. Someone has turned up."

Stephen now looked so desperate, that amused malice took hold of David. "I might come with you. We could separate there if you don't want me."

"Much better not, David. Much better."

"My dear boy! What is it? Invented a secret gambling system or something?"

"No. Not gambling. It's something I can't tell you now, David. If you'll only leave me, I'll tell you all about it when I get back."

"Good. Of course. But why didn't you say so at once?"

Without replying, Stephen turned to brush his thinning hair with hands that seemed none too steady.

There was nothing for David to do then but to close the door, withdraw to the garden and his newspaper, and spend the remainder of the day consumed by curiosity.

Chapter Seventeen

"THERE ye are, my dear. There's something that should interest ye." Arthur Moorhouse tossed a folded *Glasgow Herald* across the breakfast table.

Bel took up the newspaper. "What is it, Arthur? What do you want me to look at?" She turned to Sarah who had just come in to remove plates and to ask about fresh toast. "My spectacles should be on the mantelpiece, Sarah. Can you see them?"

Sarah found them, took them from their case, and came across to give them to her. These last weeks had left their mark on her master and mistress. This waiting for further news of Tom was a strain on all of them. Mr. Moorhouse looked thin, even for him, and his naturally deep-set eyes were beginning to have that sunken, luminous look that sometimes goes with old age. And the elegant face of Mrs. Moorhouse was showing lines that told of the lack of sleep; and now, as Sarah bent over the familiar head, it seemed to her that more grey hair was showing.

She did not, of course, express any of this. She wiped her mistress's spectacles fiercely with a table-napkin, gave them to her, looked at her master, and said angrily: "Ye havena eaten yer porridge again this morning, sir! And no' much ham ither! Have ye made up yer mind to leeve on air?"

"I'm gettin' on fine, lassie! Never *you* heed!"

With the spring of her eye-glasses pinching her nose, Bel's expression was even more severe than she intended, as she arched her brows in criticism, first of her husband, then of her maid. Must the language of the Glasgow streets invade Grosvenor Terrace? "Well, really!" she said quietly, after what she judged to be a pregnant pause. Thereafter

178

her eyes dropped once more upon the morning newspaper.

"Where is it, Arthur? How am I to know what you mean?"

"Marriages. Second from the bottom."

"Help me to find it, Sarah."

Sarah was taking a pair of thumbed steel spectacles from a pocket of her morning wrapper as her mistress exclaimed: "What! Stephen Hayburn! And the woman must be Lucy Rennie! Phœbe met her. Well, that's extraordinary! At his age! And at hers!" She turned primly to Sarah. "Sir Henry Hayburn's brother, Mr. Stephen Hayburn, has just been married in France to a lady we knew years and years ago, Sarah. That's what the master wanted me to see. It was quite unexpected."

Sarah found nothing to reply to this. She had hoped it might be something worth reporting to old Bessie, the cook downstairs. Disappointed, she put her spectacles back into her pocket, collected the plates with gestures which told more plainly than speech that for her Mr. Stephen Hayburn could marry a female Hottentot if he felt so inclined, and went off to her pantry.

Arthur smiled to himself at his wife's eagerness. This was what he had intended. Anything to tear her mind from the care that beset it. Here was a glint of the real Bel, genteelly reproving, and hard on the scent of family gossip. It was a glint that pleased him.

She laid down the newspaper. "I wish I knew more about this!" she said, looking out of the window behind him, at the trees over there in the Botanic Gardens, at the traffic on Great Western Road as it passed up and down in the pale, watery sunshine.

Arthur got up. "Oh, ye'll be hearin', my dear! David'll be back one o' these days. It's time I was away." He bent down to kiss her, a custom he had revived after many years of morning forgetfulness and hurry, revived to show he shared this tension, revived as a comfort to himself. In two minutes more he was swinging himself up the outside steps to the top of a city tram-car, still with the agility of a young man.

On this same morning David Moorhouse appeared at Bel's front door. He had travelled by night from London and breakfasted alone at a station hotel. He had looked in neither at club nor office, for he was determined to see Bel before others knew of his arrival.

David and Bel were confederates of long standing. From David's first days in Glasgow, the happy, rising days of Bel's early married life, they had been close friends, each understanding the other's point of view, in a way that the rest of the family could not. Now he had come to consult her about Robin, before he saw either Henry or Phœbe Hayburn.

Just before David left the Riviera, Stephen, who was now remaining for some time longer with his wife, had judged it best to tell David what he knew. It was better, Stephen felt, that nothing should be set down in a letter.

A pompous indecision, coupled with a nervous overdiscretion, and, too, a genuine desire to help, had been weighing upon David more and more, the nearer he got to Glasgow. Last night he had lain in his sleeping-berth as he flew northward, turning this way and that, wondering how and what to tell the Hayburns. But at last the thought of first seeing Bel had dropped into his mind as a lifebelt drops into a stormy sea.

He found her in the back parlour, which she chose to call the library.

"David! I heard you were coming home this week, but I had no idea when. Are you alone? Did Grace meet you?"

"No. I wanted to see you first. I came on the night train." He bent to kiss this sister-in-law, who had long stood closer to him than any of his own sisters.

"See me? Have you had breakfast?"

"I've had breakfast. I've come to talk to you. To get your advice." He took off his travelling coat, and was laying it over a chair, settling himself down, when the change in Bel's appearance prompted him to ask: "What about Tom, my dear?"

"Still waiting, David." She sat down by the fire, clasped her hands in her lap, looked up at him and smiled a little. "It's a strain. But we'll get news soon. Sit down and tell me everything. This wedding of Stephen's. And to Lucy Rennie, of all people! How did you feel about that?"

The colour in David's cheeks rose. So Bel remembered.

She saw his embarrassment and laughed. "I never really knew just how near you got to marrying Lucy Rennie yourself," she said. "I often wondered. I think you might tell me now that it can't matter." But as the plump, handsome man on the chair across the hearth merely stroked his head with one hand and said nothing, she added: "Well, for everybody's sake, she's much better to be married to Stephen Hayburn than to you."

But David was somehow looking as though he did not quite agree with that either.

"You wouldn't change her for Grace, would you, David?"

"No. Oh no, not now." He said this with so little enthusiasm, however, that Bel decided to give up teasing him.

But really! What did men want? There was David. He had married Grace Dermott, who had given him his wealth, his position, his influence, and everything else; in addition to her own charming and gentle self and the two fine children she had borne him! And yet he could still, it seemed, cast back a lingering regret in the direction of a second-rate might-have-been, a woman who had neither bank account nor background, a paid performer!

"And tell me about Robin," she said, determinedly changing the subject.

"It's Robin I want your advice about. That's why I'm here. He has got himself mixed up with a young woman in Mentone, and Stephen thinks I should speak to his father."

Again, for an instant, Bel wondered at the ways of men. Now David had lost all embarrassment. Now he had become

181

the serious uncle, one of the reproving family pillars upon which the Moorhouse good name must rest. That he had once been "mixed up", as he called it, with Lucy Rennie, and this, when he was years older than Robin and already promised in marriage, had already, it seemed, dropped from his mind.

But Bel's interest was caught. "Speak to his father, David? But you talk as if this were serious. The boy is only twenty!"

"It *is* serious, Bel. Even if the boy is only twenty." He got up, stood with his back to the fire, looked down upon his sister-in-law, and repeated: "Very serious, indeed."

III

A door flew open to admit David's oldest sister, Sophia Butter. "Bel, dear! David! What luck! You'll be able to tell us everything! Mary's in the hall taking off her galoshes! Anne's helping her! Fancy! Lucy Rennie and Stephen Hayburn! Of all people! And were you at the wedding? Mary, here's David! And are you just back, David? Mary, David's just back. It would be a funny French wedding, was it? I saw a picture once, and they all had on evening clothes and white ties. How are you, Bel dear? Taking care? That's right. And David's all sunburned and well! Mary, doesn't David look well?" Sophia kissed Bel and David impulsively, drew a wisp of worn fur from her neck, and was already sitting down by the table as Mary, followed by her daughter Anne, came serenely into the room, presented an ivory cheek first to her sister-in-law, then to her brother, and sat down in the chair he had just got up from.

Bel sent David a look of despair, which David acknowledged with a look of annoyance. Their niece Anne saw this, understood, and wondered what could be done. Bel had suffered these sudden invasions—on the whole good-naturedly—all her married life. But now she was angry. "I didn't hear you coming in," she said coldly.

182

"The door was open, dear. Your cook, Bessie, was polishing the letter-box," Mary said.

This did nothing to soothe Bel. Letter-boxes in Grosvenor Terrace should be polished before breakfast, not at eleven in the morning. She must speak to Cook about this. But that did not excuse Mary's tale-bearing, nor yet her smug tones. Bel, in her annoyance, decided that there would be no morning tea for any of them.

Now Mary was sitting, regal in black silk and sealskin—the sealskin a present from Arthur, who, in a fit of highly provoking generosity, had said he did not like to see his widowed sister going about shabby—placidly leading the talk. "And when did you come home, David?"

"This morning," he answered shortly.

"Only this morning, David dear? We *had* heard you were coming home this week. But I said to William, *you'll* see—"

"Sophia! Sophia, please! I'm talking to David!" Mary's voice was seldom loud, but it would be firm.

"But I just wanted—"

"No, Sophia! And, David, tell us about this wedding."

"Well? What do you want to know about it, Mary? I don't see why you should be particularly interested. They were married last week in Nice. Robin and I were witnesses." David spoke querulously. It was intolerable that these foolish sisters of his should be here to waste his time.

But Mary, her curiosity still unsatisfied, chose to disregard this querulousness. "You forget I've always known Lucy Rennie. Why shouldn't I be interested, dear?" she said, adding pleasantly: "And where are Mr. and Mrs. Stephen Hayburn now?"

"Still in Mentone, of course!"

"I don't see why you should say 'of course', David. They might quite as well be somewhere else. But I am sorry to hear they're still there. Especially with you away now. I've always thought—haven't I, Bel?—that a woman like Lucy Rennie was no kind of friend for any young man."

183

"I don't remember what you thought, Mary," Bel said.

"Oh yes, Bel, dear, surely you do!" Sophia hastened to interpose. "Mary has always thought so. And William and I have always—"

"And what have they got to live on? Lucy must have some money now, I suppose." Mary raised her voice a little, managing thus once again to stem the flow.

"I really don't know, Mary! Why don't you write and ask for all particulars?"

It was not often that David showed temper like this. The ivory of Mary's cheeks became tinted. But her smile was controlled and kind as she shook her head and said: "David! David! It was only a very natural interest in an old friend!"

"Friend!"—David was beginning, when his niece actually dared to come to his rescue.

"Uncle David looks very tired after his long journey, Mama. And I'm sure he has come in specially to see Auntie Bel. I think we should go. Don't you, Auntie Sophia?" This was a rare outburst of courage for Anne.

Sophia at once became an incontinent flood of compassion and apology, which was just what Anne had intended. A flood that swept Sophia, her niece, and her astonished sister out of Bel's front door.

IV

"Somebody should rescue Anne from that mother of hers," David said.

Bel scarcely bothered to consider this. Anne's only chance was marriage. And that chance, Bel felt, was becoming increasingly remote. "Tell me about Robin, David," she said, dismissing her unwanted visitors from her mind.

He settled down to the story that had brought him to Grosvenor Terrace. Stephen and Lucy had, he said, come to his room on his last night in Mentone and told him everything.

184

They had decided that he should share the responsibility of knowing. Now in his turn David had come to Bel.

Gazing at the flickerings of the parlour fire, she sat considering for a time. Henry Hayburn's own son. There was much in that. Now, raising her eyes for an instant, she looked at David. No. David, had never been 'mixed up' as badly as this. He was too canny, too much of a Moorhouse ever to have given way to real foolishness. But she was genuinely sorry. She had always liked Robin. "Pity to send him down there, just to be caught like that!" she said presently.

"Caught, Bel? Who's caught him?"

She raised her eyes to him once more. "That woman, of course! What does she look like?"

"Attractive."

"I thought so. Well, don't you see, David? You say he's talking about marrying her?"

"Yes. He did to Stephen. I don't think he has talked to Miss St. Roch yet."

But Bel's innocent shrewdness—the innocent shrewdness of her class, her times, and her creed—would have none of this. "David, how can you be so simple? If he hasn't talked to her, she will have talked to him! We can be sure of that! Hasn't she heard that Robin belongs to Sir Henry and Lady Hayburn? To rich people? Do you think she would have— well, gone so far, if she didn't mean to hold him? Of course! A woman like that is providing for her old age. A fortune-hunter! An adventuress!" She turned once more to the fire, leaving David time to see reason.

David got up, thrust his hands into his pockets, and paced Bel's parlour. He supposed she must be right. And yet he had not thought of this before. Lucy and Stephen didn't think there was any fortune-hunting in it. He said: "Their fear is for Robin, when she leaves him. They feel his health may suffer dangerously."

Again she looked up. When she spoke, her voice was sharp. "And who are Stephen Hayburn and Lucy Rennie, to have opinions, David? Nothing very much themselves, by all accounts."

He did not like this. Stephen was an old friend. And Lucy had once meant something to him. Why should Bel use these tones of contempt? But David still possessed the remains of an intuition. He now saw that Bel should not, perhaps, in these days of her own trouble, be asked for level judgments. "I think I'll try to see Phœbe," he said. "Have they flitted to Whins of Endrick yet?"

"No. They're still at Partickhill. They go tomorrow."

V

Phœbe sat on a packing-case in her empty drawing-room. Her brother David's footsteps resounded on the bare floor. Down below she could see the remover's men taking chairs and tables to the van. Straws and papers were everywhere: inside and outside, on the garden path, on the grass, tangled in the shrubs. Harsh spring light streamed through naked windows.

Henry and she would only sleep for one night more here in this house. Instinctive in most things, she hated leaving the place that had been her home for so many years; where Robin had grown up; from which Henry had gone each morning, striding down the hill. Tomorrow they would sleep at Whins of Endrick, where things would feel strange.

Now, as she looked at David, her mind, torn from leave-taking, was filled with what he had just told her.

"Bel is certain the girl has done this deliberately, so that Robin will be forced to marry her," David said.

"Do you believe that?"

"Yes, I daresay it's very likely."

"Why, David?"

"Sir Henry Hayburn's adopted son. A rich boy to be exploited. If not marriage, then she may hope to be bought off."

Phœbe got up, went over to the window, looked down upon

the men as they went to and fro, then turned once more to look at her brother. "What does this woman look like, David? Does she seem that kind of woman?"

"Well, she's beautiful in a queer sort of way. But, no. Not like that."

"I thought so."

"Why, Phœbe?"

"I don't know." It was her turn to walk about the room now. She had lived in Vienna once; seen other ways. It was a strange assumption in this rigid Moorhouse world of theirs that such things could only take place for gain. Moorhouses measured life in terms of hard cash. No. Such things happened for all kinds of reasons. The idea of marriage was more likely to have its roots in Robin's ignorance. She turned to David, who now sat on the packing-case. "But she must be very much older than Rob, David?"

"About ten years."

"Marriage! Bel's a fool!" She swung on her heel and continued walking about. "I wish I knew what to do!" she said desperately.

"About what, exactly?"

"Robin, of course. Robin's health. Everything!"

"What about his behaviour?"

She shrugged. Her instinct had become crudely maternal. She could only wonder how to save him from a great unhappiness, unhappiness that might so darken his days as to bring disaster to him.

David waited.

"I don't think I'm going to tell Henry about Robin," she said presently.

"Why?"

"Well, not at once, anyway. He's terribly busy with the Exhibition, for one thing. But it's not that. I must try to save him. This would—oh, I don't know—!"

David wondered why she should speak thus. Why should Henry be spared the duty of calling Robin to heel? From what

187

must he be saved? But David could not read his sister's heart. He could not see that she was seeking blindly for a way to stand between these two who were her all, to hold back each from wounding the other with a wound which might cut too deep for healing.

"Listen, David," she went on. "Say nothing about this to anyone, please. Bel won't talk. I may write to Stephen. He knows his way about better than Henry does. Henry has always been—I can't exactly explain—so innocent in some ways."

"What will you ask Stephen to do?"

Again she shrugged. "I must think. But I'll let you know."

As her brother held out a hand to say goodbye, a bell rang harshly through the half-empty house. The telephone was downstairs in the hall. Descending after her, David signed to the workmen to go more quietly, here, where everything reverberated.

"Hullo? Bel? Yes, Phœbe. I can hardly hear you. What? Tom? A wire just now? Oh, Bel, I'm glad! Oh, I see. But he's alive and coming home. That's all that matters. Yes. David's here. I'll give him the news. Yes, the house is full of people, but I'll come across at once." She turned to tell her brother. "Tom is on his way home. He's had a foot off. But he's all right in other ways. Poor Bel! She could hardly tell me!"

Phœbe stood on her doorstep watching David until he had gone. Starlings chattered on roof-tops. A blackbird kept on repeating its call from a tree misted with young green. Now the van was loaded up, and the driver was cracking his whip and shouting to the two great Clydesdale horses.

Phœbe sighed. Life was—but it didn't matter what life was. She must hurry across to Bel.

Chapter Eighteen

IT was mid-morning.

Denise St. Roch appeared on her balcony ready to go out. "Are you going to stay here, Robin? I'm going to the shops."

Robin, whose custom it now was to come up each morning just after breakfast and work beside her, raised his head. "I'm staying. I want to get on with this. Better take him with you, though." He indicated the dog, Paul Morphy, panting in the sunshine. "He always begins to get restless. He won't give me any peace."

Followed by the great wolfhound, Denise took herself downstairs and into the Rue Longue.

It was a brilliant April day. At this hour the mounting sun struck down into the old, narrow street, making its springtime warmth felt.

The foreign young woman with her boyish head, her strange clothes, and her sandalled feet, was now a familiar sight among the friendly Mentonese. Philomene had, of course, told her friends about her. These had repeated what she told them, and thus, the human hive of the old town knew everything, approving what they knew. There she was now, erect and easy in her long, rope-girdled robe, smiling good-humouredly at the little children sitting in doorways, telling them not to mind her dog, and exchanging greetings with their mothers in a French that was purer than their own.

Here and there a knot of women, having stopped their morning gossip to return her salutation, turned to gaze when she had passed them by. This American girl was unlike all other Americans they had seen. She might lead her life in a way that was not their way, but was she not a writer, an artist? And were not all such gifted people queer? Queer, but certainly beautiful. It was no wonder that slender young man with the tumbling hair and the large eyes was forever to be seen going up to visit her. Philomene said—here heads drew close together. But why not? Besides, as the eager heads were never done agreeing, it was no affair of theirs, and who were they that they should inquire?

And for the time being, indeed, Denise had found her own kind of contentment. All tension with Robin, on her side at all events, had been relaxed. She was working well, was fond of the gentle, gifted young man who had become her lover, and was glad to leave things thus for the moment. Why look to the future? When the thread was running smooth, why seek to knot it?

Now she was doing everything to help Robin with his work. The old sting of jealousy had gone. That he had been adjudged a better artist than herself no longer troubled her. She was proud of him and anxious that his short, finely-wrought pieces—she felt their fineness, now the "old man" had said they were fine—should receive due recognition. She had, indeed, sent some of his work where she thought it might be used; and they were even now awaiting a decision.

Where the Rue Longue comes down into the lower town, Denise suddenly found herself face to face with Mr. and Mrs. Stephen Hayburn.

She called to them: "Oh, hello! I didn't know you were back in Mentone. Robin never told me. Congratulations! You look just wonderful! My! My! Are we really blushing?"

All feathers and frills, the new Mrs. Hayburn held out her hand in a charmingly suitable confusion. "Don't talk nonsense, Denise! What's different about us? Two decrepit old creatures, determined to support and comfort each other in their decrepitude. Isn't that it, Steve?"

But Stephen, more debonair than ever, would not allow this. Modishly dangling his eye-glass by its ribbon, he turned to his wife. "Decrepit rubbish, m'dear! Do we look decrepit, Miss St. Roch?"

Denise's white teeth flashed in her glowing face. "Why, no! Haven't I been telling you? You both look wonderful!"

They walked along together towards the shops, telling their news. After their marriage in Nice, they had thought of going to Paris, as they had found—the bridegroom in particular had found—that there was shopping to do. "A married man wants this and that, don't you know." Stephen, forced as he was to walk behind the ladies in the narrow, noisy street, shouted over their shoulders. But feeling they were not yet done with Mentone, they had compromised, and, as neither of them had seen Marseilles, they had gone to spend a day or two there. "Honeymoon in Marseilles! Something not quite respectable about the sound of it, wouldn't you say, Miss St. Roch?" Stephen shouted again.

Lucy smiled back at him. "At our ages, I'm afraid there is nothing left to do but be respectable, my dear." As she turned back to Denise, she was surprised to find her preparing to leave them. "What? Already?"

"Yes. I can get through to where I'm going this way."

As she made her way through a narrow side alley, Denise smiled a little. Marriage at over fifty made folks self-conscious and silly, she supposed. But these two would soon get over that.

II

When Denise had gone, Robin sat sucking the end of his pencil and looking from the high balcony. Since it was before midday, the sunlight was still streaming down upon the eastern side of the town. Here on this sheltered coast, early summer, it seemed, was almost come. In the near distance he could see a cascade of wistaria falling from the wall of a cliffside garden. A puff of warm spring wind brought him the scent of roses.

He swung back on his wicker chair, put his feet against the

bars of the balcony, thrust his hands into his pockets and gave himself up to the pleasures of self-examination, a habit that had lost none of its attractions in these last days.

Was this what he had wanted? He supposed so. Happiness? He supposed that, too. An impossible hope seemed now to be coming true. He was to be a writer. Dreadful to think now how another, colder world had nearly claimed him! But yet, in spite of all, his artist's blood had forced its way. Which all went to show—he could not quite think what it showed. But one thing was certain. The world to which he belonged was the world of passion and imagination. Robin tossed the eternal strand from his brow, and smoothed it back with one hand, determining in future to let his hair grow rather longer.

Passion and imagination. Passion. Denise. A great experience had come to him. Now, with the probing curiosity of a writer, Robin sought about within himself, examining facets of his feelings, examining his experience. He was, beyond disputing, deeply in love with her. With the turn of her head, with her warm southern voice, with her gaiety, with the slim perfection of her. This, his first love, obsessed and overwhelmed his twenty years. It walked with him when he walked. It met his waking moments. It wrapped him, in their times of exaltation, in a mist of quivering bliss. He had read somewhere that the first love of a very young man was bounded only by infinity. He could understand that. Such adoration and possession could be known only to a very few. It must be made to last forever.

Robin stood up and began to pace the balcony. Halting for a moment, his eyes followed the movement of a fishing-boat as, its red-triangled sail already hoisted, the men strove to row it from the harbour into the breeze that fanned the waters in the open bay.

He had sat at the end of the sea wall down there with his Uncle Stephen discussing what he must do. His uncle had begged time for reflection. But now that Robin came to think of it, what was there to reflect over? He loved Denise and she

192

loved him. They would be married. What else? Already they belonged to each other.

Still, when it came to marriage—as soon, of course, it must—he might be glad of his uncle's help. Marriage. Boyishly, Robin shrank from the thought of this grave step. And boyishly, too, though he had not spoken of marriage to Denise, it had never once struck him that she might have different notions.

Now he leant on the rail of the balcony, staring down and pondering. Carriages with linen sun-awnings ran round the bay. The distant jetty was alive with shouting fishermen. He could just see the heads of two swimmers out in the harbour, daring the April waters.

Yes. It might be better to talk to Uncle Stephen. For Uncle Stephen could help with his father.

Remembering Sir Henry, a cold breath of doubt blew through Robin's mind. Uneasily he shifted his weight from one leg to the other, and his thin, handsome face looked glum. Would it not indeed be better to discuss all this with Denise before he went much farther? Was not that the first thing he must do? But somehow he did not want to do it. Not yet awhile. He did not quite know why. She puzzled him. She could allow him to be so much to her, could give herself so wonderfully. Still, now that he thought of it, did not those little gay coolnesses of hers, those occasional moods of enchanting solemnity, keep their relationship on her terms, force it to take the pattern she had chosen to impose upon it? The dark mop fell forward as Robin gave his head a knowing, manly nod. Of course there must be much about Denise he did not understand. How could it be otherwise, when she had been his only for so short a time? Yet very soon he must speak to her of their future.

She found him thus, still mooning on her balcony, when she returned an hour later. "Well? Got a lot of work done?"

"Not much."

"What have you been doing?"

"Thinking things out." Then, as he turned to look at her: "Hello! You seem very pleased about something."

"Yes, I am. And so will you be!" She held out an opened letter. "Look. They're publishing your story. And paying twenty pounds. That's a lot for a start, believe me! Delighted with it, and want more. Now, doesn't that make you feel good?" He snatched the letter from her, ran his eye through it, then took her into his arms in a frenzy of exaltation. Here was confirmation. Here was the answer to his problem. Here was independence. "Denise, darling! I can't believe it! Why all this—and you as well? Denise, we're going to be rich, you and I! How will you feel, with your husband a prosperous writer like yourself?"

He had said it. He had said the word 'husband'. He realised this as she kissed him then drew herself away gently and stood looking at him, a question in her face. But almost at once she came to him again and put her arms round his neck. "Robin, everything is going to be fine! But we needn't talk about what's going to be, just right away, need we, sweetheart? Sufficient unto—wouldn't you say? And of course we'll go on being very, very happy. And fix everything when the time comes."

III

In the afternoon of this same day, Mr. and Mrs. Stephen Hayburn sat drinking tea in their pleasant sitting-room. A page-boy had brought up letters.

"Here's one from Scotland," Stephen said. "It's handwriting I know, but I'm not quite sure whose." He broke the envelope open, unfolded it, and turned to the signature. "Oh, Phœbe."

"About Robin, Stephen?"

"Probably."

"Then it's sure to be full of difficulties. Put it down, dear, until you've finished tea."

194

Letting the glass fall from his eye, Stephen did as he was told. With one hand he held out his cup to be refilled and twisted his moustache with the other. "Quite right, m'dear. Sure to be full of 'em. Why sup sorrow?" He smiled approval at his wife's good sense.

But when, indeed, was Stephen Hayburn not smiling these days? And were not his reasons for smiling of the best? An amazingly short time ago he had been—well, actually the mere dependant of his friend David Moorhouse. Oh, David had always been very generous and good about it, and it had gone on for so long—over twenty years, was it?—that he, Stephen, could not really say he had much to grumble about; no iron entering his soul or that sort of thing. Still, how was he ever to get over the miracle of this? In the twinkling of an eye, or certainly in the twinkling of a mere two weeks or so, the charming, sympathetic, and highly intelligent little woman who sat there elegantly pouring out his second cup of tea had found the courage and good sense to wave a hand in his direction; and having waved it, to offer it to him, along with her heart; and what was more, a very reasonable and unhumiliating share in her excellently secured income. The balm to his pride! The relief! The dignity gained! The final arrangements must wait, of course, until, in a few weeks time, they found themselves in London; when Lucy's man of business would make everything perfectly straight and legally precise.

But what was legal precision between two love-birds? As he had so often said to this dear, newly-acquired wife of his. Let them linger here at their pleasure in this lovely place of their first meeting, until, indeed, they felt induced to move, or the increasing heat of summer drove them from it.

"Thanks, m'dear." Stephen took his cup back from Lucy. "It's pleasant here," he said.

"Yes." Lucy looked about her. The windows, half-shuttered against the sunshine and hung with loops of net, threw light and shadow among the gilt and marble of the hotel furniture. She had filled the room with roses. She was glad he found it pleasant; glad this stranger was her husband; glad her courage had not failed her. So far it was easier than she had expected. Easier for herself, and easier, too, she guessed, for Stephen, both of them no longer young, to readjust one to the other. But she had judged Stephen Hayburn aright. In their close relationship he lacked neither fastidiousness nor courtesy. In such things he was like herself. Now, as she saw it, their future might be very happy. Beneath the inevitable play-acting, they knew exactly where they stood. She had made a good investment against the loneliness of old age. Perhaps—who knew?— they might still fall in love with each other a little.

Stephen swallowed down his last mouthful, then once more he took up Phœbe's letter. "She's seen David. She feels Denise St. Roch must be mainly responsible. Older. All the experience and that sort of thing." He handed the letter to Lucy.

"What mother wouldn't say that?" Lucy said, taking it up to read. "But I daresay she's right. Oh? Hasn't told Sir Henry yet? She wants us to talk to Denise, does she? But I'm not sure that I want to. Robin! My dear!"

The sitting-room door had been thrown open. It disclosed Robin standing with one hand on the knob. Lucy folded the letter quickly.

"Come in, Robkin. Glad to see you. Had tea?" Stephen called.

"Had tea, thanks. It's only a message from Denise. She says you've never seen her studio, and she has suddenly got it into her head that you had better pay her a formal call as Mister and Missis."

Stephen took a resolution. "Robkin, come in and shut the door for a moment."

"I've got to fly, Uncle Stephen."

"You fly too much these days, if you ask me. Shut it and sit down."

Robin shut the door and advanced, looking from one to the other, as he found a chair.

"How are you getting on with Miss St. Roch?" Stephen asked, hoping, perhaps, to gain some advantage by putting the question abruptly.

Robin smiled radiantly. "She's sold my first story for me. Twenty pounds. I can't believe it! I came to tell you that too."

"Oh, Robin, how splendid!" Lucy cried brightly.

Her husband wondered if her fervour did not seem a little over-acted. "Congratulations, Robkin," he said. "But it wasn't her help with your stories I meant. How are you getting on with Miss St. Roch herself?" And then, seeing that Robin went red to the roots of his hair, he added: "Oh, don't worry. Your Aunt Lucy knows all about it. She's heard of—well—that kind of friendship before, you know."

Robin frowned in his confusion. He was still callow enough to be embarrassed that such things should be discussed before a lady. "I don't see why we need to talk about this now." He stood up.

"No, Robkin! Wait! You came to me before I went away, if you remember. You wanted my help then."

"Thanks, Uncle Stephen. And you can help. But may we discuss this another time? The main thing is that I love Denise and she loves me. Today she promised to marry me."

"Promised. Robin?"

"Yes. Why not, Aunt Lucy? Why this surprise? What would you expect?"

Lucy's face became overspread with a misty smile. "Tell her we'll be up to see her very soon, Robin."

"But don't you believe it, Aunt Lucy?"

"I'll believe whatever you tell me, Robin."

"Well, I daresay the idea takes some getting used to! I haven't got used to it myself."

Stephen looked at Lucy as the door closed. "Do you believe that?"

She shook her head. The smile was gone. She had been struck with Robin's frail look as he stood there. Why should a woman like Denise St. Roch, who had fought for her

197

independence, now tie herself to a consumptive boy? "I don't understand," she said.

"Robin, it seems to me, might as well be left to take what's coming to him, m'dear. Part of his education."

For a time Lucy sat thinking. She had much to blame herself with. Much that she really regretted. If Robin were a strong young creature, then Stephen would no doubt be right. But now? "I had better see Denise alone," she said at length. "Whether I want to or not."

IV

Denise and Lucy sat beneath the striped awning of their usual pavement café, looking across the gardens towards the casino. The stream of visitors on the pavement was thinner. Although the gardens blazed with a triumph that belonged almost to early summer, the world of fashion was beginning to move northwards towards places where finery could be flaunted in cooler comfort. The century was still twenty-five years too young for brown-skinned virility and elegant nakedness.

"It's hot," Lucy said.

"Yes. Are you and your husband staying much longer?"

"Some weeks. I'm not quite sure. Are you?"

"I don't know either. I've got some work to finish before I go."

"Robin told us yesterday he had a story sold."

Denise displayed her dazzling teeth in a wide smile. "Poor child! He's walking in the clouds about it."

"Why do you say 'poor', Denise? He's very lucky to have you to help him."

"Me? Well, maybe I can help him to sell his work."

"He's been talking to his Uncle Stephen, Denise." Lucy saw her companion's quick look. "He doesn't want to go home. He wants to stay in France writing."

198

"Yes." Denise turned to stroke Paul Morphy's ears as he sat beside her, then she turned back to Lucy. "But I didn't know he had been talking to his uncle."

"He's worried. He knows the people at home won't like it. He can't make enough to live on, can he?"

Denise shook her head. "No. Not at once, anyway." Then she waited before she said: "Still, I believe in doing what you want, whatever the consequences. Don't you?"

"I suppose so. If you're young and strong."

Denise sat considering this. "Are Robin and your husband good friends?" she asked presently.

"My husband tries to help and advise."

Denise stroked Paul Morphy again. "I wonder what kind of things Robin tells him?"

Lucy bent towards her companion. "Do you remember once I talked to you about the stuffiness of the Moorhouse family, and suggested you might educate Robin a bit?"

"Yes. Why?"

"I'm sorry I did it now."

"Why?" Denise asked sharply and, as Lucy seemed to hesitate: "Has he told his uncle about—that, too?"

"It depends on what you mean, Denise."

"No. It doesn't depend on what I mean. You know very well what I mean! That boy's tongue's too long! That I'm—?"

"Sit down again, Denise, please. He told us yesterday you had promised to marry him."

"I don't believe it!" Having sat down again, Denise considered Lucy's word gloomily. Then she went on: "Oh, I may not have denied it! What do you expect? But he can't be such a child! Or I guess he is, if he goes jabbering to everybody! But how can a woman like you—"

"My dear girl, I didn't believe you had said it. Oh, I don't know what to say! I suppose you're fond of him?"

"Of course I'm fond of him! I'm not a street-walker!"

"Then remember you hold the happiness of a foolish,

fragile boy in your hands. Please, Denise! I'm not blaming, I'm pleading!"

"Pleading for what?"

"Use him gently."

"Have I ever done anything else? Goodbye. You know how much I like interference!" She had jumped up once more and was dragging the great dog to his feet.

"Denise! But of course I see your side of it! How can you think I don't? No, please! We can't leave it like this."

"I'm sorry. I don't see how else we can leave it. I've got to go now. Look, that's our chocolate paid for." She gave a coin to the waiter, raised a hand in sullen salute and went.

Now, as Lucy sat watching Denise go, she found herself forced to ask herself what had been accomplished by this meeting she had put herself to the trouble of contriving. Disturbed and angry, she had to admit she had accomplished nothing.

V

Denise wondered at the change in Lucy, as now Paul Morphy pulled her home, ploughing, as he went, through the late afternoon rabble of visitors, peasants, fishermen, and work-people that almost blocked the narrower streets.

Lucy Hayburn, of all people! The Lucy Hamont she had known in Paris, who was admired and accepted by their friends for her charmingly broad mind and her gay understanding of their ways. Now this disapproval, these provincial family judgments!

But she must talk to Robin at once. Disabuse his mind of this nonsense. Tell him to be a man.

She had left him working on the balcony. For a moment she halted on her landing to fetch breath, then she took the large, old-fashioned key from her satchel and turned it in the lock. Released, Paul Morphy sprang into the room in front of her.

200

Robin was outside scribbling as though his life depended upon it, his hair dangling over brows that frowned in concentration. But now, the dog having run to him, he looked up. "Hullo!" he shouted. "Got back? I'll finish this, if you don't mind. Just a minute."

But inconveniently, as she stood watching him, Denise was assailed by feelings of tenderness. Lucy Hayburn's words came back to her. "I'm not blaming, I'm pleading! Remember you hold the happiness of a foolish, fragile boy in your hands." Now on the balcony, her eyes following the movement of the thin hand, nervously writing, she had to admit that her lover was no pillar of robust young manhood. But what was she to do? He had deceived himself. It had not been she.

Annoyed by Paul Morphy's large gambollings, Robin threw down his pen and got up. "Oh, look here! I can't do any more with that beast jumping about!" Then, turning to Denise: "How are we? See anyone?"

She wondered, as he blew her a young, self-conscious kiss, how, despite experience shared, Robin could still remain so immature, so uncertain of himself. Yet his nearness troubled and confused her. She turned from him, back into the room. "I saw the new Mrs. Hayburn," she said.

"Aunt Lucy? I still feel funny when I say that. Doesn't come natural." He laughed as he followed her.

"Oh, she's your aunt all right. One of the family!"

"What do you mean, Denise?"

"I had quite a little talk with her."

His colour rose. "Did you? Good."

"Yes. And you seem to have had quite a talk with her too. Or your uncle, which is the same thing, I suppose?"

He straddled a chair in front of her, leant his folded arms on its back, and looked up at her nervously. "My dearest, what is it that you want to say to me?"

She had meant to tax him with disloyalty, with lack of sense or feeling, in blurting out their secret to the Hayburns. But now, looking down upon him, she could not. On an impulse, she bent down to caress his dark head. It would be easier thus, perhaps, for what she had to say. "Sweetheart, you've been talking to them about you and me."

"Yes."

"Now, why?" She stood quite still, her hand on his hair, awaiting his answer.

"It was the first morning, after—it was before he went away to be married."

"But why?"

"I was worried. Worried how it would all work out. But that's past. My stories are selling. It's going to be all right."

"All right?" But she knew what was coming.

"Yes. I'll work hard. Soon I'll be earning quite a lot, I hope." Then, before she could reply to this, Robin added in a voice that shook a little: "My very dearest, I promise you here at once you won't ever find yourself married to a lazy good-for-nothing!" He stood up, came behind her, and put his hands upon her shoulder.

She burst into tears.

"Darling, what is it?" He turned her round, towards him.

"Robin, I can't, I won't, I never intended to marry you! No, no! Don't go away from me! I'm not hard. I'm not cruel. I thought you always knew!"

"But the other day you said—?"

"I thought that was just a game."

He sat down beside her on the sofa. So this, Denise reflected, was the firm, woman-of-the-world's talk she had determined to have with him? So this was the progress his so-called education had made? She could feel that the hand he had placed over her own was trembling. At last he got up and began to pace the room. What was he thinking? She must know. "Robin," she began, "I thought my love was helping you; that you were unhappy. That it was—oh, what can I say?—untying emotional knots. I saw us together in my mind in a wonderful kind of idyll. That was all."

202

He stood looking down on her and he said: "Pity I didn't know that." Then he turned aside as though he were struggling for calmness enough to say: "But I come from queer, puritan sort of people, I daresay."

She looked at him with curiosity, wondering even now which people he meant. The people of his adoption, or the people he believed to be his own.

"It's a pity I didn't understand either, Robin," she cried. "But must you hate me now?"

He stood before her, dishevelled and unhappy. And yet, as it seemed to her, considering what to do. "My darling! How can I hate you?" He had dropped on his knees and his face was in her lap.

VI

Robin had stayed for supper, but it was not yet late when he got back. Now, alone, in his room, he went to his window, threw back the shutters, and stepped outside. The air was warm and caressing. Lights in the garden, shining up through shrubbery and palms, made fantastic shadows. He heard the high-pitched hum of a mosquito. Looking into the shapeless blackness of the nearby pine-tree, he saw two eyes of golden-yellow fixed upon him. He called Grimaldi's name, but the eyes disappeared. Down on the promenade young men and women were walking arm in arm.

Did the loves of those down there run smooth? Were their emotions simpler? Easier of fulfilment? Less mixed, as they were at home with conscience and regret? It seemed so. Their tradition of behaviour was said to sit more lightly, to allow a wider freedom to their blood.

He thought of himself now. Was that his trouble? Had he sprung from warmer, more passionate soil than Hayburns and Moorhouses? Was his Viennese blood at war with his Scottish upbringing? This pleased him; made him interesting

203

to himself. And Denise, of course, was French. That was why—

Why what? He sighed, then turned to go inside. This did not help him in his present trouble. He loved Denise St. Roch with all the wildness of a boy's first love. He could not bear the thought of ever losing her. He had never dreamt that she did not mean to be his wife. Now she had told him that she could not. And yet, did she not love him? Not desire him? She must be shown she could not turn away like this.

He flung himself down in his chair by the window. The tensions of the day had left him very tired. But he must fight, must think of something! Work out a plan.

As he sat thus slouching and exhausted, Robin felt resourceless and confounded. At twenty the flesh may be adult, while the mind continues adolescent. Robin's feet had never yet stood on the ground. The story that Denise had sold for him would yield the first moneys he had ever earned.

He stretched out his legs in front of him. Drew them in again, sat forward, and threw back his hair. Flung himself back again, then recommenced these antics. But all this did not help. Was there to be no way out? Might Denise go at any time without a struggle? That was impossible. He could not allow that. What then?

But insensibly his instinct had been swinging on its pivot. There was one way he could take. In all the troubles he had ever known, he had turned to his Scottish parents. They had never failed to help him, even although along with help might come a sharp reproof.

There was nothing left, it seemed, then, but to beg of them to help him now. He would hide nothing. He would say exactly what had happened. He would tell them of his love for Denise; how wonderful she was; of her love for him; and how, already, and however she might see it, their lives were bound together. Tell them that somehow she must be made to see that marriage was the only thing. That this new cult of irresponsible freedom would end in breaking his heart! Now, in his pain and fear of losing her, Robin was even prepared to say that, despite encouragement and promise, he would give up all thought of being a writer; that he would come home and, without another word, try to fulfil his father's plans.

In his trouble, he had quite forgotten his romantic blood. His Viennese beginnings. These dreams were sweet and flattering to dream of. But such dreams do not always help their dreamers. They cannot force reluctance. They cannot take up pens and sign paternal cheques. Nor are they always there, when young bewilderment would turn to them for refuge.

His Scottish parents could not like his letter. His father would at first be swept by a storm of anger. But, as Robin now told himself with self-dramatising weariness, for the sake of Denise, there was nothing left for him to do but brave this angry storm. And in the end even his father would come to see he had no choice but help him.

And Denise meanwhile? He would treat her fondly, and with understanding. Gently try to prove to her that they were made the one for the other, that it was impossible to think of ever parting.

The soft night wind ballooned the net curtains at the open window. Down in the garden Grimaldi was spitting at an enemy. The clock in the Cathedral of St. Michel struck twelve long strokes. Was it as late as that already?

Robin drew himself slowly to his feet, crossed to his table, and sat himself down to write a letter to Sir Henry Hayburn.

Chapter Nineteen

AS she happened to be out in front of the new house, Lady Hayburn took the letters from the postman.

The old man was glad to have a look at this new mistress of Whins of Endrick, standing thus bareheaded in the morning sunshine. "Ye'll be richt pleased to be oot here in this bonny place, Mum, after leevin' in a dirty town like Glesca."

Phœbe laughed. "I'm very fond of Glasgow. Even if it is dirty. I've lived there most of my life. But I know all about the country. My father was a farmer in Ayrshire."

"Aye. So I've heard tell."

Again Phœbe laughed; this time to the postman's bewilderment. What, he wondered, was there to laugh at?

"Now, how did you hear that?" she asked.

He looked surprised, scratched a ruddy, weather-beaten cheek, and pulled a white side-whisker reflectively. "Och. I don't ken. Ye jist hear," he said with embarrassment.

But Lady Hayburn, having been a farm child, was remembering. Country people had ways of knowing all about you and your affairs almost before you knew about them yourself. Henry and she had been here for a very short time, yet these cottages across the fields, with their rising, blue smoke, that far-off village over there in the haze, would know all about them already.

From the front steps of the house, Phœbe smiled down at him. "I don't mind, you know," she said. "Are you the regular postman?"

"Aye."

"We'll see each other again, then." She came down two steps and held out her hand.

206

The old man took off his postman's hat as he returned the handshake. Thereafter he turned away, sturdily crunching the gravel of the drive with heavy boots, and deciding to spread the verdict that the new mistress of Whins of Endrick was "a nice like young wumman, that didna seem tae bother her heed wi' the P's and the Q's".

Phœbe examined the letters, strolling about in the sunlight. It was only ten o'clock. But Henry had gone more than two hours since. It was pleasant out here, with the lingering dew still wet upon the lawn; with the finches twittering across there among the tracery of the drooping birch branches. Inside, men were still working. There was intermittent hammering and a smell of paint.

Bills. One or two business letters addressed to herself; letters from tradespeople about this new house. Henry had left everything to her. He had enough on his hands, he said; both at the yards and on his stand in the Industrial Hall at the Exhibition. It must be ready for the opening on the second of May, and there was still much to do.

A letter with a French stamp in Robin's handwriting addressed to his father. Her fingers had almost begun to tear it open, when she remembered that Robin was a grown man now, that she had no right to read what he wrote to Henry; until, at least, Henry had given her permission to do so. It had been different when he was a schoolboy.

She walked about, wondering. She thought of the news David had brought her, and the letter she had, as a consequence, written to Stephen Hayburn. Stephen must have got it by now. Had he taken action? And was Robin writing to his father about that? She could not think so. In these days, Robin stood closer to herself than to Henry. He would almost certainly write first to her about anything so difficult.

Phœbe bent down to look at a clump of primroses growing in the moss beneath the birches. The action was mechanical. Her mind was still on Robin. But the poor boy was scarcely grown up yet! Might not his uncles, after all, be imagining? It

207

was difficult for her to believe that Robin could have the passions of a man.

A tradesman was signing to her from the doorway. She was glad to be forced to go back into the house, glad to be forced to drag her mind from nagging thoughts, glad to be forced to make decisions about such things as painting and carpets.

II

It was Sir Henry Hayburn's custom, when he got home in the evening, to drink a large and strongly-brewed cup of tea to which much cream and sugar had been added. He claimed that this whetted his appetite for dinner. He was standing by a window, still in his old Inverness, drinking this when Phœbe gave him Robin's letter. He laid down the cup on the window-sill and tore it open.

The letter was long and, for Robin, strangely humble. He had written what he had resolved to write with as much bare truth as his sense of the dramatic would allow him. He sought to hide nothing, realising, as he said, that he could not ask for his father's help so long as he kept things from him. Denise was older, but they loved each other dearly. Yet some strange scruple—he guessed an old unhappiness, or an early shock of some kind—made her quite determined against marriage. His father might not yet know this, but with Denise's help he was writing stories, one of which had already been accepted at a very good price. Thus he could look to keeping himself if need be. Yet, since he felt better in health, he would even go so far as promise to give up writing, if only his parents would help him with Denise now, for this matter of Denise could not wait. And she must, surely, after what had happened between them, come to see that marriage was the only think-able course. Thus Robin's letter went on confessing, arguing, and pleading, through several pages.

Having read it, Sir Henry put it down on the windowsill, took up his teacup and went on drinking his tea, staring out of the window as he drank.

His wife could not read his face. "Henry. What does Robin say?"

"Better read for yourself."

Phœbe raised her eyes to her husband's face at the end of the reading. She expected to find it dark with anger, but instead it was flushed and meek, and his eyes would not meet her own. Years ago she had seen this look, suffered bitterly, and at last learnt the ways of compassion. Compassion came first now. She ran to Henry and put her arms about him. "Henry! He's just a child. It's a boy's madness."

"He's my son." Henry stood stiff in her arms.

"He's my son, too. If he's yours he's mine. You've never grudged my right to him before."

"Grudged? Do you *want* him?"

Crushing his stiffness to her she cried out: "Want! Want my own son! Want Robin! Did I want him when I took your baby from you that night in Vienna?"

"He's my blood, Phœbe. Poor stuff."

She could feel his body shudder with a dry sob. Her voice softened, as she drew down his reluctant head and kissed him. "Oh, Henry! Don't behave as if the end of the world was here. Come and sit down." She led him to a seat. How well she knew that look, as he sat there. The old look of bewildered fecklessness. She let him sit thus for a time, herself walking about in the room. Presently, as she turned to him, she saw that he was looking at her. "Henry," she said, "what are we going to do?"

"Do?"

"Yes. Surely you realise you must do something."

He nodded. "Yes. Something." Again he sat pondering stupidly for a time. But to a man who is by nature decisive, decision must come. "I can still manage to get a late train for London," he said.

"London, Henry?"

"Then I can cross the Channel tomorrow."

So he was going to Robin. "Oh, Henry! I had better come with you."

"No. I'll send for you if I want you. You had better stay and tell everybody where I am. They'll be wondering. But don't tell them too much."

III

It had been easy to get a sleeping-berth on a Riviera train. At this time of the year fashion was travelling north, not south.

Henry lay heavy-headed and unable to sleep. It was his second night thus, and the intervening day had been taken up in crossing the Channel and getting himself to Paris. He was tired out.

Now, in the swaying, hurrying darkness, his thoughts revolved in circles. Robin. The boy was a fool. He must be rescued from this woman. But it must be done with care. For Robin was excitable and frail.

That rush job in the shipyard he had promised to supervise himself? What would they do about it? Would they have sense enough to grasp his long telegram of instructions, written out in the train last night and sent back from London? This unforeseen absence might cost him several thousand pounds. But then there was Robin. He must go to look after Robin.

And the stand at the Exhibition? He had not been able to give the final directions about that either. What would people think if Hayburn and Company—? But there was no choice. He must travel south to his son.

What was all this nonsense about writing? Who was encouraging Robin to write? Was it that woman who thought she had got hold of him? The boy must have been keeping low company ever to have met her.

Low company? Memory pointed an accusing finger. Henry

stirred, uneasy and restless, in this narrow bed that was flying through the night. Now, from the front, he could hear the whistle of the French locomotive; the high foreign note as the train rushed over a level crossing.

And yet if he, Henry Hayburn, had not transgressed, there would have been no Robin. None of the thousand gentle moments of his growing up. None of this present pain. But none of the joy Robin's existence had brought to them. Brought to himself and—amazingly—to Phœbe. Phœbe, to whom that existence should have been an insult. Where did wrong stop and right begin?

Round in circles. The weary thoughts of a brain that could make decisions that were unemotional and concrete; a brain that could only grope among the dilemmas of the spirit.

But he had had enough of this. He sat up, threw back the sheets, uncovered his roof-light, and found his pipe. That was better. The taste of tobacco helped to clear his thinking. He looked at his watch. It was three o'clock.

Robin. What, then, must be the first step? What was the plan of action? Henry's eyes, ranging aimlessly, caught the railway map framed there on the wall to show the route the train was taking. Marseilles. And then, thereafter, along the French Riviera through the well-known towns. Cannes, Nice, Monte Carlo, Mentone. These last two resorts lay within easy reach of each other. The train would get to Marseilles in the morning. Thereafter it took many hours to follow the coast-line to Mentone. That gave him time to wire Stephen from Marseilles. He would get out at Monte Carlo, where Stephen must meet him. He would find out how to see and talk to this woman before his son even knew he was in the south.

That was better. Something to go on. Henry smoked his pipe to a finish, put it away, and got back into bed. Soon he was actually feeling drowsy.

211

IV

It was the following afternoon.

Never did a less pleasure-seeking visitor than Sir Henry Hayburn descend at Monte Carlo's beflowered railway station. In the rush of arriving elegance, the exuberance of French greetings, it was some time before he could find his brother on the platform. He had, indeed, begun to wonder if the sleeping-car attendant had put the money for the telegram into his pocket.

But now Sir Henry saw a well-dressed gentleman moving towards him. "Stephen! So you got my wire? Good of you to come."

Stephen was always pleased to see his younger brother. There had never been a lack of warmth between them. Indulgently, he took note that Henry had cut himself with his razor in the train this morning, had not bothered to have his boots polished, and looked as though he had been sleeping all night in his clothes. "My dear boy! I never got such a surprise in my life! But why not Mentone? Why not tell Robkin?"

"Take me to some hotel. I may stay here all night," Henry said. "Robin wrote me a letter. I'll tell you about it there. Have you been at somebody's wedding today?"

Stephen raised quizzical eyebrows. "Why?"

"That flower. And all your get-up."

Stephen looked down at the carnation in his buttonhole. His smile became kindly. "My dear boy! These things grow wild round about here. And my clothes? Well? A man can't be shabby in these parts, you know."

The clerk of the unimposing hotel Henry insisted upon choosing had some difficulty in understanding that, of the two gentlemen, the untidy one with the dirty collar was Sir Henry Hayburn. The other gentleman seemed so much more like what he would have expected somehow.

"Well, Henry, what's this all about?" Stephen asked as the bedroom door closed upon them.

"Robin. He has written to me. How much do you know?"

Stephen took his grey top hat and laid it with his gloves on Henry's bed. Thereafter, he sat down and contemplatively dangled his malacca cane by its silver head. "You mean about Robin and this unfortunate flutter?"

"Yes. If you like to call it that."

"I'm sorry about it, Henry. Yes, he's been talking to me a bit. As a matter of fact, I'm deuced glad to see you. Too much worry for his old uncle." Stephen went on dangling his cane sympathetically.

Henry looked at him, grunted, drew Robin's letter from his pocket, and handed it over. Stephen put down his cane, fixed his glass, and began to read it.

While he did so, Henry took off his jacket, loosened his collar, pulled off his shirt, poured cold water into his wash-basin, soaped his entire head and his neck, then rinsed and dried them. As he took out a clean shirt, a floor-valet in a green apron appeared with a can of hot water for the newly-arrived guest, put it down, and withdrew.

Stephen looked up. "What do you mean to do?" he asked.

"I've decided to see that woman. I want you to keep the boy out of the way."

"He's in bed today, as a matter of fact. Cold—or—I don't know. The old trouble. Life upsetting him a bit, I daresay. Now don't turn and look at me like that, Henry. The doctor thinks it'll be nothing. I'll tip the old man the wink to keep him in bed most of tomorrow. You're almost certain to find the lady at home in the morning. And by the way, my dear old man, you must see Lucy. You haven't said a word to me about *my* flutter yet!"

213

Chapter Twenty

ROBIN'S talk of marriage had left Denise disturbed. It had left a sense of tension. Now the note of their relationship was forced. His desperate earnestness had shaken her, leaving her self-accusing and on edge. Her work was suffering. It was impossible that things could go on like this.

Out on her balcony this morning, staring at the boats, the people, and the come and go of traffic on the quay beneath her, Denise sat wondering what she had better do. Go away? No. At least, not yet. She could not, thus easily, bring herself to give him up. Yesterday he had sent a note that he was kept in bed; an affectionate, plaintive note that had alarmed her. Was he really ill? She did not like the idea of his lying down there, sick and unhappy. But she had not been quite surprised. In these last days he had looked strained. Yet he had said nothing to her, except to own once that he was sleeping badly.

Denise sighed. If he were still unwell tomorrow she would go down to the hotel and ask Lucy Hayburn to take her to his room. Lucy could, she felt, scarcely refuse her.

Denise looked out across the flat waters of Garavan Bay at the still, airless mountainside. It was unnaturally hot for a day in late April. Sultry.

Crossing to her table, she fingered the pages upon which she should be working. No. Something must be done. Why on earth had she allowed herself to become entangled with a young man whose ways, whose ideas were so different from her own?

But she must try to do a bit of this. She pulled over her chair.

Her woman came out. "A monsieur asking to see Mademoiselle."

214

"Who is he, Philomene?"

Philomene did not know. She had never seen him before.

"I'll come." Disinclined for work, Denise was glad of interruption.

A lean, angular man was standing in the doorway. She saw at once he was not French, that his untidy clothes had been made for a colder land. And that his expression, too, was oddly familiar. But where could she have seen this man before? His movements seemed awkward and embarrassed as he came forward into the light.

"Yes?" she said, speaking the word in English.

"Miss St. Roch?"

"Yes."

"Oh." He appeared surprised. Why? Did she look to him other than he had expected. "My name is Henry Hayburn."

"Sir Henry Hayburn?"

"Yes." He blushed, she saw, conscious of her womanhood.

"Please sit down."

"Thank you." For a time he waited hesitant, sitting erect in his chair, until, forced by her determined silence and by the question in her face, he added: "Miss St. Roch, I'm Robin Hayburn's father."

"Of course! That's where the familiar look comes from. Oh no, I'm sorry. It wouldn't. You're only his foster-father. Isn't that so?"

"Robin seems to have told you a lot of things, Miss St. Roch."

"Yes, he has, Sir Henry. He's a great friend of mine."

"I know."

She was unsure of what to say to this. But of one thing she was sure: she was sure she did not mean to sit before him listening to a paternal lecture. "I hear Robin has been ill," she said. "How is he? I hope it isn't much."

"I haven't seen him yet. He doesn't even know I'm in this town. I wanted to see you first, Miss St. Roch." Sir Henry might blush in her presence, responding to her womanhood, but he intended to say what he had come to say.

215

"See me first, Sir Henry?" She, too, felt her colour mounting.

"Some days ago, Miss St. Roch, I got a letter from my son telling me all about his very close friendship with you. Everything. He wants my help to persuade you to marry him." He stopped, obviously waiting to see the effect of his words.

Anger had begun to rise in her, but as yet she did not show it. "Well, Sir Henry?" she asked. "And now you've had a look at me, does that make sense to you?"

"No, it does not."

Despite her growing annoyance, Denise had the curiosity to ask: "Why?"

"Well, anybody could see you're too old and too clever. But if you're thinking about it, remember that my boy is very young, that he is ill, and that he hasn't got a penny of his own."

Denise jumped up. "Do you actually think I've been attracting Robin for his money, Sir Henry?"

"I haven't said so. But such things have been known." Then, because, perhaps, of her look of intense displeasure: "Oh, I'll admit I expected quite a different type of person, Miss St. Roch. Not a young woman of education."

"Thank you, Sir Henry." Her voice was icy. "But money has never entered with myself and Robin. Never! Whatever there was about the rest of it!"

Now he, too, was standing up, wondering what next to say to her. "I'm taking my son away, Miss St. Roch, just as soon as I can take him," he said at last.

A cloud crossed her face and was gone. "Quite right, Sir Henry! See that he's kept away from people like me!" Then, with a cry, as though to relieve her feelings: "Oh, I'm sick of family interference, sick of silly talk!" Again she turned to him. "But thanks for making up my mind for me. I'm getting out of here. So don't be in a hurry. Your son will never see me again! I'm disappearing today—at once." She went to the door and flung it open. "Goodbye, Sir Henry Hayburn," she said.

Coldly, she watched his awkward going; heard his hoarse goodbye as he went. And yet she was left with the awareness that Robin's father had got from her what he had wanted.

None too softly, she shut the door behind him and turning, began, mechanically and distraught, to collect her papers.

Philomene had withdrawn into the little kitchen. Now, as she reopened the door, she was surprised to see that Mademoiselle was dropping tears upon the sheets; that the hands that held them were trembling.

II

Just before lunch-time a knock sounded on Robin's bedroom door and a voice begged admittance.

"Of course, Aunt Lucy. Come in."

"How do you feel now, Robin?"

"Oh, all right. I'm having lunch here in bed."

Lucy hesitated, then she asked: "No more—unpleasantness?"

He shook his head and smiled. "Not these last two nights. Besides, the doctor told me this morning not to worry. He says I'm better. I certainly feel it. He said I had only been coughing a bit too hard. No, Aunt Lucy, I'm feeling grand."

Lucy smiled, too. "Your uncle and I have to go out to lunch. I just looked in to ask about yours before we went. What shall I tell them to bring you?"

Having shown an encouraging desire for food, Robin thanked her and saw her close the door. He wondered where they might be lunching. He did not know that she had gone to make a third at a family conference.

He lay back on his pillow and looked out at the date-palm standing motionless and hot. Beyond it there were glimpses of the sea rimmed by a line of low cloud. He wondered idly if it was storm-cloud; if there was thundery weather over Corsica. Here, certainly, it was curiously warm and airless.

217

He was glad the doctor's report had been good this morning. For although he had not liked to admit it, even to himself, the illness of the last two days had frightened him. The reappearance of red spots on his handkerchief— what his aunt had delicately called 'unpleasantness'—had been, to say the least, discouraging. But now they had disappeared, and he had spoken the truth when he had told her he felt grand. The Denise affair had put him off his sleep, he supposed. That, and the worry of writing to his father, had probably upset him. He felt a qualm now as he wondered what the reply would be. But the optimism of his illness did not allow despondency. Sir Henry would just have to understand. And as for Denise: it was impossible that, in the end, she could not be forced to see reason.

A waiter came with his lunch-tray and gave him a letter. Robin thanked him, watched him go, then opened it. It was an acceptance of another of his short stories. A mere few pages, that Denise, from experience rather than from judgment, had suggested might please this particular editor's fastidiousness. There was a line of encouragement with the acceptance and a request to see more of Mr. Hayburn's work.

Robin attacked his lunch in high glee. This, if anything, was the medicine he needed. Having gobbled it, he was too happy and excited to stay in bed. Denise must see the letter and rejoice with him. Robin got up and walked across to the window. He remembered now that the Stephen Hayburns were elsewhere and could not prevent his going. When the waiter came to fetch the tray he was surprised to find Robin almost dressed.

Taking his way now by the high road into the old town, Robin felt the oppressive languor of the weather. Women, glad to be free of their lunch-time kitchens, lounged in little terrace gardens. A boy, spraying tomato-plants, had stopped to take off his straw hat, and was leaning against the water-barrel, wiping his brown face and neck. In the Rue Longue itself few people were moving. It was cooler in their cellar-like, shuttered rooms.

Robin ascended the first flight on Denise's staircase. Here he halted. He must not go so fast as this. He had been forgetting. He could feel the quick beat of his pulses. And what if she were not in? But he must risk that. He continued upwards, taking time.

Now, the top. And the door was off the catch. He stood waiting regaining breath to call out the good news. As he stood there, the door swung open. Philomene had heard his step.

"Mademoiselle?" Robin asked.

The woman shrugged. She looked glum, but she beckoned him to come in. The studio was in the confusion of packing. In his halting French, Robin asked when Mademoiselle would return. Again she shrugged. Never, so far as she knew.

Never? What did she mean?

But Philomene had turned to the table, picked up an envelope and given it to Robin; an envelope addressed to himself. "You've saved me a walk to the hotel," she said in the Mentonese dialect. But had she spoken in any tongue, Robin would not have taken it in, for he had run to the balcony, thrown himself into a chair, and burst Denise's letter open.

III

With a numb deliberation, Robin folded the letter, fitted it carefully into the opened envelope, and put it into his pocket.

It was only after he had done this that he became aware of a feeling of nausea. The balcony began to swim round him, and he asked himself if he were going to faint. He grasped the arms of the wicker chair in which he was sitting and kept himself rigid, staring at one point, in an effort to stop this sickening spinning. That was better. His surroundings were once again becoming stable. But he must go on sitting here for a time, steadying his shocked bewilderment.

219

So Denise had done that to him? Left him without a word. Vanished. But what had his father said to bring about her going? What did the letter say? Robin drew the envelope once more from his pocket. But as his fingers held it, they shook so alarmingly that he had to put it back again. Now he merely sat staring at nothingness in a trance of misery.

At last Philomene, hearing no sound from the balcony, came to have a look at him. His aspect frightened her. He was sitting forward, wild-eyed and pale, clasping and unclasping his hands.

She had always wondered what Mademoiselle had seen in him. Why she had chosen this thin, delicate creature as a lover. But it was plain now that she had left him; and Philomene could not but be disturbed to see him suffer thus. She found a flask of wine, poured some out, and came back to Robin. He was slow to raise his eyes, when she touched his arm. But at length he drank, holding the glass with both hands to keep it from spilling. Once more, as he gave it back, he looked up. She could only shrug; gesticulating sympathy. Then presently, as she was working, she lifted her head to see him hurrying past her, making for the stairs. Fearing he might stumble, she crossed to the door and listened to his steps, then, reassured, she closed it, glad to have him gone.

Robin panted along the Rue Longue. He did not really think where he was going or what it was that impelled him. He had, perhaps, been taken by a momentary notion that Denise might still be in the town; that he might still find her.

But soon he had stopped. Where was he? At the stairway leading in an easy flight to the small cathedral square. Turning, he went up. But now he must halt and rest himself a moment.

He was sitting on the steps of the cathedral itself, when he heard his name called out.

"Robin! Whatever are you doing up here?" It was his Aunt Lucy's voice. She was coming down into the square from the higher side, accompanied by his uncle and his father.

Robin looked up. But he neither spoke nor rose to his feet.

220

"I was told you were in bed, young man," his father said not ungenially, by way of a greeting.

Now, standing over him, Lucy was distressed at Robin's aspect. But she was still more distressed at the distracted look he turned upon Sir Henry.

"I want to talk to you," Robin said.

"You can talk to me when we get back, Rob," his father answered.

"No. Here."

Sir Henry straightened himself. "Indeed? Oh, very well, then!" He turned to the others. "I'll bring him."

He said this as though his son were a naughty child. Now, but for themselves, the square was empty. Henry sat down on the steps beside his son. "Well, Rob?" He made his voice calm. "And what have you to talk to me about?"

"You know very well what I have to talk to you about! Denise has gone!"

"Who? Oh, Miss St. Roch? I saw her this morning."

"I know."

"It was the most sensible thing she could do, Rob."

His son looked away from him. "What did you say to make her go?"

Henry continued to keep hold of himself. "Rob, I don't like this unfriendliness. And remember this mess is of your making, not mine. I'm only here to do what I can for you."

"What did you say to make her go?" The young man raised his voice as he repeated his question.

His father stopped to consider, then he said: "I wish with all my heart you hadn't done this. For one thing, you're looking wretched. Worse than when we sent you here."

"What made her go?"

Henry thought of the interview this morning with very little pleasure. "I don't know," he said. "I should say she went of her own accord. She seemed very ready to go. You see, Rob—" Here he laid his hand on Robin's arm.

"Liar!" Robin shook off the hand and jumped up.

221

Henry lost his temper. He stood up to face him. However ill the boy was, these insolent hysterics would not do. Now he, too, was shouting. "That's enough! I've nothing more to say to you about that woman. You're coming home with me tomorrow."

Robin drew back, shook his head, then spoke in tones that he hoped were low and telling. "I'm not coming. I'm independent now. I'm staying in France to write."

"Rubbish!"

"After what you've done to Denise and to me, I don't see how I can have any choice. How can I ever come back to Scotland now?"

Had the boy's wits left him? Would he have to take him home in a strait jacket? Henry controlled himself. He must try reason. "Look here, Robin. Stop this crazy nonsense. I'm not going to lecture. But this lack of sense makes me frightened. Think of what you have waiting for you at home. Your mother. The new house. The shipyard. Listen, man. Glasgow and shipbuilding are in your very blood."

"Blood?"

"Your grandfather was a great engineer. And I've done well enough. If only—"

"*My* grandfather?"

Sir Henry Hayburn hesitated, then he stopped and looked at his son glumly. Had the boy's mad behaviour almost forced him to betray himself? "Well, anyway, you know what I mean," was his lame reply.

"Yes, I know what you mean. And I'll tell you, if you like. You lost your own child in Vienna, didn't you? And you took me because my parents were dead. Very nice of you. But ever since, you've gone on building a fantasy round me until you've forgotten who I am. You've forgotten I haven't a drop of your own blood in me. I don't and won't belong to you any more. Goodbye!" Robin was shouting as he had turned to climb the steps on the far side of the square.

"Robin! Your mother—" Henry ran towards him.

"Yes. I'm sorry about—Lady Hayburn. But all the same—goodbye."

His father stood watching him climb. He had caught the cracked note in Robin's voice as he had tried to say the words "Lady Hayburn" with indifference. Henry felt reassured. Things were not so bad, perhaps. Robin used to have these tantrums as a child, he reflected. Still, twenty was getting old for them. But he had better let him go. Always, in the old days, Robin had come back ashamed and purged of his anger.

Chapter Twenty-One

WHAT was he doing up here? He did not know. What time was it? He did not know that either. His watch? No. He must have forgotten it. And he couldn't see where the sun stood in the sky. Clouds had come over; heavy clouds that hung low and dense on the mountains.

It was hot—breathless. Or was it merely his own lack of breath? But he must have found some breath to toil up here. Yet he hardly remembered coming. He must have struggled up wildly, noting nothing; half-stunned, he supposed, by what had happened.

Once more a sense of nausea threatened. Robin put out a hand to gain support from an upright post, one of several that carried wire-netting round a hillside vineyard.

His surroundings heaved and fell distressingly. The mountains, the pathway, that plot of market roses, the crescent of Garavan Bay, the black rim of the sea. Better sit down, take a rest and try to think steadily. Why wasn't he down there? Down there in the quiet of his own room, instead of sitting up here, light-headed and soaked in sweat, his pulses thudding?

But hadn't he been here before? Of course! Now he knew. He had come up on muleback with Denise. On the day they went to Castellar. They had stopped at this very place to admire the view. No wonder he was puffing a bit. It must be quite high up. But why?

He tried to remember. The balcony. Denise's letter. After that for a time he had gone on sitting there. Then the Rue Longue. The cathedral square. His father. His father, who had brought this catastrophe upon him, who had driven Denise away. Robin trembled, as he pieced his thoughts together. Rage had claimed him, he supposed. He had lost all hold of himself.

The flame was fanned by recollection. No! He could not go back to his father. He could not and would not. Not yet. Not now. Never, perhaps. Robin jumped up in his renewed excitement. So that was why he was here? Why he had stumbled blindly away from them all? Stumbled away from his father, from Denise, from himself, from his misery? If this was how you felt when unhappiness had almost crazed you, then it was a relief to let your reason go.

A large drop of water fell, rolling about for an instant as a little ball of dust before it burst and sank into the pathway. The still air, heavy with the scent from flower terraces, lay like a weight upon the hillsides. Robin wiped his brow and looked upwards. The clouds were black and low above him. Lightning had begun to flash along the southern horizon. He had better go on. But where? Never mind. Just go on. So long, at least, as this burning resentment drove him. He could do it. He was all right. He could keep going. Going away from the man who waited for him down there below.

Yes. They had come this way, he and Denise. He remembered everything clearly. This part of the track that passed underneath gnarled olive-trees, where the ancient paving was broken and the mules had to choose their steps slowly. And now it became very steep as the way led straight up the face of the hill. The mules, he remembered, had climbed up through the rocks like monkeys.

No. That was too much for him. Better take this path branching off to one side. Robin turned to follow it. An old man working in his plot of vegetables called out to the thin young foreigner with sweat-sodden hair and strange eyes that seemed to burn but not to see. This was a private path, he shouted after him, a path leading round the side of the mountain, passing vineyards and losing itself at last among heath, juniper, and boulders. But his voice was weak, perhaps; or the young foreigner had merely paid him no attention.

A roll of thunder sounded in the distance. A second, nearer. Angrily, Robin pushed on. Now the heavy raindrops came more quickly, leaving dark splashes on sun-whitened stones, broken stones, rolled from the hillside lying everywhere and forcing him to go more slowly. But the rain that fell upon his head was cool and grateful to him as he laboured forward. The lowering clouds had begun to make it dark. He must be careful not to stumble.

Denise. No. He must keep walking away from the thought of her. Walking along this path. She would not have been so heartless, had she not been driven to it.

He must stop to breathe for a moment. Stop to calm the hammer beating in his throat. Funny he had never climbed so high on foot before. Hadn't liked to risk it. Was it these heights that were making his head swim? But it wasn't so high, really. Not when you looked down. Bother the rain. It had turned into a shower-bath! Should he look about him for shelter? But there was no shelter. Only some dwarf junipers. Should he go on, then? Or, after all, turn back and face—but how could he do that?

Damnation take this rain and darkness! What was to be done? If only—

A piece of rock lay upon the pathway. In his distraction, Robin tripped against it, then stumbled sideways, wrenching a foot in a crevice. As he drew it free, the pain dazzled and sickened him, causing him to cry aloud. He sat down on the hillside, rocking back and forth, while the drenching rain dripped from him.

But after a time he saw that he must stand up somehow. Stand up and try to get back down the hill. Self-preservation was now the force that ruled him. Fear and the thunderstorm were giving Robin back his senses.

He got up, clutching at a juniper bush to steady himself as he stood, one-legged upon his sound foot. If only he didn't feel the return of nausea, this lightness in his head!

Failing to balance himself, his sprained foot came down heavily. With a groan of pain, Robin crumpled senseless on the stones.

226

One of the double shutters was not secure. The morning breeze caught it. It swung back against the outside wall with a loud bang.

In the chair by the window, Henry started. He looked about him bewildered. Where—? Yes, in Robin's room. He must have gone to sleep, after the doctor went. A white-clad figure was bending over the bed. That was the nurse, of course.

She turned, saw Henry was awake, and smiled, to reassure him that the bang had not disturbed his son's drugged sleep. Thereafter she hurried out to the balcony to catch the swinging shutter.

"I've been asleep," he whispered, as she fixed it, standing near him in the once more darkened room.

"Sleep. Yes," she answered. It was about all the English she knew. If she had known more, she might have asked him why he did not go to his own room and have a proper rest.

As Henry moved in his chair, he became aware of the stiffness in his bones. But he had to go up last night. How could he have stayed down here while others searched on the hillside for his son? Now he sat, sore, and conscious of a great weariness, watching the Frenchwoman as she crossed the dim room, settled down by Robin's bed and took up some knitting.

Sitting thus, Henry began to retrace the nightmare that was yesterday. The quarrel in the square. Robin's foolish goodbye. His own annoyance, cooling to distress as the afternoon lengthened into evening and no Robin came. Stephen's wife, Lucy, had gone up to the studio. She had found a woman working. No, he had not again been there. Nor had the woman heard anything of him. They had all begun to be alarmed, himself, Henry, in particular, remembering Robin's angry parting.

The boy in the bed moved, sighing as he did so. The nurse stood up, put aside her knitting, bent over him watching, then sat down again and once more took it up.

227

Cheerful voices came up from the garden, exclaiming at the bright freshness of the morning.

Henry went on with yesterday. The thunder and the drenching rain. Robin could not have disappeared with the St. Roch girl. He must have been caught by the downpour, must be sheltering somewhere. The early darkness. The storm was over now; there was clear starlight. Where could Robin be? Fear had taken hold of him. The hotel had telephoned to the police, who had, in turn, spoken to the railway station. Miss St. Roch, in her own kind of dress and with her great dog, was difficult to miss. They found a porter who had seen her leave Mentone alone. At midday.

Then, after a dinner which Henry could not eat, the woman from the studio had come with a message. A neighbour had just heard of an old peasant having seen a young man on the hill; a strange-looking young man, who paid no attention when the peasant called to him.

The breeze blew through the slats of the shutters, rattling them gently. The nurse looked up, afraid they might again come loose, then she dropped her eyes and went on with her work.

Lucy and Stephen had waited down here. But he, his father, must go with the searchers, the little group of stocky, dark-skinned men whose rapid speech seemed to him a kind of guttural barking. They had been quick to show him kindness, lighting his steps over the stones with their lanterns and supporting his arm in rough places. One of them followed with a mule.

It had not taken long. The crazy boy had not climbed very high. The men knew, of course, the position of the peasant's plot, and thus they guessed, readily enough, the way he must have taken.

And the finding of him.

Merely to remember was to flinch and bleed—to remember the look on his face, as suddenly a searching lantern found and lit it. Robin had the look of a stricken animal, trapped and beaten, waiting for the end, however it might come. With a cry he had run to his huddled, trembling son, calling him by name.

For a moment the Frenchwoman raised her head, wondering why, in this cool room, the patient's father should be sitting over there wiping his brow.

It had been horrible. He was glad Phœbe had been spared the sight of Robin, dazed and broken, crouching up there in the darkness. But although he had not spoken, dull relief was in the boy's eyes. Relief and an instinctive yielding as he, his father, had run forward to catch and hold him.

Now, unable to sit still, Henry rose and crossed to Robin's bedside. In the shuttered twilight, he stood looking at him. He put back the dark hair and gazed into his face as he slept this sleep that drugs had forced upon him. Once or twice Robin's brow contracted as though he were distressed. He stood beside him watching for he knew not what, then at length he turned and left him, coming back to his seat by the window.

An agony of contrition took hold of Henry. An agony of self-doubt, of self-interrogation.

The woman wondered to see him lying back, his eyes shut, his hands grasping the arms of his chair.

What had he done to Robin? Had he killed him? Was this to be the end? Why hadn't he known his son better? And who was he, Henry Hayburn, to stand in judgment over this boy whose very existence sprang from his own unfaithfulness?

In the future, if Robin had a future, he must keep closer to him. Seek to understand him. Gain his confidence by giving all his own. Hold back nothing. Share his secrets. Treat Robin as a grown man. Why had he ever let it come to this? Why had they fallen so far apart?

The quarrel up there by the cathedral came again to Henry. Why, like a fool, had he lost his temper? Almost lost it so far as to admit to Robin he was his father?

Henry opened his eyes and sat forward in his chair. But had he not, just now, determined to share his secrets?

Why not tell his son the truth? Tell him everything? Step down from his stucco pillar? Robin, surely, must feel different towards him when he knew he was his father.

But would he find him ready to listen? If health came back, would mad resentment come back with it? Henry could not think so. Robin had been rational after they had found him; and plucky on that journey down.

He had almost fainted again with pain and exhaustion as the men had tried to lift him to the mule's back. But making an effort, he had been able to show them the reason, pointing to his foot. Then, taking better care next time, they had got him up and set him in the saddle.

Slowly the little cavalcade had brought Robin down the hillside, swaying and sliding, as the creature found its way by instinct and by the light of the lanterns. He, his father, had walked beside him, holding him to keep him as steady as he could. It had been the most anxious journey Henry had ever made.

A gentle tapping sounded on the door. The nurse opened, and Lucy put her head in. "Henry," she whispered, "you're awake, are you? It's ten o'clock. You must come downstairs and have some coffee."

III

They had dreaded pneumonia. But in this, at least, the fates were merciful. Yet the events of that fateful day and evening could not but take a heavy toll of Robin's strength. The ravages of the disease that had brought him to Mentone must, as his doctor feared, noting the all-too-active symptoms, be given a fatal impetus.

It was a dreary time of waiting.

Robin's days and nights were passed between an exhausted sleep and a distressing wakefulness. And yet a veil of unreality hung between himself and his emotions. He would follow those

230

who came and went in his room—the doctor, the nurses, Stephen, Lucy and his father—with eyes that were dazed and gentle, eyes that reflected neither rebellion nor dislike. He spoke little, and was, indeed, discouraged from doing so.

And while Robin lay gazing out at the sunlight of early May dancing on the familiar date-palm, his father, sitting through the long hours, patient and purposeless, would ask himself what was passing in that mind, usually so quick: would ask himself, sometimes, if his son's thinking were lowered to a mere dull consciousness.

Yet people and happenings passed before Robin as he lay there. Denise. Her face, her aspect, their love together, her laughter, her hand on his shoulder when she bent to read what he had written. "Now, would you put it just like that? Well, I don't know. Oh, I guess it's all right. Leave it, Robin. What do I know, anyway?" The reading of her farewell letter.

And up by the cathedral; his strange outburst of rage at that lean figure who now sat forever over there by the window. The mountainside. The moving lanterns. The descent. Events and people hung and floated continually; floated like fishes in a glass tank, coming to the front, showing themselves clearly, then receding into the inner dimness, while others moved forward to become clear in their turn. Yet dim or clear, they hung apart, all of them in a world that could not touch him.

But after some time things were better. Robin awoke one day to find his father by his bedside in the nurse's chair. For some minutes he lay drowsily contemplating the square, familiar profile. Curiosity had begun once more to raise its head. Allowed to talk now, he startled Sir Henry by saying: "Hullo! What are you doing over here?"

"You've had a good sleep, Rob. Better than usual. Your nurse has gone out for half an hour. All right?"

"All right."

"I've got news for you." Henry waited, but Robin did not speak. "Your mother will be here this afternoon. She and your

231

uncle and aunt are going to wait with you and bring you home. In several weeks from now; but whenever they can. The doctor says that's what to do." Here Henry stopped, remembering, suddenly, his son's hot disavowal of Scotland and anything connected with it.

But Robin was smiling. "I'm glad," he said.

"I've got to get back," Henry now added, with relief. "You won't be too excited at seeing her, will you?"

"No."

This drowsy, smiling Robin pleased him. This was the child of the old days waiting, already half-asleep, for his father to come and bid him good-night. Henry touched his hand. "Robin," he said, "you and I must never quarrel any more. What's past is past."

"Yes, Father. Past."

He bent to scrutinise his son's face, seeking to find what Robin wanted him to take from these three words. He could find neither regret nor bitterness. So he took courage. "Just before I leave you, and while I have this chance, there is something I want to tell you, Robin."

His son turned his eyes to him. "Yes?"

"I'll never mention our—that stupid talk up by the cathedral again. Except this once. But—"

"What do you want to tell me, Father?"

"You said we had built a fantasy round you. That there wasn't a drop of Scotch blood in you."

Robin's head nodded on his pillow.

"Well, there *is* Scotch blood in you."

Robin continued to watch him. "In me, Father? But I was told—"

"You had to be told something."

"But whose?"

"My own." Emotion forced Henry to stand up and turn away.

"And who—?"

"She was a Viennese girl. That part is true. I wanted you to

232

know. I thought—I don't know—that it might bring us nearer, maybe, make you feel—well—that I'm not—that I understand a bit." It was difficult for Henry to turn back and look at his son just then, yet he must see how Robin took this.

There was curiosity in the boy's face. Nothing more. "So you *are* my father, after all? And what about Mother all this time?"

Henry considered his answer. "Not the whole story now, Rob. Some time later," he said. "But your mother was—was good. You see, Rob, she insisted on bringing you—and me—back home again." It was all that he could say. He had hurried out to the balcony, and for a time he was out of Robin's sight.

Robin lay thinking about this. So his father—like himself? No. It was very queer. When they had been in Vienna. He must ask more about it sometime. Meanwhile, this was something new to lie and think about. A bright new fish to swim to the front of the glass tank.

But presently, the fish was receding into the dim recesses of a mere drowsy weakness.

Some few minutes later, when Henry felt he could return to Robin's bedside, he was much surprised to find that his son was again asleep.

Chapter Twenty-Two

WHEN Phœbe came to look back on the long, sunlit months of the year 1901, the summer of a Glasgow Exhibition, the last summer of Robin's life, its memory lay there behind her a hot, uneasy, golden dream. A dream compounded of joy and sorrow.

The early mists lifting from the valley. The distant mountains, their colours ever growing darker, richer, as sunlit day succeeded sunlit day. The birds squabbling and twittering in the silver birches over there across an early morning lawn still with the bloom of dew upon it. And then, later, when the dew was safely gone and the air had turned warm, the routine of arranging Robin's long chair and rugs, that he might spend his day in the open. The quiet hours of sitting beside him. The friends and relatives who came and went. Lucy and Stephen on a long visit. Robin's wasting aspect. A monotonous, bitter-sweet pattern.

And yet things had happened. There was that important day when Bel and Tom Moorhouse had come to Whins of Endrick to be with Robin, fetched, Phœbe remembered, by Henry's much-used motor-car after it had dropped him at the shipyard. Later, it had taken Lucy and Stephen to the Exhibition, and herself to a consultation with her doctor. A day of moment to herself and Henry, stamped forever on her mind.

She would always see the group by the tea-table over there on the grass when she returned that afternoon. Bel in a suit of white serge, its jacket thrown back over her garden chair; the choking elegance of her lacy blouse with its boned neck; her straw hat modishly draped with a white veil. She was holding up her parasol with one hand and pouring out tea with the other. A Bel whose face was smooth again, now that her son

234

was home and safe beside her. A son, Phœbe remembered telling herself, who would be able to live out the usual span now, like any other. Tom himself in a long chair like Robin's, but, unlike Robin, becoming fat a little, and with no marks of his South African wounding in a face that was brown and cheerful. Presently Tom would have an artificial foot, and his life would touch back to normal.

And Robin, lying on his cushions, watching her as she crossed to greet them, with eyes that seemed in these days to possess a quick, separate life of their own. She had sometimes wondered if these eyes knew everything.

"We must get back, Phœbe." Bel had risen after tea. Tom, too, had stood up on one foot, balancing his strong young body. Phœbe could still remember a sharp, quite primitive jealousy as she turned her eyes from Tom to Robin.

"Tom! Stop jumping about on one foot! You'll fall down. Here, take your crutches." Bel could laugh at her son's antics, as he got to the car in a succession of hops.

When they were gone away and Phœbe came back to the tea-table, she found Robin's eyes still upon her. "Tired?" she asked.

"Not specially."

"Why are you looking at me like that, Robin?"

"I couldn't be looking at a better friend."

"Bad boy. That's no answer."

"Mother, you've got a secret!"

She remembered wondering if she were blushing; and her absurd hesitation as she said: "How do you know what I've got?"

"I know the guilty look!" His detached teasing smile, there against the cushions. And then: "Tell me, Mother. Amuse me."

And indeed why not? Unless it should be that the thought of a new life he might never see would have power to vex him. Still: "Something I was once told could never be again is going to happen to me, Robin. I haven't got used to the idea of it yet. Your old, middle-aged mother is going to have a baby."

"Good heavens!"

She watched him, as his thin body shook with silent laughter there under the rug.

"Well? Will you please tell me what there is to laugh about?"

"I don't know! But somehow—no! When I think of Sir Henry—"

"What about your father?"

"I can just see him looking sentimentally down on that poor little bit of wriggling redness; then going to his writing-desk and making arrangements for his engineering course. And by the way, Mother, tell the baby from me not to send any poetry to the evening newspapers. Tell him to keep to the weeklies. Father doesn't read them."

"Robin! That's not fair!" Yet she was not quite sure what he meant. Still, she was glad at least that he had taken it in this way. Glad now, when anything amused him.

He had lain thinking for a time after that. The summer day was on the wane, a little, but the sun was still high. The birds, awakening from their midday torpor, gave a chirp now and then among the birches. A red squirrel dared to appear and to bump himself across the far corner of the lawn. Cows in a distant field gathered themselves about the gate, lowing to be milked. Midges began to dance. The parlourmaid came down the front steps and took away the tea-tray.

She had turned to him then, she remembered, wondering why he lay so quiet. He stretched out a hand.

"No. Really, old lady, I'm pleased about this. About as pleased as I could be about anything, I suppose. Pleased for you and pleased for Sir Henry. He'll get a full-blooded Scotsman this time. Not a half-bred misfit. Yes, honestly, it's wonderful! Just as it should be."

She knew what he meant. It was beyond her powers to answer him. How could she tell him that she would give up everything she had, this new hope even, if only the half-bred misfit, as he chose to call himself, the child of those far-off

236

days of her own young, bewildered suffering, could be spared to live out his life as Tom Moorhouse would now do.

"So keep up your health and your pecker, Mother. It's your bounden duty. Will you promise me?"

She had said: "I promise."

That Robin had spoken again of this, Phœbe could not recall. Nor yet, strangely, could she recall the first telling of the news to her husband. But it had been the coming of the second Robin that had shone like a lamp before them in the darkest winter Henry and Phœbe Hayburn ever hoped to know.

Henry had come back that evening accompanied by his brother and Lucy. They were full of news. Foreign royalty was to come to Glasgow's Exhibition. As people of importance, Sir Henry and Lady Hayburn were expected to be there.

They had gone indoors, she remembered, leaving her to follow with Robin.

And again she had seen the knowing smile. "Well, Robin? What is it now?"

"Aunt Lucy has a secret too. Oh, not your kind of secret! But something. I wonder what it is."

II

Phœbe was not told Lucy's secret until the thing actually happened. On the day of the royal visit she learned what it was.

That morning, she had been forced to tell Henry she would not be able to come to the Exhibition with him; that she felt sick and had a headache. Her husband, guessing the reason, had smiled and acquiesced cheerfully enough, adding, however, that Stephen, and especially Stephen's wife, must help him by taking her place. But Lucy, hearing this at breakfast, had come up to see her. Her new sister-in-law, Phœbe remembered, had seemed more than conventionally worried. "But, my dear girl! How can I leave you in this condition?"

237

"Why not, Lucy? I've been like this before, and I'll be like this again. It's nasty, but it's natural. All I have to do is to stay here in my room. If I feel like food, I'll have it sent up."

"But Robin will be left alone."

"Well? That has happened before, too. The servants will look after him. He has his books. He'll be all right."

"But, Phœbe—"

"Lucy! Please! This head of mine can't stand arguments. And Henry says he needs you." So that was that. And yet Lucy's reluctant going had left Phœbe wondering a little.

During that warm morning she had lain in a restful twilight made by lowered blinds and half-drawn curtains. The windows they cloaked were open. Now and then a light breeze caused the hangings to move. Outside noises came to her. The cackle of farm hens from across the still fields. Heavy gardeners' boots beneath her window. The snip of garden scissors. The bellowing of a bull somewhere in the far distance. Sounds of the summer. Later, she had heard a servant come from the house, heard the click as she arranged Robin's chair, heard the girl exchange a joke with the young gardener, then heard Robin's brief thanks and his assurance that he had all he needed.

What happened next she could not recall. But she must have slept for a time, she supposed, since about three o'clock she had wakened up, feeling better. She remembered the hot afternoon stillness.

She got up, crossed to a window, and turned back an edge of the blind to look down and see what Robin was doing. Usually, at this time of day he drowsed a little, his chair shaded by the birches. But now he was wide awake, sitting upright and looking about him. Phœbe was about to pull up the blind and call through the open window, asking why he was so lively, when, on a sudden impulse, she decided to leave him, turned away, and went to bathe and dress herself.

Something, she did not later remember what, had left her restless. She had wandered from room to room thereafter,

238

persuading herself that she, the mistress, must see that everything was in order.

Stephen and Lucy's room. Idly she examined Lucy's toilet silver, wondering at its luxury. It had never been her wish to have anything so expensive, so handsome for herself. She picked up Lucy's crystal flagons of perfumes and lotions, taking out the stoppers and smelling the contents like an inquisitive little girl. She had felt tepid, a little, towards Stephen and his wife. Their gods were neither her gods, nor were they Henry's. But they were easy, pleasant guests. And his brother's presence, she had kept telling herself, must be of some comfort to Henry in these days of Robin's illness.

Now her husband's workroom and study. Henry's worktable was in its usual confusion. A T-square. A drawing-board with paper pinned to it. Technical magazines. Sheets of script. Henry could not keep his work away from his home. Absently she picked up a blueprint lying unrolled on the table. She saw it had something to do with a ship's engine, but could make nothing more of it.

As she made to put it back, she saw that it had been lying over a large square envelope upon which, in pencil, Henry's impatient hand had scrawled "Robin". Reaching for it, she found it was unsealed and appeared to be much thumbed.

Making a clear space on the table, Phœbe sat down in her husband's work-chair and shook out the contents. These were pages cut from magazines containing the three or four stories that Robin had succeeded in publishing. Some poems. A few letters beginning: "My dear Father".

So Henry was keeping these things; treasuring now, in spite of all, the results of his son's unwelcome gift. Knowing her husband, she understood why. Understood, too, why he had kept them without telling her. Henry was like that. But she could read nothing now. Perhaps later. Phœbe folded them together, slipped them back into their envelope, laid it down, and drew the blueprint over it.

Robin's room. Full of everything that was Robin's. His

books, his prints, his rug of tartan rags before the fireplace. Her own photograph in the middle of the mantelpiece.

She had given him the old Viennese photograph of his real mother now that the truth had been told to him. It seemed to fascinate him endlessly. It lay, she knew, in a drawer of his writing-table, for he had taken it out more than once to ask questions about that pert, smiling girl who had given him life. Phœbe had forced herself to hide her instinctive dislike of these questions, but now she slid the drawer open.

As she picked it up, she found that it overlay yet another photograph, a photograph she had never seen before. One of an odd-looking young woman in queer monkish clothing, strangely beautiful in her way, with her cropped curls and her regular, vivid features. Phœbe hung over this for a time. She did not need to be told whose picture this was. But at last she put it back, glanced again at that Viennese girl, then she closed the drawer and went.

A bumble-bee was humming over a bowl of roses on the upper landing. There, downstairs, the sunshine, striking through the open door, made a square of white light on the rug and tiles of the front hall. The half-grown house spaniel, a present for Robin from his Uncle Mungo Moorhouse's kennels at Duntrafford, lay in the shadow, just beyond this hot square, panting and snapping at flies. Seeing her above him, he beat the floor lazily with a stump of black tail, his eyes imploring her not to expect him to go for a walk until the day grew cooler.

Now, perhaps, she might go out and have a look at Robin. Phœbe took two steps downwards, then, thinking she heard a footfall in the drive, and disliking the thought of meeting strangers, remounted, and turned back quickly into her room.

III

It was still in semi-darkness. She went once more to the window and turned back the blind, making again a chink to spy through. She had wanted, she remembered, to be sure that no one had come to trouble Robin.

It was then that she saw her. Saw the young woman of the photograph, as she crossed the sunlit lawn, her slim figure draped to the ground in clothing such as no woman would ever dare to affect here in this self-conscious country. And the photograph had given no hint of these vivid colours; of the fairness of that head; of that glowing skin.

Phœbe watched her move across the grass, watched Robin stretch out his arms in welcome, then watched her bend down to catch him up into her own.

A moment later she was kneeling by him and they were talking, happy and excited.

These pictures would forever be with Phœbe, together with the memory of how, when she had dropped the blind and withdrawn back into her room, her heart was beating quickly. She had been the unseen witness to a strange, bewildering happening. What was its meaning? Was it that she had seen Henry's son reach vainly for the things that were his birthright? Reach for a young man's morning hopes and their bright fulfilment? Hopes that now he must leave behind him? Phœbe could not define such things. But there were times when her instinct told her.

She had been strangely shaken, she remembered, sitting there in the dim light. Yet strangely, too, it was neither anger nor jealousy that had shaken her. But now, what should she do? Robin, it seemed, had known of and wished for this visit. And his behaviour towards the visitor had told of his joy at seeing her. Should she, Phœbe, go downstairs and ask her to stay for a time? Should she present herself and thus make regular this stolen meeting? And yet, perhaps, they would not want it so. They had, she reflected, expected herself to be away. And what would Henry have to say, if, coming home, he found this girl still with them?

He had not told her much about his son's adventure. There had been outlines, that was all. And she had guessed her husband's reasons. It would have exposed old scars, old unhappinesses better left forgotten.

But now, at least, every prompting told her to leave these two down there alone.

She could not remember how long she had been sitting in the darkened bedroom, but when once again she rose and crossed to the window, Robin's visitor was bidding him goodbye.

Phœbe stood once more upon the upper landing, listening until the receding steps were gone, then, having waited some moments longer, she picked up her sewing and went downstairs into the sunshine.

IV

Robin lay back against his cushions. His eyes were closed, but a half-smile came and went, and his face was flushed a little. She had crossed the lawn so quietly that he did not open his eyes until he heard the wicker chair creak as she sat down beside him.

"Hullo, Mother. Head better?"

"Yes, thanks." Phœbe took out her work. She was determined to say nothing if he did not.

Robin lay watching as she chose a coloured thread.

"Your mother is turning into a blind old woman," she said, aiming it without success at the eye of a needle.

She heard his chuckle. "Oh, don't fumble, Mother! Give it to me. You're not blind. It's impatience that's always been your trouble!"

She looked about her as he threaded it. The birches with their pale, slim trunks and their frail branches, hanging motionless in the breathless afternoon. She looked across at this house that had not yet had time to feel like home. She watched Robin's young spaniel, who had decided, after all, to leave the cool of the front hall, and was now flouncing joyfully towards them.

"There, Mother."

"Thank you." She received the needle from him, took up her work and bent over it.

"I had a visitor this afternoon," she heard him saying presently.

"Yes," she said without raising her head to look at him. "I saw her from the window."

"Uncle Stephen and Aunt Lucy met her at the Exhibition. She's been sent by an American paper to do descriptions. She's a writer. She's the friend I had in Mentone. But I daresay you've heard about her."

Phœbe continued to sew. "Yes. I've heard about her," she said. And as Robin lay saying nothing more, she added: "Is she coming again to see you? Do you want me to invite her?"

He thought a little before he said: "No, Mother. She came to say goodbye." And presently: "No. Everything is finished." And then, as though to reassure the troubled eyes that had been turned to search his own: "But I'm glad she came. Now I feel quite happy."

She had bent again to her work, she remembered, with feelings of relief. Whatever he had felt, Robin was now contented.

V

Yes. It was difficult, later, to recapture quite completely the mood of that long, almost Italian, summer. A procession of sun-drenched days moving at last towards a golden autumn. Days that seemed to wait, suspended in time, which, if they could not be happy, still seemed to hold their own strange peace.

243

But she could recall how the web of her existence had been shot with bright threads of joy for the child that was to come; with dark threads of pain at the thought of Robin's going.

And the visitor who came to him on that still afternoon? Whose coming, he had said, had left him happy? And the part that she had played in Robin's sorry story?

There was, of course, the harsh, the Moorhouse answer.

But Phœbe's untamed heart refused this rigid judgment, even though it might at the same time refuse to tell her why. Nor did it tell her why she had chosen to cloak Denise's coming in silence and compassion; schooling memory to see her forever kneeling there by Robin as a haunting, summer dream.